GANTS

Richard K. Abshire
&
William R. Clair

GANTS

Richard K. Abshire
&
William R. Clair

A DELL BOOK

Published by
Dell Publishing Co., Inc.
1 Dag Hammarskjold Plaza
New York, New York 10017

THIS IS AN SOS Publications, "PRIVATE LIBRARY COLLECTION BOOK."

Dell ® TM 681510, Dell Publishing Co., Inc.

ISBN: 0-440-12797-1

Reprinted by arrangement with The SOS Publications' Private Library Collection

Printed in the United States of America

February 1987

10 9 8 7 6 5 4 3 2 1

WFH

To
Lloyd and Bill
Who Would Have Been Great Friends

To
Lockie and Lois
Who Loved Us

To
All Of Our Families

Contents

PROLOGUE

THE COOL BLUE-BLACK MUZZLE BRUSHED AGAINST the old man's ear. With a dull pop, the slug slammed into his skull, and his brains compressed. Arteries ruptured, skin and bone bulged but did not burst. The impact spun him backward and to his left from a sitting position on the edge of the narrow bed. He did not seem to stop falling when he flopped on the bedspread, but felt himself still spinning inside a deafening roar. A dark tunnel rose to meet him; he was flying incredibly fast into the tunnel's mouth. The grinding roar filled the small space, reverberating around and around him, faster and faster. And then nothing for a while.

When he stirred, the old man looked down on his own crumpled body.

Police came, uniformed officers at first, then detectives. A single word slipped through the heavy air to the old man, "Suicide," and for the first time a sickening sense of panic swept over him. My God, they don't understand!

The room dimmed. A sound the old man had never heard before washed over him. Lighter and lighter, he felt himself rising, as the sound, soft and comforting, called him away. It was drawing him out of the bloody little room. Leaving . . .

leaving . . . no! Not yet, not before someone understood. He fought the tow, fought to shut out the sweet siren sound, to stay. A powerful, quiet tide was carrying him out to sea, and he held onto the little room, keeping shore in sight by the force of his will. The sound rose and broke around him like breakers in the shallows off a dark beach, drawing him away to a welcoming sea. Even against the sweet ache of exhaustion, he held on. He could not go . . . not yet. Not yet.

1 | THE CROCKETT HOTEL

POLICE OFFICERS CHARLIE GANTS AND WES Braverman walked off the creaking old elevator into the dark hallway of the seventh floor. The wallpaper bore an ornate faded floral pattern. Wall lamps burned dimly in dirty yellow globes and the hallway lay in dark stretches between them. The carpet was threadbare and the floor moaned under their feet as they made their way toward the room at the end of the hall.

Nursing homes and hospitals smell of antiseptics and medicine. In the Crockett Hotel there was that same odor of Lysol mingled with a musky dankness. There had been no fresh air or sunshine inside in years. The windows were all closed, with heavy velvet curtains drooping before them. The Crockett had once been something of a Dallas landmark, but it had fallen on hard times.

The occupants of this floor were all elderly pensioners. Too independent for nursing homes, they kept to their shabby rooms. Gants had been here before, as a patrolman, when the transients who rented by the day or week on the floors below found their way to the old folks' floor, usually around the first of the month. They pilfered possessions from a room or two at a time, making off with pension checks, radios, and an occasional nest egg before moving on.

Now, at almost midnight, the floor was quiet. Somewhere behind a bolted door hymns were playing on a radio. They reminded Gants of home, years ago, in East Texas, when hymns could be heard lilting out of radios late at night, from houses where old people lived with their sons and daughters. Then one old frame house sheltered three or four generations. That was before Gants had moved to Dallas and lived in apartments where kids and pets were not allowed and before he had ever seen a nursing home.

They followed the hallway around the corner to the right. Whoever had died, he was one of the more ambulatory, Gants thought, living this far from the elevator. He knew from his earlier visits that the most decrepit residents lived nearest the elevator. They moved gradually, as their health failed, to rooms closer and closer to the elevator. Finally, in their last move, they would be loaded onto the elevator by uninterested ambulance attendants and taken away. Tonight, someone had broken in line.

In the dark stretch before the last door, two young ambulance attendants waited with their stretcher. The shorter of the two leaned against the wall, smoking, while the larger heavier set man sat passively on the stretcher, his feet dangling. Beyond them, the light over the last door spread an amber shawl over two old women, in bathrobes, as they huddled together, stooped and silent. At the door itself, a uniformed officer stood guard.

Sergeant Burden was in the doorway, nervously wiping his forehead with a handkerchief. He stood half in the amber overhead light and half in the shadows of the room in his wrinkled suit, his belly hanging over his belt. He turned toward Gants and Braverman as they edged past the people in the narrow hall.

Braverman spoke first, his pleasant smile in place, as if he had taken no note of their dark passage. "Hi, Sarge. What'cha got?"

"It's Captain Jonas," Burden whispered as if the corpse might hear.

"Yeah? I heard he was staying up here after he retired. How's it look?"

Braverman maintained the same easy style, whether he was looking over a corpse, or sitting down to lunch. His dark hair swept back from a broad handsome face with a smile that never went away. He took in the room as he stood against the doorjamb, his thumbs in his belt.

Gants stepped past the fat sergeant and glanced into the room. Two lab men were at work, one taking pictures, the other dusting for prints. Gants fished his glasses from an inside jacket pocket. They annoyed him, and he was too vain to wear them all the time. It seemed bad enough that he was losing his hair. But he needed glasses in the dark room.

A single bed stood in the far right corner. The room was so small that the bed left only enough space for a nightstand between it and the near wall. There was just enough room for a man to walk between the foot of the bed and the dresser that stood against the left wall. Opposite the door, in the corner between the foot of the bed and the dresser, another door opened into a bathroom. Gants leaned farther into the little room, where he could see a closed window in the left wall and beyond the dresser.

"It's a suicide," Sergeant Burden stood behind him. Gants turned away and faced his partner and the sergeant. "At least that's the way it looks. Nobody was seen going in or out. Neighbors thought they heard a shot. Well, they thought at first it was the captain's television. Then they remembered he didn't have one. They got worried about him and knocked on his door. No answer. They knew he was in here, so they called the desk clerk. He got in with a pass key, found the captain just like that, with the gun on the floor. It's his gun. The department gave it to him when he retired."

Braverman shook his head. "Looks pretty open and shut to me, Sarge." He had taught Gants that a good detective should suspect the obvious. Most of the really tricky stuff is in the movies.

"Window there faces the fire escape," Burden went on. "But it's stuck, ain't been open in a long time. I couldn't budge it."

"You did real good, Birdie. I think you've covered just about everything." Braverman smiled. It was usually his job to get to the scene first and brief the sergeant. Technically, Burden was the boss, but they had worked together for years and enjoyed a comfortable rapport. "You must have been right on top of this deal when it came out."

"Yeah, I was just around the corner."

"Well, Charlie and me were pretty close ourselves. I bet we were within half a mile or less, right up the street. I was in looking up one of my snitches, with Charlie waiting in the car. He heard the call come out, and came looking for me. By the time he found me and we got up here, it couldn't have been more than just a few minutes."

"Yeah, like I said, I was just around the corner."

"Anything else you want, Sergeant Burden?" The photographer loaded his gear and turned to leave.

"Nah, looks like you covered it."

"Not a hell of a lot to take pictures of in here." The cameraman eased past them through the door, followed by the print man, snapping his kit shut. Gants stepped further inside the room with Braverman behind him and noticed for the first time that he was wringing his hands. Surprised, he held them up as if for inspection. He saw Braverman looking at him, and shoved his hands deep inside his pockets.

Braverman leaned over the corpse and pointed at the entry wound. "The old man knew what he was doing. Square in the ear lobe. No reflex, no waiting around to see if it took."

Like an ear piercing in a Gahan Wilson cartoon, Gants thought, and shuddered.

The old man lay on his left side, his left arm extended past his head, his right hand dangling over the edge of the bed. He must have been sitting on the side of the bed, facing the wall, when it happened. Then his head kicked backward and to the left, turning him so that he fell on his left side. His head was lopsided from the force of the slug. There was nothing on the nightstand but a telephone and a lamp.

Captain Jonas had been a cop for over forty years. At mandatory retirement age, he asked for extensions. When they ran out he wanted more, but the department was through with him. Burden and Braverman had worked for the old man. Gants knew him only by reputation. Cops talked about him over coffee or a late-night beer. He was a legend, a bigger-than-life figure from the old days. The ruined little man on the bed was less than Gants had imagined.

14

Gants looked down at the chalk outline of the death weapon the lab men had taken away. A chill came over him suddenly, and he jerked his shoulders upright. It was as if an icy hand had brushed the nape of his neck.

"You okay, Charlie?" Braverman had noticed.

Gants nodded and smiled, "I just felt the damnedest chill." A second chill froze the smile on his face. He cupped his hand over his neck and laughed.

"Rabbit running over your grave." Braverman smiled.

"Yeah, I guess so." Another chill. "Feels like he's tap dancing on the damned thing."

Gants moved to the window. It was shut tight but not locked, just as Burden had found it. The room was warm and close. Gants could not shake an eerie feeling, something ominous. Christ, he thought, am I the only one in here who feels it? Burden was still at the door, talking to someone in hushed tones. Burden certainly felt no chill. He wiped his forehead again and again, and still the sweat glistened in the dim hall light. Inside the room, only the little lamp was lighted. Gants flipped on the overhead bulb, erasing the shadows at the foot of the bed and in the corners of the room.

The assistant medical examiner came in, brushing past Sergeant Burden, who pointed toward the bed. Gants knew the examiner from other calls, other corpses. He was a nervous little man who moved in quick, darting motions and always smoked a cigarette. The butt dangled, neglected, directly under his nose, with a tail of ash that never seemed to fall. He wore thick glasses and mumbled between clenched teeth. Gants knew that a lot of homicide cops smoked cigarettes to combat the stench that usually goes with violent death. He had tried it himself, but gave it up because it did not seem any better to gag on the smoke.

The little man worked briskly, scribbling in a notebook that he drew from his pocket. He touched the body gingerly, turning the head enough to see the purplish color of the left side of the face. He rose and faced Braverman.

"What's the approximate time? Any witnesses?"

"The sergeant has 'em. People heard the shot, about two hours ago." Unlike Burden, Braverman made no attempt to shield his comments from the dead man. He took out one of his cards to write out the information the medical examiner would need.

Gants, standing beside the window, heard his name called softly. Again. He looked at the other men, who were paying no attention to him. The voice he heard was faint and muffled. He sensed the little room closing in on him and fought back a wave of nausea. That voice . . . Charlie . . . Charlie . . . .

"Charlie!" Gants started at the touch of Braverman's hand on his arm. "Where have you been, partner? Let me see your pen. Mine's out of ink."

Gants handed him a pen, trying not to tremble, and heard the medical examiner say: "Two hours. That fits, all right. Post-mortem lividity's setting in on the left side of the face. Two hours ago sounds right to me. I'll have some details for you tomorrow."

With that, the nervous little man turned and hurried off down the hall.

"You know," Braverman laughed, "Sometimes I think our M.E. don't like dead people. Now that's a hell of a note."

The ambulance attendants came in with the stretcher between them. It was close quarters around the bed, and Braverman joined Gants at the window. The old man was lifted and laid on the stretcher in almost the same position. They drew a sheet over the face and left.

Sergeant Burden stepped aside to let them pass. Then he came into the room for the first time. He shook his head sadly.

"I never figured Cap Jonas for it. Not him. He was a Catholic, too. What they call a practicing Catholic."

"Well, you just can't ever tell." Braverman stared at the gory bed. "Some you think never would, do, and some you'd bet money on, don't. I just don't believe I'd ever have the guts."

"I know I wouldn't." Burden was pale and still sweating.

"Hell," Braverman looked around at them, smiling again, "if I ever turn up like the old captain, don't you believe none of this suicide bullshit. You just round up all my ex-wives and put them on the damned lie box."

It was a little ritual of reassurance that Gants did not take part in. At first he had not felt the need for it. Later, he found no solace in it. He could see through it, and it did not work for him. He knew that any one of them might end up like the captain. It was a matter of statistics and circumstance. Guts had nothing to do with it. He caught himself squeezing his hands again. His fingers were cold and stiff and he held them at his sides, clenched into fists.

"We both worked for him. And I'll have to admit, even if he was the toughest sonofabitch in the department, he was always fair," Burden said.

"I guess," Braverman agreed. "I didn't have any complaints. But, you know, it's these guys who make the department their lives who wind up like this. Time comes when they have to leave, and then what have they got? Nothing, that's what."

Gants stood beside the bed, trembling. He felt eyes on him and choked back a scream. Slowly, affecting a calm that was the opposite of the prickly panic he felt, he turned and strode out of the room. He walked until he was well down the hall, past the waiting old women and almost to the corner where the hall turned and led back to the elevator, before he stopped and looked back. Burden was coming out of the room, closing the door behind him.

Braverman shouted down the hall at him, "You going down to talk to the desk clerk? I'll visit with these ladies, and meet you downstairs in a few minutes."

Braverman and the women disappeared into the room next to the captain's, as Gants waited for the elevator. He pushed the down button, then pushed it again. Burden and the uniformed officer were there when the door finally opened.

Gants said nothing during the bumpy ride down to the lobby. Burden was talking to the patrolman about the report that he would write. When the door opened at the lobby, Burden turned to Gants as the patrolman walked away.

"Charlie, are you all right?"

"Yeah, Sarge. Why?"

"You're white as a sheet."

"I'm just a little under the weather. No problem."

"It wasn't . . . upstairs? I mean, a year and a half in homicide, you've seen plenty of that. I figured you were used to it by now."

"It's not that, really. I'm just off my feed a little."

"Okay, I'll see you back at the office. I gotta get hold of the lieutenant. He'll need to call the duty chief on this. This is sad, really sad."

The sergeant walked through the lobby, between the phony rubber plants and out through the double glass doors. Gants looked down at his hands. They were not shaking anymore. The old hotel felt sticky and warm again.

2 | THE SLASHER

·

THE WALLS OF THE HOMICIDE OFFICE WERE GREEN,
with fluorescent lights overhead. Typists and clerks sat near the
glass doors at grey steel desks. Detectives and investigators sat
in back, around the sergeant's office. A side door marked "Lieutenant" opened into the office shared by the three shift com-
manders. On the opposite side, three smaller doors were
marked "Interrogation." Bulletin boards plastered with memos,
rosters, posters, and cartoons covered the walls. The captain's
office was at the back of the room.

Gants sat typing the desk clerk's statement. At the desk beside him, Braverman leaned back in a swivel chair. He had
dictated his reports to a typist.

Sergeant Burden was in the hall just outside the door, talking
to two detectives. After a brief, hushed conference, he ushered
them into the office, straight to the lieutenant's door. He
knocked and pushed inside, followed by the two detectives.
Braverman nudged Gants, who had not looked up from his
typing.

"Looks like something else is brewing, partner."

Gants looked up as the lieutenant's door closed. "What is
it?"

"Burden and the second string just blew into the lieutenant's office. Birdie looked plumb overwrought."

Gants continued to type, and had just finished when the lieutenant's door opened and Burden motioned for them to come in.

"I knew if it was much of a deal they'd have to call in the varsity," Braverman drawled.

Gants admired the older man's casual attitude. For his part, he still had not shaken the strange chill of the captain's room. He was thinking about it when he and Braverman were ushered into the lieutenant's office. The sergeant's shirt was soaked now, plastered to his beefy belly. He looked like one of the old tent preachers Gants remembered from revivals he'd gone to as a kid. His black hair lay in damp strings across his head.

The lieutenant spoke softly. There had been a high-profile murder earlier in the evening and the two detectives Braverman called the second string had been working the case. High profile meant press coverage, heat. This one involved a sixteen-year-old boy, found with his throat cut and multiple slashes over his upper body. It was the third such murder in just over a year. The papers had nicknamed the killer the "East Dallas Slasher."

In contrast to Sergeant Burden, the lieutenant was smooth and cool. He was a lean, sharp-featured man only a year or two older than Gants. There was an ivy plant on his desk, and a framed picture of his wife and kids. His college degree hung on the wall behind him, along with his certificate of appointment to the rank of lieutenant.

"As you all know," Lieutenant Moss reminded them, "we have had similar cases before. Young boys slashed. The first one was over a year ago. Another a few weeks ago, almost on the anniversary of the first. We got plenty of heat from the press on those, because of the ages of the victims. One of the papers ran a piece a few months ago on unsolved murders in Dallas, and the "East Dallas Slasher" was the lead. Now it looks like our man is stepping up the pace, hitting more frequently." He delivered a detailed lecture on media relations. Gants thought ahead to the time when they would huddle with Burden and decide what to do next.

Burden's office was smaller than the lieutenant's, and he shared it with another sergeant. Burden did not have any degrees or certificates but in a corner of the bulletin board, in front of his desk, he had a Polaroid snapshot of his youngest son, in football gear. It was next to a black-and-white picture of him and his wife, both wearing baseball caps and holding stringers of sand bass.

"Well, I guess we need to do some kind of background on the victims to see if we can come up with a tie-in with the others. Also, I'll get a hold of somebody in the Shrink Shop," Sergeant Burden began. "Maybe they can give us some kind of profile of a likely candidate for this thing. If we can run it through the computer, maybe pick out some known offenders."

Gants knew Burden was guessing about the shrinks. Like most of the older officers, what Burden knew about the Psychological Services Unit was what he read in the paper.

"Lane and Franklin, y'all get back out to the scene. Start a good house-to-house. We'll get you some help out there as soon as we can shake somebody loose."

The two rose wearily and left. Burden turned to Braverman. "You two get a hold of the boy's family."

"The family, Sarge?" Braverman protested, "It's after one in the morning. We're supposed to get off at eleven P.M."

"I know, but we can't wait around on this. It's high profile. I am sending you, Wes, because you can do this without upsetting them. You know what I mean. You're smooth."

"Bless their hearts, Sarge, they've probably been right in the middle of making arrangements and everything all evening, and now they're trying to sleep . . . ."

"Well, by God, you've talked to people at bad times before, and you're going to do it again. And personally, I don't give a shit if you do have a date waiting for you. You oughta be married anyway, a man your age. And what you may not know is that this poor little victim of ours liked to hang out in bars where he wasn't supposed to be because of his age, and he got picked up a couple of times for beating up drunks, and a queer or two for good measure. And he came by it pretty honest, too, if you know what I mean. Now, I don't mean anything against his folks, but I really don't think they've been up all evening making arrangements. And I don't think this'll be the first time the po-leece have come to see'em late at night. Or the last."

The streets were quiet as they drove to the East Dallas address. Braverman was at the wheel. Ordinarily, the junior man drove, but not with Wes Braverman. He liked to be in control.

"Charlie, you looked awful up there."

"What? When?"

"In the captain's room, Cap Jonas's room. You looked like you never seen a stiff before. I thought you were going to throw up, man."

"I don't know what it was, Wes. Dead people don't bother me, you know that. But there was something else . . . I felt strange. I can't explain it."

"Maybe I can. That wasn't just a dead body up there. It was a cop. And a suicide. That got to you a little. It gets to all of us. Maybe it makes us think about it happening to us some day. I don't know."

"Wes, you worked for Jonas a long time, didn't you?"

"Yeah, he helped break me in. Why?"

"Well, his death didn't seem to affect you that much, not as much as it did me, and I never even knew him."

"Charlie, the old man was a po-leece, and we went back a long way together. Now, if somebody had walked into his room and blown his brains out, I'd be assholes and elbows on the case until I caught the sonofabitch. But that ain't what happened. The old fart did it to himself, and that don't rate any sympathy from me. Understand?" Braverman's smile disappeared.

"Sure." Charlie knew that he wasn't the only one who had thought about how a retired cop might end up. Wes just dealt with his fears in a different way.

The apartment house was in a rundown part of East Dallas. Gants wondered why he never got to call on people up in North Dallas. Don't rich people ever get mixed up in killings? Seniority. The twenty-year men worked up there, except for Wes. He seemed to like it down here.

Wrought-iron steps led up onto a dark balcony. Each door had a light fixture overhead, and every one of them was dark. The stucco walls were generously autographed and initialed. Here and there particularly graphic graffiti had been painted over.

They found the apartment. A dog was barking below. Gants

remembered the old farmhouse where his grandfather lived, with tractors and farm implements standing in the moonlit yard, like hulks of junk cars in the dim glow of the street below. It was not moonlight on the farm, and the people who lived in apartment houses like this one in East Dallas were not on the farm any more, either. They had left the farms, sharecropping and hiring themselves out to cut hay and work on other people's places, to move to Dallas. In the country, sixteen-year-old boys from sharecropper families spray-paint obscenities on a school bus, or shoot the headlights off tractors with their .22's late at night after sneaking a few beers. In the city, they hang out in bars and beat up on bums and fags, or get into brawls with poor city brats who dare to call them "white trash" under their breath. And, sometimes, they wind up in the basement of Parkland Hospital with tags on their toes. It's a different league, Gants thought.

After Braverman's second knock, the red door opened to the stench of cigarettes and beer. A tousled blond head appeared at shoulder level.

"Wha'chall wont?"

"Po-leece," Braverman answered, with his smile. "I need to talk to Mister Estep."

The face disappeared behind the door as it closed. There were muffled voices. The door opened again a minute later.

"Yeah? Wha'chall wont?"

There were the same features, only older, and the teeth were much worse, brown and gapped. The scrawny body was clad in faded plaid pajamas, the top open on a bony chest.

"Po-leece, Mister Estep. I need to talk with you for a minute." Braverman smiled again.

Estep unchained the door and showed them to the couch. It was made down into a bed with four or five small children sprawled apart and hugging each other there, under a flowery cotton sheet.

"We won't bother you for long, Mister Estep," Braverman promised. "We know you are in a time of mourning, and we wouldn't have disturbed you at all, except that we need you to answer a couple of questions if you can, so we can find the one that brought harm to your boy."

Estep looked confused at first, and then smiled. Gants

thought that he was not often the object of that much concern, certainly not from the police.

"Aw, he wudden mah boy." Estep shook his head, still smiling. Missing teeth gave his lips the wrinkled-up look of a very old man. Gants guessed that he was only about fifty. The old man rumbled through trash on an end table by the crowded couch and found a cigarette, which Braverman promptly lit for him. "He'us mah wife's by her fust husband."

"Your wife?"

"Well, you know," Estep lowered his voice to a whisper, "I call her mah wife." He seemed to wink, there in the dark, foul-smelling room, with his ragtag brood of kids sleeping on the couch and the light from the street lamp falling through the empty window on them.

"I see. Well, what we really need to know is, do you have any idea who might have done something like this? Was your boy having any trouble with anybody, any of the guys he ran around with?"

"Never said nothin' to me 'bout no trouble. 'Course, him 'n me, we di'n talk too much ennyways. Lessee. There was a kid name Louie summinother. An' a meskin boy name a Peppy. Tha's whut they all called him. They hung out downair at t'em clubs. Mostly at ol' Dub's place. Dub might know more about it. I don' know."

The detectives thanked the old man and left. Such questioning depressed Gants, but they seemed to cheer up Braverman. People like Estep made Gants doubt some of his ideas about mankind and the human condition in general; they confirmed all of Braverman's.

The club was dark, with scattered red light overhead and pool tables along one side. Jukebox country music bounced off the walls, while men in greasy work clothes sat hunched over their beers in twos and threes at little tables littered around the floor. A short stage squatted at one end of the bar. A smell of beer and sweat hung in the air, with a fog of cigarette smoke. The front door stood open in the early morning muggy heat. There was no air conditioning.

A man called Dub might be called Dub because his real name is any he does not care for, or because his first initial is a W.

This Dub, a fat balding man behind the bar, wore a greasy white shirt, and kept a pencil behind his left ear. Gants made a note of that and watched Dub's left hand as he and Braverman talked. Braverman usually did the talking.

Dub allowed as how a hell of a lot of people came into his place, and he couldn't hardly be expected to remember all of them. Besides, he surely wouldn't allow no minors in his place. No, he couldn't help them.

"Tell me, Dub, you say this is your place?" Braverman's tone was friendly, and he was smiling.

"That's right."

"So your name is on the license, isn't it?"

"Yeah."

"How long has it been since the Liquor Board was in here?"

"What's that got to do with anything?"

"Nothing at all, Dub. Do you know Mister Johnson? He's the head man on the Liquor Board here. Johnny T. Johnson."

"I don't know nobody down there. I never had any trouble with no board."

"You've been real lucky, Dub. I've known people to get shut right down, lose their licenses, for stuff I thought was just piddling. Johnny was saying to me just this morning at breakfast . . . we went to school together, Johnny and me did . . . he was saying just this morning that he was getting a lot of complaints about some of the places in this part of town. Asked me did I know any places that needed a real close going-over. I told him I didn't, but I'd sure keep my eyes open."

"You say this meskin kid's called Peppy?"

"That's right Dub."

"Yeah, seems like I did see him a couple a others 'round here. They's too young, so I run 'em off, a course."

"Of course."

"Him and two white boys. I haven't seen 'em around for quite a while."

"You have any idea where they might live?"

"No, I don't. And that's the truth."

"Tell you what, Dub. Here's my card. If you see either one of those boys, or if you find out where one of them stays, I'd appreciate it if you'd give me a call."

"I'll be sure and do that."

On the street again, Gants watched the lights going off in the little dives across the street. He yawned. Dub was shooing his customers out and closing up, too.

"Two o'clock A.M." Charlie yawned.

"Yeah. Tell you what, partner. I think I'm gonna take the old cop car home with me tonight. I'll drop you off at your place."

"What about Sergeant Burden? Wes, did you check with him about taking the car home?"

"Investigator Gants, you worry too much. I'll give old Birdie a call when I get home. My guess is he'll be calling us in early in the morning. This way we'll save ourselves a little time."

Gants was too tired to care. He was asleep before Braverman got him home.

3 | THE RHAPSODY

CHARLIE GANTS LIVED IN ONE OF THE HUNDREDS of single adult apartment complexes that stretched in a belt along either side of Northwest Highway, north of White Rock Lake. His ground floor efficiency faced Southwestern Boulevard near Greenville Avenue. It was within easy walking distance of the Old Town Shopping Center, home of the all-night Tom Thumb Supermarket, several chic shops, and a number of Dallas's trendy singles bars and clubs. One club across the street from the Tom Thumb featured male strippers, and there were several cowboy discos. There was also a twenty-four hour, walk-in first-aid shop, where people went to be patched up when the partying got out of hand.

When he closed his door behind him, Charlie thought at once of the dead captain's room. Unlike the captain's room, Charlie's had plants. It was full of them. They stood shoulder to shoulder in the front windows that faced the parking lot. A big one whose name he could not remember hung from the ceiling; it was a gift from a stewardess who had been into plants before she got on the Far East run. She was into Zen now, and Charlie had not heard from her in a long time.

The plants gave the apartment the appearance of being furnished. Actually, there was not a piece of real furniture in the place except for the sleeper couch in the middle of the room and a cheap kitchen table with a pair of mismatched chairs. Efficiencies usually rented furnished, but Charlie only paid half-rent because he was a cop and the managers liked having him on the premises. For half-rent, he made do with a sleeper couch and whatever he could rustle up.

His divorce had cost Charlie a houseful of furniture, as well as a house, a car and almost everything else. It left him with his daughter four days a month, the first and third weekends. She was five. He had thumbtacked a dozen snapshots of her on a little bulletin board on the wall opposite the door, so that she seemed to greet him when he came home from work. "Hi, Bit," he would say, "How's my girl today?" Her name was Elizabeth, but he called her "Bit." Sometimes he called her "Little Bit." The only other picture in the room was a framed poster from the Joffrey Ballet, a gift from another stewardess who was married now.

A cheap little stereo with speakers the size of shoe boxes sat on an unfinished plank resting on stacked bricks. In the space under the plank, his mixed and meager collection of albums lay in disarray. In a corner, four plastic milk crates he had spray painted, two red and two blue, sat one on top of the other. They were brimming with books. The bottom carton was full of text books on crime and criminals, left over from his police science courses. The other three held the books he liked to read, paperback editions of Faulkner, Proust, Vonnegut, Conrad, Dashiell Hammett, and Raymond Chandler. A tattered, second-hand copy of *Crime and Punishment* lay open, face-down on the top carton.

Charlie closed the door behind him. He breathed deeply, relieved, and a welcome sense of solitude rose to greet him in the darkness. Being alone felt good after a double shift of too many people with too many problems without solutions and too much misery. He pretended he could see Bit's face grinning at him from the bulletin board. She was all the company he wanted. He kicked off his shoes and let his jacket fall to the floor, things he could not do without remembering his ex-wife. Living alone was not all bad. Loosening his tie, he made his way across the room. It was half-dark, and half-lit by parking lot lights that shone in through the front windows. He fished a handful of ice cubes out of the Tupperware bowl in the freezer and dropped them into a water glass, which he filled with cheap Scotch and milk, in equal portions. His stomach hurt. Walking slowly, he found the couch, still turned down to serve as his bed. He slouched down on it. For practice, he closed his eyes and pictured his room as if it were a murder scene. What does this room say about the man who lived here? That was the part, the only part, he still liked about working murders, the challenge of the puzzle. You start with a body and the bits of debris that lie about it, sort out the clues from the trash, and use them to reconstruct the fatal chain of events. Bringing the murderer to justice had been his favorite part at first. Now it was the process itself. Wes Braverman dismissed the whole idea of physical evidence as bullshit. Informants solve crimes, pure and simple. That was his philosophy. Like a reporter, a detective is as good as his sources of information, no better and no worse. But Charlie begged to differ.

What did this room say about Charlie Gants? He pictured the milk-crate book shelves and his battered old black-and-white television with a twelve-inch screen (a concession to his Little Bit; Charlie seldom watched it). It said that he was broke and he lived alone, he thought. It said that he read a lot. That was all. In his mind he saw the dead captain's room again. A few books whose titles he had not noticed. That was unlike him, not to read the titles, but he had wanted out of that room desperately. Broke and lived alone, and died alone.

Charlie flipped the stereo on, and the tone arm fell onto a well-worn album, a "Best of Beethoven" special from the Tom Thumb. He knew nothing about classical music, but he liked some of it. It soothed him when he was alone at night, which was often. The piece began softly, and he lay back on his bed and sipped his Scotch and milk. He wanted the music to help him unwind, to slow him from his cop's gallop to his own, more comfortable pace. It was his way of decompressing.

When he got up to freshen his drink, he remembered Captain Jonas's room again, and a clammy chill passed over him. He half-heard a sound in the dark part of the room. Silence. The music stopped. Charlie froze, glass in hand. Seconds ticked by. Someone was there. He saw by the light from outside that the rear sliding glass door was still closed, held in place by a piece of broom handle placed in the runner. And the front door had been locked.

With a click an ice cube shifted in his glass.

Someone *was* there. There, in the shadows near the curtains by the sliding glass door. Charlie opened his mouth wide to breath more quietly. Not a sound. He gingerly shifted the glass from his right hand to his left. His right hand reached his holster, then found and cleared the strap. Barely breathing at all now, straining with every cell to hear any sound in the room, he heard nothing, no one else breathing. But he felt as if someone were there. With a quick step he reached the wall and slapped the light switch on, drawing his revolver. Nothing. He checked the bathroom quickly, then both doors, then the back door again. He stood listening for a long time. Finally, he holstered his revolver and turned to the still-revolving turntable, where the needle was scratching on the spent record. For some reason, he did not turn it over. Instead, he laid it aside and squatted by the homemade shelf. An album jacket caught his eye, it was one he could not remember ever playing before. Not until he heard the opening clarinet of Gershwin's *Rhapsody in Blue* could he even recall its contents.

It had a strange effect on him. He imagined the notes dancing, disjointed and brokenhearted, in the dark air, and in his mind, he could see a spectral ballet: dancers in black, *en pointe,* their faces expressionless. Ordinarily he liked Gershwin, but the *Rhapsody* had never seemed so melancholy, and he suddenly felt maudlin. Elizabeth. Momma and Dad. His father had passed away with things unsaid between them. Lost chances. He mused about the dream woman of whom he had despaired as his hairline receded. He thought of these things, and when the melancholy piece ended, he played it again. It was precisely the music he wanted, no matter how or why he had chosen it. He turned out the lights, and his mood darkened even more. Still holding what was left of his drink, he closed the drapes over the front windows and lay back in the dark on his rumpled bed. A police siren shrieked outside.

Someone was standing silently behind his head, where he could not see. Without turning to look, he drank the last of his Scotch and milk.

And then he was in the captain's room.

He stood for what seemed a long time beside the bed, looking down at the dead man. The obscene little hole, macabre in its symmetry. Blood stagnant on the pillow. With a creaking of springs, he sat on the small bed beside the corpse, mesmerized by the wound, as if it were the eye of a cobra. He sat silent and still.

He felt a soft tremor as the dead man rose and turned slowly toward him. Charlie was transfixed, unable to look away, to shut out the hypnotic picture of the cold eye sockets turning toward him . . . . Charlie could not move. Captain Jonas faced him, his mouth agape, slack-jawed. The gray old face, its left side puckered and livid, fixed Charlie with its sightless stare. Charlie's heart screamed in his chest as the old dead man suddenly slumped toward him. That face fell toward him as he pulled his head back, away, and he smelled the hot putrid stench in his nostrils. The old man was upon him, bearing him backward, onto the crumpled sheets. The corpse was alive with tiny beasts that Charlie felt but could not see.

Charlie shot bolt upright in the bed in his small, dark room and screamed. And screamed.

4 | THE SHRINK SHOP

THE DOOR DID NOT SAY "PSYCHOLOGICAL SERVICES." It said "Personnel Services," and it was next to the men's room in the grubby little tenth-floor hallway in a building four blocks from the Police and Courts Building. Sergeant Burden had picked Gants to check with the Shrink Shop on a suspect profile, because he was the only one who would admit he knew where it was. Cops do not go to shrinks; when they do, they do not admit it.

The door opened into a cluttered little office filled with two gray metal desks, several battered file cabinets, and a clerk-typist. She was matronly and stout, with rimless glasses, and a bun at the back of her head. She was typing, and smiled pleasantly.

"May I help you?"

"Charlie Gants, to see Sergeant Pomeroy. I called."

"He's in conference, but I'll tell him you're here."

There were three closed doors along the opposite wall. She went to the one nearest her desk and tapped lightly before easing it open and leaning in. After a whispered exchange, she motioned for Gants to go in.

"Can I get you some coffee?" she offered.

"No, thank you."

Still smiling, she returned to her desk.

Gants found the sergeant behind his desk, lying back recklessly in a broken swivel chair, with his feet resting on the desk, beside an ashtray piled high with cigarette butts, some white and some brown. There were two straight-backed chairs on the near side of the sergeant's desk. A blond woman rose as Gants entered. She was about thirty, tanned, with a smile that revealed even white teeth. Her blue eyes fixed Gants with a direct and appraising gaze.

"Charles Gants, this is Sam Cartwright. Doctor Cartwright is doing some consulting work for us."

They shook hands. Her scent was subtle and expensive.

Gants handed the sergeant the package on the slashings. Pomeroy sat up and spread the contents of the envelope over his desk. He scanned each report and laid it to one side. The pictures he passed to the woman.

"Here you go, Sam. This'll give you some idea of what the troops have to deal with. This kind of stuff is one of the reasons cops need people like you. You can imagine what eight hours a day of looking at crap like this can do to somebody."

The pictures were of the three boys who had been killed. Gants watched her face as she looked at them. Her eyes widened a little, and her lips tightened.

"Charlie brought the file up here so we could maybe look it over and give him some idea of who he's looking for, a kind of a profile. Since our full-time staff psychologist hasn't come on board yet, I thought you could help us out. What do you think, Sam?"

"Well, this is a little out of my line, Sergeant Pomeroy. My field is psychological testing. I know about job stress, not homicidal maniacs."

"You're a doctor?" Gants asked. "A psychiatrist?"

"Not an M.D. I'm a psychologist."

She gathered the stacks of papers from Pomeroy's desk and laid them in her lap. Then she took each in turn, scanning the narrative from each offense report and its supplement. Gants waited for her to finish, trying not to be so obvious about looking at her tanned thigh. The slit in her skirt opened as she moved, showing her leg and the lacy border of her slip. When she had finished reading, she went through the photographs again, studying each one more carefully.

"Officer Gants, what do you know about the victims?"

"All about the same age, all from East Dallas. Other than that, there aren't many similarities. We haven't found a common denominator."

"Were they gay?"

"Not as far as we know. Why?"

"I was just wondering."

She held one of the pictures. "I remember some cases. Men who lured young boys with promises of dope and money. As I recall, they were found slashed like this, at least some of them."

"The last one, Estep, had a record of beating up drunks. He and couple of friends beat up a gay outside a bar they are known to frequent. At least one time they pulled a strong-arm robbery on a gay victim."

"Strong-arm?"

"No weapons. Two or three of them would rough a guy up and take his money. Usually, the victims wouldn't make a police report."

"Why not, Charlie?"

"They think that cops are prone to harass them," Gants explained, looking into her clear blue eyes. "Well, cops do harass. A lot of the gays don't want anything to do with us. They figure there's no sense in making a report because we don't care if they get robbed."

"Is that true, Charlie?"

"Sometimes, I guess. Some of us care."

She looked closely at him, until he felt uncomfortable. Then she returned to the picture in her hand. "As I said, this is out of my line. If I come across a client or applicant who shows excessively violent tendencies, I refer him to a psychiatrist. That's what I'm trained to do. If you had a roomful of suspects, I could give them all tests and probably pick out your man. But starting out with the end result like this and working backward is new to me. One thing, if I were going to guess about this, I would guess the killings were sexually related."

"Why?"

"Primal urge, basic drive. Whoever did this was in an absolute frenzy, and expended an awful lot of energy. Obviously, it was meant to do a lot more than just kill the victim. I'm guessing, but I think I'm right."

She reminded Gants of a teacher whom he had known a long time ago, when he was a little boy. She was attractive and a little intimidating. It was the way she looked at him.

"Tell you what I'll do." She put the pictures and the reports back on the desk. "I have a good friend who is a psychiatrist. He's on the faculty at Southwestern Medical School and heads a research institute here in Dallas. He's tops in his field. If you don't have any objections, I'll show him this stuff and see what he says. You can trust him to be discreet. I know you don't want this talked around."

"I don't have any objections, Doctor. We need all the help we can get."

"Please don't call me 'Doctor', Charlie."

"I'm sorry."

"Oh, that's all right. It's just not necessary. Everybody calls me Sam."

"That's right, Charlie," Pomeroy laughed. "Sam. Just one of the boys. She's catching on pretty fast around here, and she's only been with us for, what is it now, Sam, three weeks?"

"Three and a half."

"How much longer will you be here, Sam?" Charlie did not like the idea that she might be leaving soon.

"A month, maybe six weeks. As long as it takes. I'm designing a series of tests for police recruits."

"That's right. Hey, Charlie, you can be her guinea pig. We're looking for a few good men."

"He's right, Charlie," she joined in, "I could always use a good man."

"Gee, I'd like to help out," he said, thinking that he was not really kidding. He would like to spend some time with her, for more than one reason. For one thing, he wondered if she knew about dreams. That one last night had been different from any he had ever had before. He would like to ask her what it meant.

"I guess I'd better get back to the office. I hate to leave them short-handed when they're so busy," he said in a flat voice.

"And you're working partners with old Wes Braverman, aren't you?" Pomeroy said as he stood to shake hands with Gants. "Yeah, I guess you'd better get back over there and keep him out of trouble. Tell him I said hello, Charlie. He and I used to work a squad together."

"You bet. Sam, I appreciate it."

"Call on me anytime, Charlie. I'll get this stuff to my friend. I should have something for you in a few days. I'll call you."

Charlie nodded and shook the hand that she offered. As he left, he looked back and was disappointed to see that Sam had already forgotten him. She was on the phone before the door closed. Gants left Sergeant Pomeroy's office and headed for Homicide. There was a lot to be done, a long day ahead.

Wes had been right about taking the car home the night before. Sergeant Burden had called them in early this morning. That meant a double shift, which meant a long day and no chance to sit down and eat a decent meal. It meant his stomach would hurt. He could remember not too long ago when the prospect of a double shift had been exciting, had meant a big case. Now he found that he thought about his stomach more than he thought about the big cases. Nine years on the job and nearing burn-out, he thought. Wes was not like that. After twenty years of it, he still rolled out of his bed smiling every day, raring to go. My trouble, he thought, is that I think too much.

On the way back to the office his quick sure gait slackened, and his mind drifted. At first he thought of Sam. He liked the name. The ID card clipped to the collar of her blouse read Dr. Samantha Cartwright. He was almost sure the blouse was real silk. It was hard to tell without touching, but it looked real, and she seemed the type. He saw her in his mind as he walked. Not a glamorous face particularly, but straight, clean features he liked. Her eyes were disturbingly clear. She looked at him and listened when he talked. Maybe it's the training, he thought, and remembered that she was a shrink. A psychologist. He wondered if her friend the psychiatrist was more than a friend. "Tops in his field," she had said.

Without any conscious thought on his part, he found his mental image of Sam replaced by the cadaverous face of the dead captain. The old man had crept up without warning and forced himself into Gants's thoughts. Now he could not force the old corpse out. Whatever you do, don't think about a red polar bear. Once you think that, red polar bears are all you can see. And dead captains. Once the old man was there, he would not go away. Gants fought the picture of the dead man with the more recent and definitely more pleasant one, of Samantha Cartwright. He remembered her subtle fragrance, but at once the stench of putrid flesh overwhelmed him. He could not block out the dead captain. He remembered the dream without effort. It was replayed in his mind like an endless tape, from beginning to end and then over again without stopping. He was sweating. It was still early morning and the sun was not high, not the hot part of the day at all. But his sweat bathed him, soaking his shirt. He pulled his collar open and breathed deeply, hungrily. He felt lightheaded and stopped. He leaned against the nearest wall to catch his breath. When he looked beneath his hand he pulled it back as if it were burned. He had laid his hand for support on a tarnished brass plaque mounted in a granite arch that stood over double glass doors. The gothic lettering read, *Crockett Hotel.*

Gants looked around at the bright morning sunlight winking and sparkling off bustling cars. People rushed or meandered by on all sides, happily absorbed in their business. It was a beautiful day. Through the glass doors, the hotel's interior looked dark and forbidding, like a great tomb. He decided resolutely not to go in, then pushed on one of the doors and found himself in the lobby.

The air-conditioning was working, but the coolness was clammy and numbing. The smell of the little flower stand was funereal. The place felt and smelled of death to him. People buzzed around the echoing lobby, some of them even laughing as they came and went, but it was as if a shimmering curtain had been drawn between him and all others. Their laughter was hollow and distant, mirthless and macabre.

Gants had no intention of going up to the captain's room. He could not imagine it. He went into the coffee shop in hope of finding somebody, anybody. It was empty, except for a grizzled waitress with no front teeth. She brought him coffee without asking and offered him a menu, which he refused. Three refills later, he was still alone at the counter, alone in the whole cafe. He rose to leave. Turn right at the lobby and out the door. Through the double doors he could see people in the warm sunlight. His strides lengthened as he fought an impulse to run.

But with every step the freedom and safety of the outside seemed to slip farther and farther away. He looked over his shoulder and saw the elevator, its doors open, waiting to take him to the seventh floor. With a tiny shudder of panic, he turned back toward the double doors. Just short of the doors and the sunlight beyond, he bumped into the desk clerk, who recognized him.

"Wasn't that something about the captain?"

Gants next found himself, passkey in hand, alone in the elevator. Going up in the hotel was like riding a falling anchor deeper and deeper into a cold black lake. He had waded around on the ground floor to steel himself against the morbid chill and stillness. Now the dive.

He stepped off the elevator into the long, tawdry hall, walking as if dazed. Seeing nothing, he had the clear impression of a figure preceding him around the corner of the hall. When he turned the corner seconds later, no one was there. He heard no closing door.

Before opening the captain's door, Gants noted with detachment that he drew a deep breath and held it. Once inside, he immediately grabbed a magazine off the top of the dresser and jammed it under the door, to wedge it open. He turned into the room, which seemed even smaller than he had remembered it. With a glance, he saw that the bed had been stripped to its springs, but he did not look at it again. The window still would not open. It was stuck. He made his way around the room, and stopped in front of a murky mirror over the dresser, because the face there alarmed and fascinated him. It seemed old and ashen as it returned his curious stare. There was a hollow, haunted look in the eyes. The cheeks, his cheeks, were drawn and creased.

What had he come here to see? He had no idea. From habit, he opened the drawer of the nightstand, careful not to touch the skeletal bed. He did not want to hear the springs creak. There was nothing in the drawer.

He looked down through the bed springs and saw a cheap little phonograph. He had not noticed it the night before. Atop the phonograph, an album jacket lay empty. It was the only one in the room. Without looking, Gants knew what it was. He opened the lid of the phonograph, spilling the empty jacket to the floor. The record he knew would be there lay waiting on the turntable. He did not play the record, yet could hear the clarinet begin its lament. He stared at the motionless record as the *Rhapsody in Blue* filled the little room.

The feeling of numb compulsion that had carried him from the street into the hotel and from the coffee shop to this room began to ebb. As it receded, he felt a tingling, helpless panic taking its place. Oddly, the ebb and flow began, not in his extremities, but in his chest. The ache of panic gutted him as it spread and he slumped forward, his leaden legs tottering beneath him, his dead arms dangling lethargically at his sides. The open door danced at the edge of his dimmed vision, unattainable as he stumbled and almost sprawled, screaming and slavering, upon the bed itself. As the searing white panic spread through him, licking at his faltering heart, he realized that the heavy senselessness that had filled him from head to toe was not lessening. It was pouring into his helpless, useless arms and legs. The rhapsody grew louder and louder, engulfing him. His legs were snarled in it as it spun a web around him. In desperation, he threw himself toward the door, and his face smacked against the facing. He could see out, down the hall to the corner far away. In the distance, he heard the complaining elevator working, like an old scow bobbing on the surface of a dark lake, oblivious to the drowning man below. A white-hot flood of panic overwhelmed his heart when he heard the creaking bed springs behind him! Cackling insanely, he flung himself through the door into the hall. The rhapsody followed him, chased him, as he lumbered brokenly down the hall. He willed each step with a frantic, silent scream. His heart went into spasms and seemed ready to burst a dozen times, until, after an eternity of running as if in a dream, he gained the corner. He did not look back at the open door.

Incredibly, it was still morning when he stumbled through the double glass doors and fell in a heap on the warm sunlit sidewalk, like a spent swimmer washed ashore at the edge of a cold black lake. He waved away the pedestrians who stopped and squatted beside him, offering to help. After a time, the blood pumped into his arms and legs again, his heart mended its pace, and he hoisted himself to his feet.

5 | THE FUNERAL

WHAT LITTLE COFFEE WAS LEFT IN THE POT WAS thick and bitter, but it took the edge off of the chill. Gants was cold now, and the sweat that had soaked his shirt outside the hotel felt like ice water on his back.

"Charlie, what did the Shrink Shop have to say?" Sergeant Burden scrutinized him over a pair of reading glasses that rode low on the bridge of his nose.

"Nothing definite, Sarge. I talked to Doctor Cartwright. She said it was out of her line, but she's going to check with somebody and get back to us."

"Okay. Cartwright? Is that the one that Pomeroy brought through here the other day on the guided tour?"

"I guess. I wasn't here when they came through."

"You would have remembered her. Let me know as soon as she comes up with anything. By the way, I'll be riding to the services with you and Wes. Don't get off without me."

"What services, Sarge?" Gants felt the chill again.

"Captain Jonas's funeral."

"Today? He only died last night, for Pete's sake. What's the rush?"

"Not much family. What there is all live here in town. I guess they wanted to get it over with as quick as they could."

"Well, Sarge, I was thinking." His stomach tightened. "I didn't even know the man. Why don't I hold down the fort here so that one of the other guys can go?"

Burden shook his head as he turned to walk away. "Captain Sharp's orders, Charlie. We're all going. No exceptions."

St. Michael's Church was near downtown, within walking distance of the Crockett Hotel. Except for the two dozen cops, the sanctuary was empty. Captain Sharp was there, with Lieutenant Moss, the chief of detectives, and the Big Chief and his driver. They all looked out of place and uncomfortable. Just before the services began, two women and a man walked down the center aisle and sat together in the front.

"That's Cap Jonas's daughter and granddaughter," Burden whispered to Charlie. "The man is Edmund Copeland, the daughter's husband. He's got more money than the government."

Charlie could not tell much about the women. They wore formless black suits and opaque veils that hid their faces completely. Edmund Copeland was a tall, slender man with silver hair and a cold thin face. The two women leaned on each other, while he sat erect beside them. He did not put his arm around either of them.

The priest was a short, stocky man with a sad face. He moved and spoke solemnly, and Charlie liked the dignity and ritual, the feeling of tradition. It was different from the little church he remembered from his childhood.

Then it was time for last respects. Charlie was surprised that the casket was open. He held back, and was among the last of the mourners to pass by the old man. In the line ahead of him, he saw Sergeant Burden wiping his eyes with his handkerchief. The fat sergeant said something to the dead man and reached into the coffin to pat his folded hands. Wes walked past without stopping, and Charlie could not see his face.

Charlie swallowed hard as he drew nearer the corpse. Someone had done quite a job on the old man, on his ruined face. There was some symmetry to it now, and the bulge was almost gone. It was not him anymore. It was an effigy, a wax doll, puffed and powdered. Charlie looked at the thing and wondered: is he in there? Is he here now? The line moved on, and he was glad to leave the body behind and walk outside into the sunlight.

Charlie, Wes, and Burden were the only cops who went to the cemetery. All the brass went home for the day, and the other detectives and investigators went back to work. The priest, the two women, and Edmund Copeland were there, too.   .

The dour priest said a prayer for the dead: "Eternal rest grant unto them, o Lord, and may perpetual light shine upon them . . . ."

With his head bowed, Charlie raised his eyes. He saw Wes standing next to him at a kind of parade rest, his head up and his face expressionless.

"Absolve, o Lord, the souls of all the faithful departed from all bonds of sins . . . ."

Charlie heard Burden sniffling, and watched the fat man shake his bowed head slowly.

". . . and by the assistance of Thy grace, may they deserve to escape Thy avenging judgment and enjoy the happiness of eternal light . . . ."

The two women stood silent and still, each holding the other. Edmund Copeland stood slightly apart. As Charlie watched, the tall man flicked something off one leg of his trousers with a nonchalant hand.

"Grant, we beseech Thee, Almighty God, that the soul of Thy servant which this day departed out of this world, may be purified by our Lord Jesus Christ's sacrifice, and delivered from his sins, and may receive forgiveness and eternal rest. Amen."

The priest blessed the casket and crossed himself, as did the two women. Edmund looked at his watch.

As the priest spoke to the two women, Charlie followed Burden and Wes as they moved toward them. When the priest walked away, Burden, who was crying unashamedly, spoke briefly to each of the women in turn, and took the granddaughter's hands. The women thanked him. Wes followed him, and took the granddaughter's hands in his.

"Jessica, if there is anything I can do . . . ." Jessica hugged Wes, and he held her tightly for an instant. Then he eased her away, ". . . please call me." He turned to Julia. "Julia, I want you to feel . . ."

"Julia," Edmund called. He had left the grave and walked halfway to his car, where his chauffeur waited, holding the open door. "It's time to go."

The women turned without another word and followed him, leaving the three cops by the grave. Charlie had not spoken to either woman, and it didn't seem they had taken notice of him. He had not seen their faces through the heavy veils. They walked back to their car. As they pulled away, Wes driving, Charlie saw the grave-digging crew with their equipment, waiting for them to leave.

"It's a shame. It's a goddamn shame." Burden was still crying. "I don't understand it, not for a minute."

"That asshole Copeland," Braverman muttered. "Did you see that scumbag? I hope to hell it didn't screw up his schedule, having to show up for this."

Burden nodded in agreement. "He looks like a very cold man. It didn't seem like he was giving Julia much comfort."

"Julia's the captain's daughter?" Gants asked.

"Yeah. I don't know why she ever married the guy," Burden said.

"The prick's loaded," Wes offered. "That's all there is to that. Julia never had much, and she didn't want her daughter growing up like that. That's all, she just wanted the best for her kid. You can't blame her for that."

"There oughta be more to it than that." Sergeant Burden sniffled and blew his nose with a loud honk. "Money's no good at a time like this. There oughta be more."

"Sarge, you and Wes knew them pretty well, Julia and her daughter?"

"Oh, yeah." Burden smiled. "We kinda watched them both grow up. The way the captain was, we were just about like family, I guess."

"Yeah," Wes laughed bitterly. "The old man would get so wrapped up in one of his cases that he'd forget things like birthdays, or if his kid was in a play at school or something. Sometimes we'd remind him, or me or Birdie would cover for him. You know, pick up a little something, make excuses for him."

They rode for a little while without talking. Then Burden

said, "I'm glad they had a church service, with the priest and everything."

"Why wouldn't they?"

Wes knew. "Because he killed himself, Charlie. That's one of their cardinal sins, or whatever it is. It's supposed to mean he went straight to hell, on the express."

"I asked the priest about that," Burden said. "He said that nowadays they kind of take each case on its own merits. In the old days, suicides didn't get the full treatment. They couldn't even be buried in ground that was blessed. He said now they figure that most of the time a person don't have his wits when he takes his own life. It ain't a decision he's held accountable for, not down here, anyway. In a case like that, they go ahead and do the service. I'm glad, for the girl's sake."

"It's all bullshit anyway," Wes spat. "Dead is dead. Period." He pulled to a stop at the corner where the cemetery road met the pavement. "I don't know about you two, but I'm hungry. What do you say, Sarge, you want to eat with us before you go back?"

"Nah, I better not. I've got too much paperwork to catch up on. You better drop me off."

Fifteen minutes later, they eased down the ramp from Main Street into the basement of the Municipal Building, and Burden climbed out of the car on the spot where Ruby shot Oswald. He slammed his door and Wes gunned the car up the opposite ramp onto Commerce Street, where he swung left and merged smoothly with the one-way traffic. He went east on Commerce to Exposition, skirted Fair Park, and went down East Grand to Samuell Boulevard. Charlie looked in the window of a tattoo shop as they passed, at the sample designs on display. A mile or so down Samuell, Wes pulled into Keller's Drive-In, an East Dallas institution: old-fashioned hamburgers, ice cold beer, and some of the last real car hops in America.

"Two hamburgers all the way and a couple of Buds." Wes smiled at the car hop, a cute lady Charlie's age who had worked at Keller's since high school, except for taking time off to get married and have kids. "Oh yeah," he added as an afterthought, "and a waitress to go."

"Sorry, sugar, no carry-outs on the car hops. You gotta eat it here." She grinned and turned away.

44

"Charlie, that little ol' gal has a nice ass on her."

"Cellulite."

"Love handles."

"Do you think that it was a good idea, ordering beer? She knows we're on duty."

"Partner, you worry too much."

She was back already with their drinks. "I thought you boys might want these in Coke cups." She winked.

"Honey," Wes laughed, "you are all right." Wes took a long drink and passed the other cup to Charlie. "There's nothing like a cold beer on a hot day like this."

"Speaking of cold, I can't get over the way Copeland acted at the funeral," Charlie said.

"Don't get me started on that sonofabitch." Wes took another drink. "What galls me is that those two girls have never known anything but cold-blooded men. First Jonas and then Copeland. They deserve better."

"What did the captain do that was so bad?"

"It wasn't so much what he did as what he didn't do. Like me and Birdie were saying back at the cemetery, he just neglected both of them, even when Julia needed him the most, when she was trying to raise Jessica by herself. He always put his job ahead of them."

"Then Copeland's not Jessica's father?"

"Hell no. I don't think he's the type. Jessica was in school when her mother married." Wes laughed wryly. "But who am I to talk? I don't even know where my kid is."

"Are you serious? I didn't even know you had a kid."

"And grandkids, for all the hell I know. My boy oughta be twenty-four or -five now."

Charlie waited until the car hop hooked the tray onto the window sill, took Wes's money and left, then he gazed at Wes. "You never told me you had a son."

"Yeah, by my first wife. I was nineteen."

"What happened?"

"Typical deal. I knocked her up, so I married her, but it didn't last. We broke up, I went off to the Navy, and I never saw much of the boy after that. Only time I heard from his mother was when I was late on the child support."

"Twelve Ten, call your office. Twelve Ten, call your office." It was the radio. It had been sputtering with intermittent traffic all along, but they had learned to ignore everything except their call number.

"Ten Four." Charlie answered and replaced the mike. "Wonder what they want."

"Whatever it is, it can wait until we finish eating."

"You didn't get the boy on weekends?" Charlie couldn't get the idea of Wes as a father out of his mind.

"For a while I did, after I got out of the service. Little bastard had no idea who I was. All he did was cry for momma. And my second wife didn't like kids, so I just kinda gave up on him. She was something else, my second wife. She was a nurse at Parkland. That didn't work out either."

"Wes, I'm sorry about your boy." Charlie was thinking what it would be like to never see Little Bit again.

"Don't aggravate your ulcer over it, Charlie. It's old news now." Wes honked and the car hop came for their tray.

"Y'all come back now, boys."

"You bet," Wes smiled. "How about around the time you get off?"

"That'd be neat, sugar. I'll introduce you to my husband, the big game hunter."

"Think I'll pass."

Wes drove to the fire station at Beacon and East Grand to call in. When he came out of the phone stall, he was grinning and shaking his head.

"What's up, Wes?"

"Another double shift, partner. Our little captain's having a pep talk at three, and he wants us there."

6 | THE SUSPECT

BY THREE O'CLOCK, HOMICIDE WAS FULL OF DE-
tectives and investigators, all of the evening crew and most of
the day shift, who, like Gants and Braverman, had been held
over for a double shift. All the chairs were taken, and cops sat
and leaned on desktops or milled around the coffee pot. The
room buzzed with their razzing and conversations.

"All right," Burden hollered, waving his arms. "All right,
everybody, let's quiet down. Come on people, listen up." The
buzzing of voices slowed and finally stopped. "The captain has
a few things he wants to say."

Captain Sharp strode to the center of the room as if he were
about to sing. He was a nattily dressed young man, the shortest
in the room. He stood ramrod straight as he inspected his
troops. Braverman, leaning against the wall at the back of the
room, craned his neck from side to side, and whispered to
Gants, "Wish somebody'd get the little bastard a box to stand
on."

"Wes, do you have something you'd like to share with the
rest of us?" the captain asked.

"I was just telling everybody back here to quiet down so we
could hear you, captain."

"Thank you, Wes. I appreciate that."

The little captain paced a step or two in each direction, his head bowed as if in prayer, his thumbs hooked in the pockets of his banker's gray, pinstriped vest. He was one of the youngest men in the room, too, and took himself very seriously.

"Men," he started, then remembered the female investigators scattered around the room, "and ladies, you all know why we are here. It's this East Dallas Slasher business. I don't have to tell you that this is a high-profile investigation. Everybody . . . ," he stopped pacing and looked up at them for emphasis, "and I mean everybody, is watching us on this one. The press, the Big Chief, everybody."

The captain paced again, and Gants looked at Braverman, who was rolling his eyes and shaking his head.

"What has made this case so tough to crack is that the victims don't seem to have anything in common, except that they come from poor families in East Dallas and that they have all been killed before two A.M., which is when the bars close. The last one, Estep, was a little character. No telling what he might have been involved in. The first one, Roy Lee Frazier, was an ambitious kid. He had a job and was going to summer school. The other one, Simpson, was still new in town when he turned up dead. As far as we know, he had no particular hangouts and no friends. It looks like our boy, the slasher, picked these kids at random, possibly in or near bars." The little captain planted his feet wide apart, with his hands on his hips. "Now, what I want all of you to do is to put the heat on. I want results, and I want them tonight. Talk to every snitch and character in East Dallas. Call in all your favors, because this is the deal you've been saving them for. Turn East Dallas upside down, and don't quit until we crack this damned case!" His face was flushed and his eyes flickered. "Any questions?"

The roomful of cops responded with a collective groan.

"All right, then. Let's get out there and do it!"

As they filed out, Gants heard the officers around him bitching.

"That little son of a bitch watches way too much television."

"He looks like Wally Cox doing his impression of John Wayne."

"God, he's short."

More disrespect was lavished on Captain Sharp at the city garage, where the evening crew signed out their cars. Braverman led the disparagement with an air of keen delight, while Gants took their car for its second tank of gas for the day. When that was done, he slid out from behind the wheel and Braverman got in. He drove out on to Wood Street and turned right, away from the afternoon sun.

"You don't think a hell of a lot of Captain Sharp, do you?" Gants asked, as they waited for a traffic light to change.

"I don't think much of the way he does things, like wasting our time with a silly-assed pep talk, when we could have been out working on the case. Like we used to say in the navy, I've gargled more salt water than that little fart has sailed on. Everything he knows he read in a book."

Braverman knew East Dallas well. He had worked there as a patrolman before making detective. In the fifteen years he had worked cases, first burglaries and then robberies and killings, he had seen the area go through a number of changes. As he drove, almost every street reminded him of a story.

"That place right there," he said, as they cruised past a shabby, red-brick apartment house where Chicano kids played in the grassless yard, "is where a gaggle of stewardesses used to live before they moved out by Love Field. We had some of the damnedest parties I've ever seen. Right along here and up on Gaston Avenue used to be Party City."

Gants waited in the car while Braverman went inside a little cafe with a handpainted sign in the window that read *BBQ Homestyle.* The owner gave Braverman information from time to time, for reasons of his own. It was a matter of etiquette for Gants to wait outside. Whatever there was between his partner and the man in the cafe, it was personal, and Braverman protected his sources. It would work the other way if Gants called on one of his snitches, if he had any.

Braverman returned to the car in a few minutes. "He's not here. We can check back later."

He drove leisurely north, and then west, along secondary streets, watching everything as he drove toward his next stop.

"Unless you've got a better plan, Charlie, I thought I'd just run my traps, see if any of my people have anything for us."

"Whatever you say."

"We were talking about wives awhile ago. The nurse was the one I probably should have held onto, but we just couldn't get on the same page of the hymnal, if you know what I mean. We both worked odd hours, never wanted to do the same thing at the same time. But, at least, she never tried to get me fired, like my last wife did."

"Wes, how many wives have you had?"

"Just three. When the nurse finally ran me off, I swore I'd never marry again, and I meant it. I was thirty-one years old when the divorce was final, and I partied steady for almost four years after that. I mean, no skirt was safe."

Gants listened to his partner as he watched little frame houses go by. Some of them reminded him of his house when he was a kid, and he decided that this was because their doors and windows were open, so that he could see and hear the people talking and living inside, and the screeching slams of their screen doors as kids went in and out. Here and there, they passed a corner bar and he could see inside, where working men were shooting pool and drinking beer before they went home for supper.

"Then I met a damned old gal and up and married her. She was a stripper."

"A stripper?"

"Yeah. I knew better when I did it, but I got her pregnant, and there I was."

"You say she tried to get you fired?"

"Nearly did, too. She lost the baby not long after we got married, but I still figured I'd give it a try." Braverman's eyes narrowed as he remembered. "Then I caught the slut running around on me, and I lost my cool. The thing is . . . now, Charlie, damned few people know this part of it, so . . ."

"I won't tell anybody."

"Well, the thing was, she was running around on me with another woman!"

"You mean she was gay?"

"That ain't what I call it. Anyway, me and this fat-assed bull dyke of hers got into a free-for-all, and I kicked the living shit out of her. So my darling bride complained on me to the chief, and I got suspended for thirty days. He came close to firing me."

Braverman eased the car over a curb and into the gravel drive of a one-story apartment house with a faded green roof and window-unit air-conditioners.

"And that's why I say there are only three kinds of women: virgins, mothers, and sluts. It's also why I never lose my cool anymore." He shut off the engine but left the keys, so Gants could listen to the radio. "I'll be back in a minute."

Gants watched his partner knock on the door marked "Manager." A heavy-set white woman in her fifties came to the screen door with her phony red hair done up in curlers. She opened the door and invited him in.

Braverman had only been inside with the woman for a few minutes when a patrol officer came on the radio and asked for a Homicide unit to meet him at Buckner Park, a city playground less than a mile away, on Carroll Avenue. Gants honked to signal Braverman, but another team, the one Braverman called the second string, answered. When Braverman heard about the call, he climbed into the car and drove toward the park.

They were still a few blocks away when the other Homicide unit radioed the office: "Twelve Fourteen, the patrol element is en route with a suspect on this cutting. You might notify Nineteen." Nineteen was Captain Sharp.

"That means they think it's the slasher," Braverman said.

"Too early for him," Gants answered.

The uniforms were gone when they pulled into the park. Braverman rolled the car up near the two investigators who were talking to a white man in his early twenties. Paramedics were working on the man's arm and his side.

"Whatcha got, Lane?" Braverman called out.

Lane walked over and leaned on Braverman's door. He was grinning.

"Could be our boy," he said. "Our victim here lives with the man who cut him. They're boy friends."

"Did the cutter use a straight razor?"

"No, he used a box-opener, the kind with a razor blade in it. Victim says his attacker works at a grocery store and he carries the cutter with him everywhere he goes. He also says the man has a very bad temper and stays out all night sometimes."

"Reckon he picks up boys in bars?"

"I wouldn't be surprised. I think he's our man, Wes. That's why I told the office to notify Captain Sharp."

"Well," Wes said, "you know what they say about the blind hog finding an acorn every once in a while."

"Now, Wes don't be sore just because we broke the case of the year. If you behave, we might show you how it's done."

The radio broke in, "Twelve Ten, call your office for a phone message."

"You better get that, Wes," Lane laughed, "it could be one of your famous snitches with a clue."

"Bite me on the ass, call-jumper. It was the patrol unit that caught the sonofabitch."

When Braverman got off the pay phone at the store down the street from the park, he told Gants that it was a snitch, who said he did have a clue. It was early dusk when they walked into a little neighborhood grocery run by a man who had moved to Dallas from the Middle East. He and Braverman disappeared into a back room and left Gants looking at a case of sandwich meat. He asked the woman behind the counter for a Polish sausage on white bread with mustard. She was wrapping it in white butcher paper when Braverman reappeared, headed for the front door.

"Come on, partner, no time to stop and eat now."

Gants gulped down the sandwich as Braverman drove. His empty stomach's nagging gave way to a rumbling protest. He wanted to go home. He wanted a hot bath and a tall glass of Scotch and milk.

"Saj says he had a customer, a Mexican lady, comes in his place every Saturday. He thinks she's an illegal. She told him she saw something. She's scared to death, scared if she talks to us cops we'll send her back to Mexico."

Braverman parked in front of an apartment house that had once been a fine one-family home. Nobody knew how many people lived there now. The two cops walked up the drive past the big house to the servants' quarters in back, and up a rickety flight of stairs to a latched screen door. The wooden door stood open in the warm summer night. Smells of cooking met them as they reached the landing and looked inside. Three small children froze in midstride, their noisy game of tag halted by the sight of the two Anglos in suits and ties. The oldest of the children ran toward the back of the apartment, yelling in Spanish. The other two stood still, their eyes wide and unblinking.

Mrs. Aguero came to the door, drying her hands on her apron. She did not look into the men's faces. She was afraid. Braverman spoke to her in Spanish and she unlatched the screen door, motioning them inside.

Gants sat on the couch beside Braverman as the older man spoke quietly and earnestly, in Spanish, to the frightened woman. Gants guessed that she was fifty. These would be her grandchildren. Their father and mother were not home from work yet. Riding buses and car-pooling to faraway jobs made their work days long. When Braverman had finished talking, Mrs. Aguero sent the oldest child, a girl of perhaps ten with soft dark eyes, down the stairs and across the yard to the big house.

"I think I've convinced her we don't want to send her back." Gants nodded.

"The kid has gone for somebody to stay here until her folks get home. Mrs. Aguero is coming down to the office with us to give us a statement. I want somebody to take it all down that speaks Spanish better than I do. We don't want any misunderstandings."

"What does she know, Wes?"

"Partner, I believe she saw our slasher! She had a cleaning job at a place just down the street from the motel where the Estep boy was killed. She was waiting for a bus the night of the murder. She saw a man leave the murder room a few minutes before the body was found. She says she remembers his face very well. She didn't come forward because she was scared of us. Thing is, she's scared of the killer, too. Thinks he may have seen her there at the bus stop. She quit the cleaning job . . . scared to be out at night. Never leaves this house except to go to the grocery store on Saturday."

"Could she identify him?"

"Says she'll never forget him, had a damned strange look on his face. We'll see what the artist can come up with."

They radioed the office on their way downtown. An officer who was fluent in Spanish and an artist were waiting for them when they arrived. After her statement was typed and signed, Mrs. Aguero went to work with the artist.

It was an old, tired face, with desolate eyes. Gants stomach churned as he watched the face come to life on the pad. The eyes looked at him from the page, and he almost thought he heard a voice calling his name. He had seen enough. He found Braverman in conference with Sergeant Burden and told them: "It's the captain!"

Somebody found a photo of the captain in the files. It was mixed in with a handful of pictures of other men of the same age and general description. When Braverman showed them to Mrs. Aguero, she did not hesitate. It was the captain. They all thanked her profusely and she was sent home in an unmarked car.

Captain Sharp was there. He and Sergeant Burden huddled with Gants and Braverman in his office with the door closed. Outside in the squad room, the interpreter and the artist waited. The receptionist manned the radio, telling the far-flung detectives and investigators, team by team, to call the office. They were told by phone to secure the operation. The day-watch people were sent home. The evening watch went back to work on other cases. Quietly and discreetly, hoping the press would not find out, the investigation of the slasher murders was closed. Lane, the senior man on the unit that had arrested the man in the park who used a box-opener on his lover, knocked on the door of Captain Sharp's office.

"Come in."

"Excuse me, captain. I just wanted to let you know about our suspect. We checked at the store where he works. He has alibis for two of the slasher murders. He was at work those nights, stocking shelves. For the other night, there's only his boy friend, the guy he lives with. They've made up now, and the guy doesn't even want to prosecute. He says our subject was home with him the night of the third slasher murder. I just thought you'd want to know."

"Yes," the Captain waved him away, "thank you." The little captain stood up and paced as best he could in the crowded office. He stood with his back to his men for a long time, then he turned on them and announced, "I have a theory."

Captain Sharp speculated that the old captain had led a secret life. Then, for some reason, he had killed one of his boyfriends. Maybe the kid tried to blackmail him. Maybe the old man's particular aberration was a progressive, sadistic one. He told Gants to check with Sergeant Pomeroy first thing in the morning, to see if that scenario made sense to the shrinks.

Captain Sharp called the duty chief at home and explained the situation. The Slasher Murders were unofficially to be considered closed. Homicide would go back to business as usual. Technically, the murders would be carried as unsolved. No point in telling the press everything, for the good of the department.

7 | THE PSYCHOLOGIST

THE SMELL OF FLOWERS WAS SUFFOCATING, THE sweet fragrance heavy all around him. He opened his eyes and saw only whiteness. They surrounded him, the whiteness and the smell of flowers. Wherever he was, he lay on his back in a small tight place; he could not move. Looking down, he saw his hands folded upon his chest. When he raised his eyes, he saw that a soft light shined down on him from a recess in the ceiling. It was a pale spotlight. A murmuring of voices, an opening door. Somewhere someone, a man, coughed quietly. An organ played softly, unseen, and Charlie heard muted sounds of movement, footsteps on carpet.

Captain Sharp's face appeared above him, cool and uninterested. Then Sergeant Burden, who was crying. Burden said, "He was such a young man. How could he do a thing like this? He had a little girl, too. Didn't he think about that?" The sad sergeant shook his head slowly, his eyes closed. He bowed his head and his lips moved silently. Then he and Captain Sharp moved on. Julia Copeland wore the same black dress, but not the veil. Her face was lovely but cold. As she looked down at him with passionless eyes, he felt a chill. She moved on.

Another face appeared above him. At first, he thought Julia

had returned, but this was a younger, warmer face. Jessica. She shook her head sadly and breathed a heavy sigh. With her fingers at her lips, she seemed to choke back a tear, and then she was gone.

In a slow parade, faces came and went above him. There were other detectives from Homicide. Then he saw a few cousins, aunts, and uncles. Some of his uncles' faces were red and sunburned up to the lines that ran across their foreheads where their straw hats protected them. They were country men who worked outdoors, dressed up now in suits they only wore to funerals. They did not understand, either. Charlie heard two of them talking:

"He'd oughta stayed at home."

"Damned straight. Don't know what he expected to find out over here in Dallas anyhow."

"Read too many of them books, I reckon."

"Damned straight. This'll kill poor Janie."

Janie was his mother, who had lost his father within the last year.

His ex-wife was next. She had been crying, and a man Charlie did not know stood close beside her, holding her. The man was about Charlie's age, with a banker's haircut and a three-piece suit. Charlie's ex-wife leaned on the man, who did not look down at Charlie. He looked at Charlie's ex-wife, and his little watery eyes blinked behind his rimless glasses. She bent down. When she stood up straight again, Elizabeth was in her arms.

"Hi, Little Bit. How's my girl?"

Elizabeth did not hear him. She hugged her mother and looked down at him, her lips trembling. She was about to cry.

"Mommy, is Daddy Charlie sleeping?"

Charlie's ex-wife sobbed aloud, which made Elizabeth cry, too. The man in the rimless glasses led them both away. Elizabeth looked over her mother's shoulder at Charlie.

Wes came next, with Samantha Cartwright beside him. Her eyes were moist.

"I only met him the other day, but he seemed like such an interesting man. There was something about him. He had a kind of haunted look. If only he had talked to me . . . if he had told me what was going on behind those sad eyes, I might have helped him. Oh, Wes . . ."

She laid her head on Wes' shoulder, and his big hand held her to him.

"There's always a lot of 'ifs' when something like this happens. Whatever was bothering him, if only he had told me about it. I was his partner, he could have told me. There was no need for this, no need to take his own life."

Samantha cried and Wes comforted her.

"Wes, what the hell are you talking about? Wes, I'm not even dead!" Charlie screamed the last part. He screamed and screamed, and his voice rattled and echoed through the room over the low background of endless, sickening organ music, but no one heard him. Sam looked at Charlie one last time, and Wes led her away.

Then no one came for a while. Charlie screamed again, and tried to sit up, but he could not move at all for some reason. He closed his eyes and tried to shake himself awake, but he could not. When he opened his eyes again, he was still in the tight box. And there was another face above him.

It was a ruined face that had begun to decompose. The flesh of its lips was drawn back from the teeth into a sardonic smile. With one hand the old corpse described the stations of the Cross on his hollow chest. The shriveled dark sockets, where his eyeballs had been before they rotted away, looked down on Charlie, and the right one gave him a knowing wink. His dead smile broadened, and the shrunken old head reared back in a silent laugh as the coffin lid slowly closed on the screaming man.

Samantha Cartwright was early to work the next morning, and she found Charlie Gants waiting for her.

"Good morning."

"Good morning, Ms. Cartwright. I'm Charlie Gants. I was here yesterday about the Slasher case."

"Yes, of course. I'm afraid I don't have anything for you yet. I told you it might take a few days."

"That's all right. That's not why I'm here. We've had some developments I need to talk to you about."

"Fine. Come in and make yourself at home." She showed him into her office, stopping to check her mail.

"Charlie, would you like some coffee?"

"Yes, that sounds good."

"How do you like it?"

"With cream and sugar, if you have it."

"Just give me a minute."

While she was gone, Charlie looked over her office. What does this room tell me about the person who works here? There were no diplomas or certificates on the wall, which surprised him a little. Just a cute kitten picture and a framed poster that announced a long-past performance of the Dallas Ballet. He thought about asking her to the ballet. While he was thinking about that, she returned with a cup of coffee in each hand.

He stole a look at her over his steaming cup, and thought that she looked bright and alive and sane, and he was glad that he was not dreaming. Would he ever sleep soundly again? She looked the same as she had the day before, the way he had remembered her.

"Charlie, how long have you been in Homicide?"

"A couple of years. Eighteen months, actually."

"Do you like it?"

"Do I like murder, you mean?" He smiled and she laughed softly, but said nothing. She drank her coffee and waited, letting the silence grow. This is not what I came here for, he told himself. But she was listening, her eyes blue and determined.

"At first, I liked catching the killers. It's not always like it is in books, naturally. In fact, I don't think it's ever the way it is in some books: all the suspects standing around in one room while the detective explains how he solved the mystery. It's never like that. A lot of the time, the killer is already in jail. Either the uniforms who get the call arrest him, or else a patrol officer catches him driving the dead man's car. You'd be surprised how undramatic a lot of murder arrests are; just a matter of changing the paperwork on somebody who's already in jail. Patrol officers probably solve more murders than we do."

"Yes, but you do work on the hard cases, where the murderer isn't known."

"I guess I'm not the first detective you've talked to." He drank his coffee, deciding whether to go on. "When I started out, I felt like . . . I don't know, an agent of justice, you know? It sounds silly, but it was like in some of the old movies, where murder outs. There was symmetry. In those old movies, the killer never got away. One way or another, things balanced out in the end, like in *The Postman Always Rings Twice,* and *Double Indemnity."*

"Is James Cain your favorite?"

"Have you read him?"

"Of course."

"You're the only other one."

"And Dashiel Hammett and Raymond Chandler."

"No wonder you came to work for the Police Department. I hope you haven't been disappointed."

"Not yet." She smiled in a way that might or might not have meant something. "You said you liked the symmetry."

"Yes, the sense of balance."

"How do you feel now?"

"That that was an illusion. Now I just like the process, solving the puzzle. The justice part . . . I don't know any more. It doesn't always make sense. We feed killers into the system, and it's like a game show sometimes. Unless there is a lot of press, a lot of heat, anything might happen. Plea-bargaining. I don't know."

"How do you feel about capital punishment?"

"I guess it's Biblical, isn't it? 'An eye for an eye.' But it's not that simple. Money is the key there, just like in everything else. We don't execute the guilty, just the guilty poor. And sometimes they're only guilty of not being able to afford good lawyers."

"And the black?"

"The poor. Poor is the main thing. Not being white is part of being poor. I understand that. But race by itself isn't the factor. A lot of white men have been executed in Texas, but damned few rich ones."

Her face showed real interest and she listened carefully, occasionally sipping her coffee as he talked. Charlie reminded himself that listening was her job. He stopped talking and drank his own coffee. These were things he had never talked about with anyone except Wes, who did not think much of them. Wes saw the same senselessness, but he was not offended by it, because he did not expect anything more. Wes took things as they came and concentrated on controlling the things he could.

"What is the worst part of it, Charlie?"

The way she said his name unsettled him. It made him too comfortable with her. But he answered her, telling her things that he had never even told Wes. Some of the things he told her were only notions he had wrestled with privately, but he found words for them as he talked.

"If it's a kid, the victim is the worst part, always. Nobody gets used to that. More than the overall senselessness, the cheap harm, it's violence done to a child. That is *the* worst part. Other than that, sometimes it's not the victim, it's the ones who are left alive and damaged. Sometimes it's even the killer. Most people don't live in a vacuum, alone in the world." He saw in his mind the ravaged old face, winking at him. "Murder is not an attack on an individual. It assaults a whole network, the little universe the victim was part of. And the aftermath destroys the killer. I still believe that, I guess. Killers don't live in vacuums, either." He remembered the captain's room, its musty smell and closeness.

"How do you cope with that?"

"I don't." That slipped out. Too nonchalantly, he added with a nervous laugh, "But I'm working on it."

"What about your personal life, Charlie, your 'little universe'?"

"My father died last February. My mother still lives in the house where I grew up, in Sulphur Springs over in East Texas. She's in good health, and I see her whenever I can get away. I'm divorced."

"Do you have kids?"

"Elizabeth." He smiled. "She's my little girl. This was taken just a few weeks ago." He showed her the studio photograph he kept in his badge case, behind his I.D. Bit was sitting on his lap in that picture. She was a radiant child, and he was proud of her.

"She's lovely, Charlie."

"I call her Bit for short."

"She lives with her mother?"

"Yes."

"Do you see her often?"

"First and third weekends. Sundays and Mondays, actually my days off. She's not in school yet."

"How are you handling the divorce?"

"It's okay now. It's been just over a year. My ex and I had some problems at first, but lately she's seemed calmer, and more reasonable." He remembered the man in the three-piece suit at his funeral, the man on whom his ex-wife leaned. "Maybe she's found somebody else."

"That would be progress, or do you want her back?"

"No. I hope she has found somebody, a square nine-to-fiver who comes home for lunch. That's what she wants, and I'd like her to be happy."

They sat without talking for a few minutes. Other people were coming into the office ready to go to work.

"Charlie, why do you answer all of my questions?"

He did not answer.

"Why don't you tell me it's none of my business? A lot of cops do. I think they're afraid I may have a hidden tape recorder or something. They seem afraid to discuss their feelings. Maybe they're afraid I'll tell the Big Chief or something, and they'll get in trouble. Why aren't you afraid, Charlie?"

"Marginal burnout. I'm getting to the point where I don't care any more. That's part of it. You're easy to talk to, and I need to talk to somebody once in a while. I think too much, and that isn't good."

"I think I understand."

Charlie wondered what she thought of him. He wondered if he should tell her about his dreams. He noticed he was drumming his fingertips on her desk in tune with part of the *Rhapsody*.

"Charlie, is there anything else you'd like to ask me?"

"Yes."

She laughed. "What? You can ask me anything."

So he asked her what he had been sent to ask her, none of the things he wondered about now.

"It's about the Slasher killings, and it's supposed to be top secret." He closed her office door. "Last night we found a witness, a woman who saw a man leaving the scene of the last slashing a few minutes before the body was found. And she identified Captain Jonas as the man."

"A police captain?"

"Retired. He was found shot to death that same night. It looked like a suicide."

She leaned forward in her chair and shook her head, but said nothing.

"Captain Sharp, my captain, has a theory about it. He thinks maybe Captain Jonas was living some kind of secret life. For whatever reason, he killed the three boys over a period of time. The guilt was too much for him, so he killed himself."

"That's quite a story."

"I know, but it would explain everything. Why else was he at the murder scene that night? Why else would he commit suicide?"

She fished a pack of Nat Sherman cigarettes out of her big, cluttered purse. Charlie lit a cigarette for her and accepted the one she offered him. She was not a dilettante smoker, a puffer. She drew the smoke in deeply and held it, then exhaled a long thin stream of gray mist. When Charlie inhaled, he choked and coughed.

"They're a little strong, Charlie. All tobacco."

He reddened and coughed some more. Probably can outdrink me, too, he thought.

"Captain Sharp's theory makes sense to me," she said. "At least, there is nothing I know of that would eliminate it as a possibility. Did you know Captain Jonas? What kind of man was he?"

"I only knew him by reputation. He was a devoutly religious man, with no real vices. He never showed an interest in women after his wife died in childbirth. He was fanatically devoted to his job. He finally had to retire because of his age. They tell me he was hard-nosed, with a strong sense of right and wrong, of justice."

"And guilt. It sounds like he might be the least or the most likely to do what Captain Sharp thinks he did. Least likely if his feelings were genuine, most likely if they were just defenses against the other side of himself that he tried to suppress. Interesting. What do you think?"

He looked away from her clear eyes, down at the smoldering brown, all-tobacco cigarette.

"I don't know."

She seemed lost in thought, and Charlie studied her. He saw lace under her white blouse, but the contours of her breasts were absolutely natural and exquisite. He remembered that his fantasy lover always wore a chemise. And stockings, not panty hose.

She faced him again, then scribbled notes on a pad. "I'd like to go over this with someone, a psychiatrist, and see what he thinks. But you tell Captain Sharp that, as far as I'm concerned, his theory sounds plausible." She seemed to sense there was more. "Was there anything else you wanted to tell me, Charlie? Or ask me?"

"Why do you say my name after almost every sentence? That's a trick of my trade, to throw a person off his guard. Is it a trick of your trade, too?"

"Your name is just a favorite of mine. I like the sound of it."

"So your answer is yes."

"You're an interesting man, Charlie. Let's talk again sometime."

"I'd like that."

8 | THE PRESS LEAK

SERGEANT BURDEN LOOKED UP FROM THE REPORTS on his desk when Gants walked in.

"Well?"

"She seemed to think Captain Sharp's theory makes sense. Said she couldn't eliminate it. She's going to run it by a psychiatrist friend of hers to see what he thinks."

"I thought she was a psychiatrist."

"No. She's a psychologist."

"What's the difference?"

"Basically, her friend can prescribe medicine and commit people, and she can't."

"A shrink is a shrink, that's what I always thought. Wes said to tell you he'll be right back. I think he went to check out a car. I'd better tell Captain Sharp what the shrink said."

"You know, Sarge, I've noticed something. You always call him Captain Sharp, never just captain. Is that because when you say 'the captain' you mean Captain Jonas? Kinda like he was the only *real* captain?"

"By golly, I never noticed that. I guess you're right, though. Old habits are hard to break. I worked for him for a long time, and I'll tell you one thing: they don't make 'em like that old man any more."

Braverman walked in, smiling. "Partner, let's get out there and fight some crime. You're not gonna catch any crooks hanging around our beloved sergeant here." If he noticed that Burden was upset, he did not let on.

"Yeah, you guys go solve a crime," Burden said. "I gotta talk to Captain Sharp."

"Come on, Charlie. I've got us a clean car laid up down on the lot. Let's get out of here before that nice attendant gives us a ticket for violating the five-minute zone, or whatever the hell it is."

While they waited for the elevator, Gants opened his accordion file, which bulged with offense reports and supplement forms.

"Where do you want to start, Wes? The pool hall shooting over a three-dollar bet, or the husband who shot his wife because she wouldn't let him watch Monday Night Football?"

"Why don't we decide that over breakfast at the Farmer's Grill, Charlie? I can't face all that suffering on an empty stomach."

"Hold on a minute, I've got something for y'all." Burden caught them as the door opened. "A cutting call out on Columbia. The victim is the right age for it to be the slasher deal."

"Hell, Birdie, I thought that case was closed."

"Captain Sharp wants us to check out any cuttings with victims who fit the profile, just in case."

"Terrific."

They went east on Main Street past garages, warehouses, and used-car lots. As they neared Carroll, where Main doglegged to the north and became Columbia, they passed a number of bars that were boarded up. Some of them had been closed and later reopened with Spanish names. They were patronized by many of the thousands of illegal immigrants who had settled in Dallas. There were so many that the cops did not bother to arrest them any more.

Braverman parked behind the ambulance and the squad car at the curb in front of a little house with aluminum siding and a flower bed. As the officers went up the sidewalk to the house, they met a paramedic coming out.

"Hell of a deal," the paramedic said, with a grin that curled the end of his drooping mustache.

Inside, in the living room, they found two uniformed officers and a young man standing in the middle of the room, with his legs spread apart and a pained look on his face. The man's even-younger wife sat angrily upon a littered couch, her fists on her knees.

Braverman knew the older patrolman. "John, what's the deal?"

"Just a light-running little spat, Wes. His girl friend called here, and his wife answered the phone . . . ."

"She's not my girlfriend!"

"Shut up, boy. I'm telling this. Anyway, they had words and the wife went out to the kitchen and got a butcher knife. Husband did the smart thing and hauled ass. Only he didn't haul it fast enough. She sliced it for him as he went out the door. He went next door and called an ambulance. Paramedics called us. He doesn't want to press any charges."

"Ma'am, is that true?" Braverman asked in mock amazement.

"Next time the bitch calls over here, it'll be his balls!"

"That sounds fair," Wes nodded solemnly. "John, you don't need us. I'll see you later."

"The course of true love," Gants said, on the way to the car. "How about stopping at the 7-Eleven up there at Carroll and Columbia, so I can pick up a bottle of Maalox."

"Your stomach eating you up again?"

"No, Wes, I've just developed a taste for the stuff."

"Partner, I swear you are just about the youngest ulcer farm I have ever seen. When I was your age, all I worried about was pretty women and fast cars. What in the world have you found to get ulcers over?"

"I don't have an ulcer, Wes. And you're not that much older than I am. I just happen to have a nervous stomach."

"Bullshit. I know what your problem is. You carry the weight of the world around on your shoulders, or in your gut. If a waitress tells you her old man ain't paying his child support, you get depressed over it for a week."

Braverman stopped the car with a jerk in front of the 7-Eleven, and Gants went inside. He came out with the bottle already half-empty. He leaned in the car.

"Wes, you want me to call Sergeant Burden and tell him about the cutting call?"

"Nah, we might as well go on in and tell him in person. I'm gonna have to pick up another car anyway. I've put all of twelve miles on this one and the brakes are grabbing like hell. That's par for the course."

Braverman drove slowly on his way back downtown, but he was not through with Charlie, yet.

"I'm telling you, man, learn from the old master here. Observe and grow wise. Don't worry about anything you can't control. There's no point in it. I'll grant you we've got a screwed-up job. We always see people at their worst, and we go around cleaning up after them. People are crazy, and the world's all screwed up. Big deal! You can't change that, so don't, there's no point in worrying about it. Just worry about the things you can control, like making your brakes work, and staying out of the chief's office. Let the rest of it slide. All this crap was here before we came along, and it'll be here long after we're gone. None of it's worth getting an ulcer over."

"Wes, I really don't have an ulcer. And you know, you're right about not taking the job seriously. Look at Captain Jonas."

"What's he got to do with anything?"

"Well, everybody says the job was his whole life. When he lost that, he lost everything."

"Have you been talking to Birdie about the captain?"

"Not really. I just told him what Sam . . . the shrink, said, and the subject naturally came up."

"Who's Sam?"

"Samantha Cartwright. She's a consultant with the shrink shop."

"Yeah? What does she look like?"

"She's all right, but she's not your type."

"Why not?"

"She's kind of highbrow, Wes. Thinks Waylon Jennings was vice president under Hoover."

"No!"

"I'm serious. Wouldn't know a cotton-eyed joe from a water moccasin."

"Gawd. Sounds like somebody you'd take to one of those fag square dances."

"You mean the ballet?"

"Anyway, what did she say?"

"She said Captain Sharp's theory about Jonas being the Slasher sounded 'plausible' to her. She's going to check around and get back to us."

"Old F Sharp ought to be good with theories about crap like that. He's some kind of head case hisself."

"What do you think, Wes? Do you buy his theory?"

"Charlie, you were there when Mrs. Aguero picked out his picture. You saw the artist's sketch."

"She could have been mistaken. Besides, she didn't actually see him do anything. If he was there, maybe he had a reason. Maybe he was working on the Slasher case on his own."

"Then why did he kill himself?"

"That's another thing. A man with his religious beliefs . . . ."

"Goddamnit, Charlie, why are you so hung up on that old man? Why not just let him lay?"

"Look, Wes, I understand you were friends. If you don't want . . ."

"Friend's ass! I don't honestly think that old man knew what a friend was. And as far as him being a religious man, I don't know about that, either. I don't claim to know a damned thing about religion, but I say he carried it beyond all reason. He acted like he thought him and God had a direct line or something. He always knew what was right and wrong, and there was no two ways about it. I've heard him talk about retribution and God's Justice and all that crap, like he thought it was all up to him. Maybe that's how you get if you take this job too serious. You ought to bear that in mind, Charlie."

Burden was on the phone when Gants and Braverman walked into his office.

"Okay, honey, I gotta go. Somebody just walked into my office. I'll see you later. Yeah, I'll take care of it when I get home. Just make sure the kids use the one in our room. Okay.

Me too. Bye-bye." He hung up and looked at them. "Kids. Why does anybody want kids?"

"What did they do now, Sarge?" Braverman asked.

"It's the grandkids this time, my oldest daughter's twins. Margie's not sure what, but they tried to flush down something big, and now the toilet's stopped up. She said water's all over the place."

"Did you tell her to take a head count and make sure none of the kids is missing?"

"All of them are accounted for, but she can't find the cat."

Braverman laughed. "Really makes you miss married life, don't it Charlie?"

Oddly enough, it did.

"Enough about my home life. How about your cutting?"

"Nothing to it, Sarge. Just a lover's quarrel. I could use a cup of coffee. Y'all want any?"

Both men shook their head, as Braverman walked toward the coffee urn.

"You know, Sergeant Burden," Charlie began, "I've been thinking about what you said. 'They don't make 'em like Captain Jonas any more'."

"That's right, by God. They don't."

"Does that mean you don't believe Captain Sharp's theory?"

"No disrespect to Captain Sharp, but his theory is a bunch of bullshit. Man, I tell you what! Some wetback washwoman pops up out of nowhere with a story like that and bang, they're all ready to write off a man like the captain as some kind of perverted mad dog. Bullshit!"

"Do you think she was lying?"

"She didn't have to be. We see eyewitnesses all the time up here. You know most of them are worthless. Two of them see the same killing, and one of them describes a jockey, and the other says it was a linebacker. Happens all the time."

"Do you think he killed himself?"

"You were there, Charlie. What else can I think? I was on the phone with his priest the night we were up in his room, and even the priest was shocked. Did you ever wonder why Cap Jonas lived in that little room? On a captain's pension with forty years? Because most of the money went to the Church, that's why."

"As a matter of fact, I had wondered about that."

"But there's things nobody knows, Charlie, things a man keeps inside. Maybe I should have gone to see him more often, you know? I should have made time to go see him. I thought I was too busy a lot of times. Now it's too late." Burden stared at the blotter on his desk as he thumped a pencil against it. "This job was all he had. I've seen it before. He just didn't feel like he had anything to live for, I guess. I don't know. It wasn't his health. He was still in great shape for a man his age. Better shape than me. Never owned a pair of glasses in his life. Never took a drink or smoked a cigarette. I just wish I had gone to see him more, that's all."

Braverman returned with his coffee, and heard the last of this. "Sounds like y'all are talking about Jonas. Charlie, you are really fanatic about it, aren't you? And I guess Birdie here told you what a saint he was."

"I told him they don't make 'em like that any more."

"I'll go along with you there." Braverman took a seat, and his voice was pleasant, not challenging. "Birdie, you were the captain's right-hand man. He liked you. I just think you have a kind of rosy picture of him. Take his reputation, for example. Jonas of Homicide, right? Charlie, do you know how long Jonas actually worked in Homicide?"

"Twenty or thirty years?"

"How long was it, Birdie, about five?"

"About that."

"The only legend we ever had in this office was Captain Frederick, the man Jonas replaced. He took over Homicide back in the thirties, when we had bootleggers and gangsters, when times were really hard. Jonas worked all over CID, and he had a few stories told about him, but he wasn't no legend, by any means."

"He was a good, old-fashioned cop," Burden protested.

"Which means he came up back when there weren't so many rules, and the police could get away with a lot more than we can now. Jonas had a lot of people buffaloed around here, all right, and some of them were chiefs. A lot of it was just because he had been around so long." Braverman eyed Gants hard, and leaned in close to him. "Why are you so geared up about the old man, Charlie? Are you holding out on us?"

"What do you mean?" Gants thought about the dreams, but he knew he could not tell them that.

"I mean do you know something we don't know? If you've got something, spill it. Tell us if you've come up with something, and we'll reopen the whole damned case. Right, Sarge?"

"Damned right. What about it, Charlie?"

"Really, I don't know anything. I was just curious, that's all."

"Well, why don't we . . ." Burden was interrupted by someone opening the door to his office. The look on his face caused the other two men to turn around.

"Cecil Burden, I want a word with you." It was Julia Copeland who looked beautiful, wealthy, and very angry.

"Julia, come in," Burden said, rising from his chair.

"I want to know exactly what is going on here."

"I don't understand."

"I don't believe you. I thought you were my father's friend and mine. How could you?"

Gants and Braverman excused themselves.

"Julia, you're upset," Burden said. "Let me shut the door and we can talk in private."

"Don't be ridiculous. It's going to be in the evening paper, on television, everywhere. There is no point in pretending to be discreet now."

"We must be leaving, Julia. Come on Charlie," Wes said, as he and Charlie escaped, closing the door behind them. They could hear what she was calling the poor sergeant even with the door closed.

"Wes, what is she mad about?"

"I don't know, but I wouldn't be in Birdie's shoes right now for anything." Braverman said something about going to check out another car and left.

After several minutes, Burden's door opened and Julia stormed out. Gants saw Burden on the phone, his face flushed and damp. Without knowing what he would say to her, Gants followed Julia out of the office and overtook her in the hallway.

"Mrs. Copeland?"

"Yes, what is it." She did not break stride as she continued toward the elevators.

"I . . . I'd like very much to talk to you about your father. I think it's important."

She stopped and wheeled to face him.

"Who are you?"

"Charlie Gants. I'm Wes Braverman's partner."

"Yes. You were at the funeral."

"That's right."

"What do you know about my father?"

"Mrs. Copeland, I'd really rather not discuss it here."

She eyed him suspiciously for a moment.

"Very well, I will see you tomorrow evening at five o'clock. But, I must warn you, Mr. Gants, I'm in no mood for a lot of nonsense. I've been through a lot in the past few days and my patience is growing very thin."

"I understand. Five o'clock."

"You have my address?"

"I'll find it. Thank you."

She turned and walked away.

"Goodbye, Mrs. Copeland."

She did not answer. As the elevator door closed, she fixed him with a steady gaze, and the familiar chill shot through him.

It made page one of the evening *Times Herald,* and it was the lead story on the six o'clock local news. Someone had leaked it. The headline read: Slasher Named. The story was basically Sharp's theory, and it ended on page seven with a disclaimer by a "police spokesman," who insisted that the Slasher case was still open.

9 | THE COPELAND MANSION

THIS MONTH CHARLIE AND WES WERE SUPPOSED TO be working the evening shift—three to eleven. They had worked those hours until the captain's death. After that, they had come in early so often and stayed late so many times that Charlie was not sure any more what shift they were on. The day after the story about the captain broke, they were ordered in early again. Everybody involved in the case was ordered in early, and every one of them had to write a special report, a "Dear Chief," about the case, setting out what he knew, how he knew it, and anybody he had told about it. Captain Sharp was trying to find the leak, but Charlie knew it was a lost cause. There were just too many people involved. When all reports were typed and signed, Charlie asked Burden if he could take off in time to take care of a personal matter at five o'clock. Burden understood. He did not want to be around the office today either.

His old VW squeaked to a halt in the driveway of the Copeland mansion. It was a circular drive, and Charlie looked back the way he had come, a hundred yards back from the street and the wooded lot beyond. The house itself sprawled in either direction and towered above him like a fine hotel. Charlie had known or imagined that there were houses like this, but he had never been in one. As he mounted the steps to the porch, he thought about the Estep and Aguero kids. They could romp and play to their heart's content in one wing of this place and hardly be noticed.

As he stepped onto the porch, the door opened, and he was met by the most beautiful woman he had ever seen. It was Jessica Copeland, just as he had envisioned her. Her dark eyes and long black hair were stunning.

"Are you a reporter?"

"No. I'm a policeman. My name is Gants. Mrs. Copeland is expecting me."

"Show me your badge, please."

He did.

"I'm Jessica Copeland. How do you do?"

"Fine, thank you."

"Please come in."

He suddenly felt scruffy in his wrinkled shirt. His jacket was wrinkled, too. He had left it on the floor overnight again. His car had no air-conditioning, and sweat streamed down the small of his back. When he straightened his tie, the back of his hand brushed his bristly chin.

"You were at grandfather's funeral, weren't you?"

"Yes."

She showed him down a long hall lined with framed photographs. He finally realized that she was the girl in all of the pictures. Some were magazine covers. She noticed that he was studying them.

"I model."

"They're very nice."

"Thank you. You seem very uncomfortable. Can I get you anything?"

"No, I'm fine. I've just never seen anything like this house. And you are very beautiful."

"You're sweet." She stopped at the end of the hall. "Mother is in the green room. Through the arch and bear to your right."

"Thank you."

She turned to leave, but hesitated, then turned back to him and almost whispered, "Are you here about grandfather?"

"Yes, in a way."

"Did you know him?"

"No, but I've heard a lot about him."

"Everyone has by now. The reporters hounded us all night."

"I'm very sorry about that. I had nothing to do with it, I promise you."

"It was suicide, wasn't it?"

"That's the ruling."

"Well, it was, wasn't it? I mean, you haven't turned up any new evidence, have you?"

"No. No evidence."

"Oh. Well, through the arch and bear right."

"Thank you."

"Good-by."

The room was easy to find. Before going in, Charlie stopped to look out a window at the grounds. He saw an enormous flower garden. Beyond that there was a swimming pool shimmering in the late evening sun, deserted. Beyond that, two tennis courts. Still farther away, he could see servants' quarters, two cottages twice as big as the house he had grown up in.

Inside the green room he stopped a few steps beyond the threshold. The roof was a huge skylight, and lush exotic plants filled the room from wall to wall and from floor to ceiling. Sunlight filtered through the foliage, casting everything in a patchwork of light and shadow. It was a jungle in miniature.

Julia appeared in a patch of light. Her hair, long and black like her daughter's, was done up, and she was dressed in a gold lamé evening gown that smoldered in the jungle sunlight. The effect was striking.

"You wanted to see me about my father?"

"Yes." He was not sure where to begin.

"I understood until yesterday that the case was closed. Now the reporters tell me that the police believe my father was a murderer and a pervert. What do you have to tell me?"

"I don't think he committed suicide."

"That was difficult for all of us to accept. What evidence have you uncovered?"

The distance between them seemed a chasm. He had imagined that he would sit beside her on a divan. He imagined comforting her, talking to her personally, unofficially, about her father. She was unapproachable.

"I don't have any hard evidence yet. To tell you the truth, Mrs. Copeland, all I have is a feeling."

"Did you know him?"

"No ma'am. I guess I might as well just tell you. I know this will sound strange, but I have had dreams."

"Did you say dreams?"

"Yes ma'am. Two of them. There's no point in going into the details. I've never believed in that sort of thing, but I think your father is trying to communicate with me. I feel as if he is trying to tell me that he was murdered."

Even as he spoke his words sounded to him to be those of a lunatic. What must she think, he wondered.

"And is that what you wanted to tell me?"

"Yes." He had not known what to expect, but her coolness surprised him.

"Then I must ask you to leave."

"But . . . ," He started when a man appeared noiselessly at his side. Charlie recognized him as Edmund Copeland's chauffeur.

"Have you discussed your . . . intuitions with your superiors, Officer Gants?"

"No ma'am. You're the only one I've told."

"Then I suggest that you do discuss the matter with them. James will show you out."

She melted into the shadows.

His phone was ringing when he walked into his apartment. It was Burden: "I'm at the office, Charlie. Get your ass down here right now!"

Burden led him into the empty captain's office and closed the door.

"Sit down, Charlie." Burden was more nervous than Charlie had ever seen him. "Charlie, my phone was ringing by the time I got home this evening. It was Captain Sharp. He had just got off the phone with the Big Chief himself, who had just got off the phone with a city councilman who had just got off the phone with God only knows who, although my guess would be Edmund Copeland. Now, can you imagine what all those people were talking about? I'd like you to tell me."

Charlie waited silently.

"They were talking about you, Charlie. You and me. Do you know the Golden Rule, the rule I live by, the rule I have lived by every day of my twenty-six years in the department? 'Keep your name out of the papers and your ass out of the Chief's office.' In other words, don't rock the boat. Keep a low profile! The only time I want a chief, any chief, to know my name is when he shakes my hand at my retirement party. That's coming up in a few years, Charlie, if my kid ever graduates and finds a job, and I don't want to start drawing any heat this late in the game. Do you understand?"

"Yes, sir."

"Good. Now why don't you tell me your side?"

"My side of what, Sarge?"

"Okay. Okay, Charlie, I won't hold that against you. I know you're not trying to be cute. 'Never cop out to anything' is a good rule, too. I understand that. Let's approach this from another angle. Let's just say it involves Julia Copeland. Okay?"

"Yes, sir."

"Julia was supposed to attend an important committee meeting this evening at six. Something about fine art and charity, stuff like that. Important stuff, Charlie. She got all dressed up and everything. Did you know she had a meeting at six?"

"No, sir."

"Well, she didn't make it Charlie. They had to start without her. Do you know why?"

"No, sir."

"Well, according to our captain, who got it from the Big Chief, who got it from some city councilman, who got it from God knows where, she didn't make it because she was hysterical! Do you know why she was hysterical, Charlie?"

"No, sir."

"According to her, she was hysterical because a member of the Dallas Police Department, a member who happens to work for me, showed up at her house this evening and told her he was in communication with her dead daddy. Seems this fellow who happens to work for me has been talking to her daddy in his dreams." The sergeant ran a wadded handkerchief across his face. "Now, Charlie, here's the thing: this guy who went out there and told her all this crap used your name. Follow me? He told her he was Officer Gants. What I want you to do is to tell me where you really were around five, so I can call Captain Sharp and tell him that guy was impersonating an officer."

"It was I, Sarge."

"What the goddam hell do you mean, 'It was I'? Can't you even talk right, goddamnit?"

"It was me."

"Oh, Jesus. Sweet, sweet Jesus."

"Look, Sarge, I realize I may have been out of line, going out there. And I understand how all this business about the dreams must sound to people. I used bad judgment. But I did it on my own time. Nobody can blame you. You're not expected to supervise me twenty-four hours a day, are you?"

"Man, you just don't appreciate the situation. When these people make these kinds of calls, nobody is safe. Do you have any idea how many lawyers a guy like Edmund Copeland keeps on his payroll just for deals like this?"

"I'm sorry."

"Well, hell, that covers it. What am I worried about? When I finally get home tonight and tell my wife and my lard-assed boy I'm not a sergeant any more, they won't mind because I'll explain to them that you said you were sorry." Someone knocked on the door and Burden screamed at them to go away. "Charlie, do you have any teeny-weeny scrap of evidence, anything at all, no matter how small, that a sane man would take seriously, that I don't know about? You know there's nobody in the department that would like to clear the old man more than I would."

"No, sir."

"Just dreams?"

"Yes, sir."

"Wait outside."

Burden called him back after ten minutes.

"I'm not sure I understand any of this, Charlie. I'm not sure I understand it at all."

"What?"

"I talked to Captain Sharp and so on up the line. Then right back down the line, and he just called me back."

"And?"

"And . . . you still work here. And, I'm still a sergeant."

"That's good. I'm glad."

"You're glad? You just stumbled through the Valley of the Shadow of Death, dragging me along behind you blindfolded, and all you can say is 'I'm glad'?"

"I'm real glad."

"Okay, okay. Two things: first, you are overworked, you're punchy, and you probably have an ulcer. Right?"

"Whatever you say, Sarge."

"Right. So what you're going to do is take some time off. The City owes you for the overtime you've been putting in. It's on the books. You take some time off and rest up. Don't come back until I call you. That's important. Do you understand? Don't come back until I call you. Right?"

"Right."

"Off the record, I will say this to you: you have been to the Shrink Shop a couple of times lately, so you should know your way around over there. Personally, I think it might be a good idea for you to pay them a little visit. Just as long as you don't come around here. Don't come back here . . ."

"Until you call me."

"Not for anything. I'll mail you your paycheck."

"Yes, sir. Do you want my badge and gun or anything?"

"No, Charlie, you haven't been suspended. You're just taking a little comp time, that's all. No disciplinary action, nothing on your record, understand?"

"I'm not sure."

"Me neither. Just get the hell out of here before the phone rings again."

"Yes, sir. Sarge?"

"Yeah?"

"I am sorry about getting you in trouble. And I appreciate whatever you did for me."

"Get out of here. And don't come back . . ."

"I know, I know."

10 | THE CLIENT

    CHARLIE LAY BETWEEN SLEEP AND WAKEFULNESS until the midmorning sunlight walked across the room and edged up onto his bed. The lighted digits on the little clock radio read 9:52. He stretched himself awake and rolled over to sit on the edge of the bed. For the first time in the three days since the captain died, he had slept without dreaming. He had lain awake the night before, afraid to sleep, to dream. When at last he slept, he slept through the morning hours. Good, he thought; the department has kicked me off the case, maybe the old man has too.

    He stood up and slowly stretched again. Another pretty summer day, what he could see of it through the drawn drapes. And me with nothing to do, he thought.

    While the little pan of water heated on the stove, he opened his front door and peeked outside. No dice. His neighbor down the way had already picked up his paper. That's what I get for sleeping so late. Charlie did not usually steal all his neighbor's morning paper, just the part with the crossword puzzle. The guy probably never missed it. He didn't look like the crossword-puzzle type. No puzzle today, and it was just as well. Charlie had a lot on his mind. First of all, there was Julia Copeland.

Charlie thought about Julia Copeland while he made coffee. She was beautiful. Her daughter was too. But, God, she was cold. "My father and I were never close." That woman missed her six o'clock meeting because she was hysterical? Not likely. She must have been on the phone before I got out of sight, he thought, or Mr. Copeland was. Either way, it got results. That wasn't the strange part. The shocker was that nothing had come of it. No disciplinary action, nothing in his file; just kicked off the case. It seemed a lot of trouble to go to, a big mess to stir up, just for that. He knew there was at least a suspension in it for him, if the Copelands had pushed it. Why hadn't they? He thought that over for a while and decided to believe that they were just good-hearted folks who did not want to make any trouble for him. They just wanted him kept out of their way. Nobody who has lost a father, close or otherwise, would want a crazy man coming around conjuring up the old man's ghost. Especially after all the publicity in the papers.

Anyway, he was off the case now. He had done all he could. Like Wes said, just worry about the little things you can control, like staying out of trouble. He had not done a very good job of that, and he knew how lucky he had been. The old captain would have to find somebody else to run interference for him now. Charlie decided to take advantage of his mandatory vacation. He would rest up, and he would forget about everything that upset or worried him.

That resolution did not last long. By the time he had rinsed out his coffee cup, the dead captain was on his mind again. He recalled the night he and Wes made the call in the Crockett Hotel, the eerie feeling of being watched; and the chills, as if a cold hand were reaching out for him. He remembered the first dream, the dead man's face, and the next day back in his room, his own dream funeral. As he thought of each of these things, they all came back to him brand new again. Every touch and chill and aching degree of terror he had felt replayed themselves perfectly in his mind. They were more real to him than the real-life things he did every day.

Around ten-thirty Charlie began to consider the question of his own sanity. If I were losing my mind, he wondered, would I know? He was accustomed to living with a minor melancholy, especially when he was working on a case that bothered him.

The ones involving children bothered him the most. He knew that he had not learned to leave things at work; he knew that good policemen, the survivors, learned to wear a shell as they went about their work, to keep the hurt and misery from infecting them. And he knew that they also learned to leave the shell behind when they went home, so that the disease did not go home with them and infect their families. Charlie had never learned to do that. As a result, he was the same person on and off duty, lugging the malaise and the disease back and forth with him. This had cost him his marriage, and had taken his Elizabeth away for most of his days. So he was accustomed to a persistent depression that did not quite disable him. He had learned to live with his complaining stomach.

What he felt now, about the captain, was different. Many a night he had lain and wished for sleep, and dreamed, but never like this. These were not just dreams, they were sent after him. They were as real as death. Captain Jonas was behind them, reaching out to him. That was real; he was sure beyond any proof. As long as you know what is real, he told himself, you are not crazy. That is the key. A psychotic did not know, he was out of touch with the real. He might think his skull was shrinking, or that he had pumpkins growing in his intestines. Charlie had known such men. We know better, but the psychotic doesn't. His shrinking skull and the growing pumpkins are as real as death to him. Like the dreams are to me, he thought. And the music in the captain's room.

Is it true if you think you may be insane you are not? Do the insane assume their sanity, without questioning it? They do, of course. He decided he was not losing his mind, but as soon as he decided that, he was not questioning any more, and he began all over again.

Forget about the captain. Forget about the dreams and the *Rhapsody*. He was off the case. What case? Jonas was the Slasher, and he killed himself because he couldn't live with the guilt. Like Wes said, that fit the facts. Mrs. Aguero, the reluctant witness, had no reason to lie. Even Burden admitted that there were secrets in the hearts of men that no one else could see. Especially lonely old men with nothing to live for. But he could not escape the pictures in his mind, the feelings they awakened. And he knew, as surely as night would come, that he would dream again.

There was someone who could help him. A second opinion was what he wanted now, from someone who knew about sanity, melancholy, and dreams. Just after eleven, he dialed the number of the Psychological Services Unit and asked for Dr. Cartwright. While he waited for her to answer, he found himself thinking of other things than his sanity. Lace under silk. Firm, unfettered breasts.

"Sam Cartwright."

"Hello. This is Charlie Gants. I was in to see you yesterday."

"Hi, Charlie. Did you think I had forgotten so soon?"

"Well, I hoped not. Are you busy?"

"Not too busy to talk. What's on your mind? Another theory?"

"No, not exactly. Actually, it's me. It's me I'd like to talk to you about."

"That sounds interesting. I think I'd like to talk about you. Do you want to stop by this afternoon?"

"I'd rather not come down there. If you don't have any plans, we could have lunch somewhere."

"I like to get away from here for lunch when I can. Let's make it Andrew's."

"That's fine. In about an hour?"

"Let's make it around one. I have a few things to do here, and we can miss the worst of the lunch rush."

"Andrew's at one. I'll see you there."

"Bye, Charlie."

Everything about the captain ran through his mind again as he showered and shaved. But as he put on his last clean shirt, he thought of her again, and remembered her perfume.

Andrew's was on McKinney Avenue not far from downtown, near the middle of a two or three block strip that for years had been known for its antique shops. Some of them were still there, in converted old houses. The in spot for antiques now was a part of Oak Lawn, south and west of Andrew's, which sat like a wedge tapped in among several different parts of the city. Oak Lawn, East Dallas, the downtown business district, and the Park Cities, University Park and Highland Park, were all within a brisk walk. Oak Lawn tried to be Greenwich Village; the Park Cities tried to be Beverly Hills; East Dallas tried to be a lot of things.

Charlie remembered his first patrol beat in East Dallas. It had been in transition from partying white singles to low-income families; later, blacks and chicanos came, many of them renting rooms in old, one-family houses. Now "urban pioneers" had rediscovered East Dallas, and were buying and restoring the old houses. Near the downtown, developers had torn down cheap little houses to build big expensive ones. Charlie wondered where the poor people would go when all the cheap housing was gone.

A row of store fronts faced McKinney. Two of the several doors opened through an archway into a courtyard full of little tables with umbrellas. Most of these were unoccupied; what was left of the lunch crowd was inside the restaurant proper.

She came a few minutes after one, breezing into the courtyard with long confident strides. Her blouse was gauze, her skirt longish with a slit up one side. The same big purse hung from her shoulder. Her smile was warm and her eyes sparkled in the bright sunlight when she lifted her sunglasses to the top of her head.

"Hi, Charlie. How are you doing?"

He rose and stood behind her chair. Not very charming or polished, he did try to remember his manners. If you can't be suave, at least be polite.

"That's what I want to talk to you about."

"I beg your pardon?"

"I said, that's what I want to talk to you about." He returned to his corner seat. "About how I am."

Looking at her across the little table, he did not want to be just a client to her. "I've been thinking this morning that I may not be sane anymore." He winced.

"That's an interesting opening line at lunch, Charlie. Are you trying to intrigue me?"

"Uh, is this table all right?"

"Fine. The sun feels good. I was thinking how nice it would be to lie out by the pool."

"What apartments do you live in?"

"I live in a house."

"With a pool?"

"A little one."

"Are you married?"

"Never been married, Charlie."

"And you have a house with a pool?"

"Yes, but we're not going to talk about that now. You didn't strike me at first as a devious person, Charlie, but I see I may have been wrong. Now, you invite me to lunch to talk about you, and the first words out of your mouth are some nonsense about losing your mind. Then you start in on my pool and my marital status. Playing mind games is part of my job, but I'm on my lunch hour. So stop acting schizoid and let's order lunch." She said all of this with no edge to her voice. They ordered two spinach salads and a carafe of the house Chablis.

"Sam, can I talk to you off the record?"

"There is no record as far as I'm concerned. Anything a client tells me is confidential, if he wants it to be."

"A client?"

"Don't you want to be my client? Then why did you say you were crazy? Is this business or personal, Charlie? Make up your mind."

"I didn't say I was crazy."

"You said you spent the morning thinking you weren't sane any more."

"Might not be sane any more. The idea is that I was questioning it. You were supposed to say that as long as I was questioning it, I was all right. Then I could stop worrying."

"And we could have gone on to something else. To what, Charlie?"

"This isn't working out . . . the way I thought."

"Have I made you uncomfortable? You feel threatened?"

"I feel confused. I have a lot on my mind, and I need help sorting it out. But I'm not sure I want to be your client."

"I don't know why not. Some of my best friends are clients. I've had lovers who started out as my clients."

He nodded. He was sweating in his last clean shirt. "Look, to be honest, I am attracted to you. But I'm not trying . . . I'm not playing any games with you. That's how I spent the morning."

"That's better, Charlie. You are attracted to me and you need my help. But you're afraid to ask for it because you don't want to screw things up romantically. Ambivalence. I like it."

"You do?"

"It's better than all the 'Hey babe' macho stuff I get from the other cops. Strong men are dull, Charlie; give me vulnerable and sensitive every time." She stared at him in frank appraisal until he looked away. "I'll tell you one thing, if this is a line you're handing me, it's the right one. And you're very perceptive."

"Wait a minute. You . . . I'm not . . . ."

"I know how you feel. An assertive woman can be a pain in the neck, if you're not used to them. Are you on the level?" He nodded. "Why don't you tell me what's bothering you, and don't worry about what I'll think."

He finished his wine and poured another, his salad untouched. She ate as he talked.

"It started the night Captain Jonas was killed."

"You said it was suicide."

"I said it looked like suicide. That's part of the whole deal. That night I had a weird dream about the captain." He described the dream in detail, reliving it.

"Have you had dreams like that before?"

"Never. Sometimes I have trouble sleeping, and I have dreams like anybody else. But never like this. You know, usually I can't remember a dream the next day. I remember this one, all right."

"What else?"

He told her about going to the captain's room after leaving her office the first time, about hearing the *Rhapsody* and feeling the dead man in the room. He related what Wes and Burden had told him about the captain, and about his meeting Julia Copeland, and being taken off the case that wasn't there. He left out the dream about his own funeral.

"So now you're on holiday for awhile."

"Yes, and I'd really like to forget all this crap and relax. I think Sergeant Burden was pretty close to the mark when he told Sharp that I was punchy."

"But you can't forget about it?"

"He won't let me."

"The captain?"

"Yes." After finishing her salad, she held her glass out for more wine.

"My first reaction is that the dream itself is probably not anything to worry about. If you are preoccupied with the captain's death for some reason, it isn't surprising that you would dream about him. The part about hearing the music when you were in his room is interesting. You think you actually heard the music, you didn't just remember it?"

"I heard it. I'm sure."

"And the record player was off?"

"Yes."

She fumbled through her big purse and produced two of her infamous brown cigarettes. Charlie let her light her own, then declined the one she offered him.

"What else, Charlie? There's something else."

"The night before last, I had another dream. I was in a casket and I couldn't move. People passed by and looked down at me. They were talking."

"What were they saying?"

"That I had committed suicide."

"Had you?"

"I wasn't even dead! But I couldn't move. I don't know for sure, maybe that's what dead is: you still hear and see things, but you can't move. And nobody can hear you."

"Who was there?"

"Cops, some relatives. My ex-wife was there with a man I didn't know. Elizabeth, my little girl, was with her. And Wes Braverman."

"Anybody else?"

"You. You were there with Wes."

"Did I say anything?"

"You said I was interesting. You said I had sad eyes."

"You do. Anyone else?"

"The last one was Captain Jonas. He didn't say anything, he never does. He crossed himself, then he winked at me and laughed." It was impossible to tell her how real the dream was, to make her feel it with him.

"Then what happened?"

"The lid of the coffin closed over me and I screamed."

"And then?"

"I woke up."

"Why did you leave this dream out at first, when you were telling me about all the other things?"

"I don't know. Because you were in it."

"What do you think that means, Charlie?"

"I don't know. You tell me."

"It's interesting that your daughter was there. How did that make you feel?"

"Oh, my God!"

"What is it?"

"My daughter. I was supposed to pick her up today. Her mother asked me to keep her this morning and I completely forgot about it. Excuse me."

One of the waitresses showed him to a pay phone, and he dialed frantically. There was no answer. He made his way back outside to the table, a pang of guilt burning in his chest. He imagined Bit waiting for him, forgotten.

"Is everything all right, Charlie?"

"They weren't home."

"Are you all right?"

"I feel terrible."

She stubbed her cigarette out and exhaled thoughtfully. "Let's go to my place, Charlie."

He hid his surprise, paid the check, and they left without another word.

11 | THE SESSION

IT WAS NOT THE COPELAND MANSION, BUT IT WAS a very nice house, just a few minutes from Andrew's, in Highland Park. A two-story colonial, it sat back from the tree-lined street in a comfortable mantle of ivy. Inside, Sam showed him through double doors to the right of a handsome staircase, and he found himself in the den. Charlie used the phone there to call his ex-wife again, first at home and then at work, just in case. There was still no answer.

Hours later, he sank back against the stuffed leather couch. On the coffee table in front of him lay half a dozen crumpled sheets of paper and a pair of lead pencils he had blunted with writing, along with a half-empty tumbler of Scotch. He was tired. She had tested him, something called the Minnesota Multiphasic, and two or three other things whose names he did not know. There had been ink blots and pictures to make up stories about. She had been gone for some time now, upstairs somewhere. Evaluating his results. He finished the Scotch and walked to the bar, stretching as he moved. It was evening. He poured his third or fourth drink, and was looking around the room when Sam came in.

"I like your house."

"Thank you. I grew up in it. Mom and Dad left it to me and my sister. It's too big, but we couldn't bear to sell it."

"I'm sorry. I didn't know your parents had passed away."

" 'Passed away.' That's quaint. They died in a plane crash three years ago. Dad was a land developer, and they were coming back from a business meeting in Lubbock when their chartered plane went down."

"I'm sorry."

"Thank you, Charlie. Anyway, there were trusts and Mom's antique shop. We did sell the shop. And that is how I happen to live in a house with a pool. No marriage, no divorce."

"I didn't mean to pry."

"I know. But if you were the prying type, you would ask, 'What's a modest heiress like me doing in a place like the Police Department.' Wouldn't you?"

"I suppose so."

"It's not the salary, Charlie. That's for sure."

She poured herself a Scotch and led him back to the couch. She patted a seat at arm's length away. Barefoot, she tucked her feet under her, careless of the way her skirt moved up over her thighs. Charlie saw the top of a stocking, tan flesh above it.

"Well, Doctor, am I crazy or not? Before you answer that, tell me something. Can you be crazy if you think you might be? I mean, is it true that, as long as you think you might be, you're not?"

"I don't know, Charlie. What do you think?"

"If you don't know, I sure don't."

"Are you disappointed in me? That's the second time you've brought up that question, and you still haven't gotten an answer."

"I just thought that was one of those basic things a shrink would learn in shrink school. You know, like how many feet it takes to stop a car going fifty miles an hour on dry pavement. It's basic. Cops learn things like that in rookie school, all of them. Even if you see a guy and he's been a detective for years, you can bet he knows that."

"How many?"

"What?"

"How many feet?"

He grinned dumbly. "I forgot."

She laughed and he felt good. He laughed, too, remembering he was wearing his glasses, and took them off. They were only for reading. Bad enough he was losing his hair. He laughed and drank.

"Would you say you're a pretty heavy drinker, Charlie?"

"No. I like a Scotch or two at night. Helps me sleep."

"Are you sleepy now?"

"No. I slept last night. First time since Jonas died. Why?"

"You're putting it away pretty well, that's all. I just wondered."

He put his drink down. "I'm sorry."

"Don't be silly. I don't care, and I'm not running low on Scotch. It was just a question, Charlie. I ask a lot of questions."

"I know. What do the tests say?"

She lit a cigarette and fanned the papers out in her hand like a deck of cards.

"I went over all of them myself, and I called a friend of mine, a psychiatrist."

"The same one you were going to talk to before, about the Slasher profile and Captain Sharp's theory?"

"Yes. He's a good, good friend, and I called him for a second opinion about you. He's the soul of discretion, it goes without saying, but I didn't give him your name. Do you mind?"

"Of course not." But he did. He figured he knew what that good, good friend crap meant. It meant the psychiatrist was his competition for Sam's attention. And they had just spent the better part of an hour going over his tests.

("I'd watch this guy if I were you, Samantha darling, he's crazy as a bed bug, and he'll do or say anything to get in your pants. You know how cops are.") He minded that, all right. "And what did the two of you decide?"

"Boiling a whole lot of stuff down to the bone, we agree that you are quite upset and preoccupied with thoughts of death."

"Sounds reasonable, for a man working Homicide."

"Good point. We also think that you are in touch with reality."

"I'm not crazy? I really thought I might be. It's scary when you're not sure." He saw her smile at him, and hoped he saw meaning in the smile.

"It's hardly as clear-cut as you make it sound, Charlie. But I think we can rule out full-blown psychosis at least. Crazy and sane are relative concepts; they're not like on and off on a light switch. Almost everybody is a little bit crazy at one time or another, a little neurotic. Picture a scale, with Ozzie Nelson on one end and Rasputin on the other. Most people would fall somewhere around the middle, but we can all be bumped out toward the Rasputin end if we are stressed enough. That's normal, and it usually only lasts as long as the stress does."

"Where am I on the scale?"

"A notch or two farther out than most of us. Make that three notches. Having dreams doesn't mean much. Being obsessed with them is worth a notch. Hearing music that isn't there, anything that happens like that when you're awake, that's another notch. The third notch is for your visit to Julia Copeland, actually acting on the basis of the other stuff. It's not severe, Charlie, not at this point. I think what you need to do is what you said you wanted to do, relax and forget about it. Avoid the stress."

Charlie did not say anything. Three notches sounded like a hell of a lot to him, like three strikes.

"Another thing that will help is for you to understand what is happening. Based on what you've told me, your tests and my observation of you, my friend and I have decided there are a couple of possible causes for the way you've been feeling and behaving. To be honest, I think there is just one probable cause. But to be absolutely fair about it, we'll talk about both. First, there is the possibility of what we'll call a psychic phenomenon. This, I think, is highly unlikely. But there are some people, a rare few, who seem to be able to pick up signals of some kind, psychic disturbances or whatever. You hear about psychics all the time, but there have been a few who were studied and seemed to be legitimate. If you had come to me a year ago, I would not even have mentioned this possibility. But I happen to know of a man here in Dallas who did some work with a research team. Apparently, he has this ability. It's as if he gets messages from the other side at times. He had episodes of precognition, and some other things, for years before he came forward to be a guinea pig. And you have never had anything like this happen before, have you?"

"Never."

"Did any of your dreams demonstrate any external validity? Did you find something as a result of either dream? Were there clues in one of the dreams that led you to a discovery that seemed to prove the dream was valid?"

"No."

"There. That's why I'm almost sure that there is nothing psychic going on in your case."

"What is going on?"

"I think it's a kind of hysteria."

"I'm hysterical?"

"Not screaming and jabbering hysteria, like in a fire or a train wreck. I am talking about the kind of hysteria that can make a person blind or crippled when there is no physical reason for it. A part of the mind takes over and tells you something is real when it isn't. The thing is, if you believe it is real, it may as well be, because it's real to you."

Charlie finished his drink. His ears were warm and his cheeks were numb.

"Or, you could be as crazy as a bed bug."

"What?" His tongue was thick, too.

"Well, these tests aren't infallible, you know." They both laughed. All that stuff about the three notches and hysteria had depressed the hell out of him. But now she laughed and he started to feel good again.

"You know what interests me about all of this, Charlie?"

He shrugged, and made his way to the bar again.

"It is this thing, whatever it is, in your personality that makes you susceptible to the hysterical reaction in the first place. I think it's your sensitivity."

"I don't understand."

"You are a compassionate, caring man in a brutal world. You live with killers and victims, all fouled up in a tangle of bureaucratic trappings. You understand what other people feel, and you feel it, too. You don't depersonalize the people in your world, and the violence and misery offends you.

"Something about the captain's death, either it was especially brutal, or he reminded you of your father, or it was just one too many; something about that particular violent death offended you so deeply that you rebelled. Subconsciously, you tried to reach him, to bring him back. You convinced yourself he was murdered because you could not accept the fact of his self-destruction. As I said, maybe he's your father, or maybe you see yourself in him; he is you as an old man. Have you ever considered suicide?"

He stopped midway between the bar and the couch, a fresh drink in his hand. "Yes."

"Ever threatened it?"

"No."

"Ever tried to do it?"

"No."

"Why not?"

"Elizabeth, mostly."

"Charlie, that is one of the things I find most attractive about you."

"That I'm suicidal?"

"That you are honest with yourself and with me. Compassionate and honest. You have absolutely no business being a policeman."

"I know. I think too much." He sat on the couch.

"Does your stomach hurt?" He realized that it did, had been, and that he was holding it with his left hand, unconsciously.

"Do you have an ulcer?"

"Not yet, but my internist is counting down."

She stood beside him and hugged him. "You're a good man, Charlie, that's your problem."

He smelled her perfume and felt her breast against his cheek. She turned his face up to hers with her hand.

"You okay?"

He nodded.

"Do you feel up to trying something?"

"What?"

"Just a minute." She walked across the room to an elaborate stereo setup and opened a sliding door. Charlie saw a hundred or more records stacked neatly in the cabinet. "I'm sure I have it."

"Samantha, I'm not in the mood for any music, really." Charlie's stomach tightened; the pain was real.

"Call me Sam. All my friends do. You said you wanted my

help, so just relax and trust me a little. Here it is." She held the album cover up for him to see. "Look familiar?"

"Sam . . ."

"We call it confrontation therapy. If you came to me with a fear of tall buildings, I would take you to a tall building and help you work your way to the top. You have a fear of *Rhapsody in Blue,* so I'll play it for you."

"I'm not afraid of the music. It's just that when I hear it, I'm reminded of the captain. He's the one I'm afraid of."

"Same thing. It has an effect on you. The thing to remember is that I'm right here with you and nothing bad is going to happen. I want to play it for you to show you that it's just a nice piece of music. Minor chords, a little bluesy, as the title would lead you to expect, but that's all. Sit back and get comfortable. Have you ever heard it all the way through?"

"Yes."

"Then you know it runs about fifteen minutes."

"Sixteen and a half."

"Even more reason to get comfortable."

The music started. Charlie was rigid, every muscle tensed; his body and mind remembering the night of the first dream as the clarinet riff gave way to the piano, then the orchestra. Sam's voice was nearby, above him.

"Relax. Just relax and listen."

She kneaded his shoulders and the back of his neck. He was warm with the Scotch and the sound of her voice. The music seemed less melancholy this time. His eyes closed.

12 | THE CAPTAIN'S ROOM

HE WAS ALONE. THE RHAPSODY ECHOED IN THE enormous empty theater. At the center of the stage a lone pianist played in a pale blue spotlight, while an unseen orchestra accompanied him. In top hat and tails, his back to Charlie, the pianist played with brittle urbanity, his head keeping time as his fingers blended with the dingy ivory keys.

Charlie rose slowly and made his way down the center aisle to the stage. He found the steps and mounted them slowly, the knot in his stomach tightening as he took each step and paused. Finally, on the stage, he advanced soundlessly toward the pianist, holding his breath behind clenched teeth.

Just short of the circle of light at center stage, he stopped and watched the hands as they swept over the keys. Bony hands, rotted flesh loose and flopping as they played. The figure turned and Charlie saw the face, top hat at a jaunty angle above a crooked smile. Decaying flesh drooping over the starched, impeccably white collar. The dead man raised his right hand and tipped his hat to Charlie, bowing elegantly from the waist. Charlie edged back, away from the old man and the spotlight. There was a door in the shadows at the edge of the stage, and Charlie threw himself upon it, and dashed headlong into a small, dark room. The music stopped. He turned, and the captain's bony silhouette filled the doorway. There was no way out. The two of them stood face to face for three beats of Charlie's heart. Then the dead man's scrawny fingers lashed out and closed like talons around Charlie's throat. With both hands he tried but could not pull the choking hand away. The dead man's left hand grabbed Charlie's right wrist and pulled him toward the dresser. Charlie could not break away. The old man forced him down, onto his knees in front of the dresser. Charlie felt himself dying and knew his time had run out, when the hand left his throat and pointed. He saw the bony finger, like a dagger, pointing at the bottom of the dresser. There! There! Remember, promise to remember and he'll let me go. I promise! I swear I'll remember! My time is up, let me go. I swear I'll remember! He was dragged to his feet and found himself face to face with the dead man, their cheeks touching. I swear I'll remember! The old man shoved him backward and he fell . . . fell . . . .

He jerked awake on the couch, screaming, "Remember! Remember!"

Sam was there, her cool hand on his wrist. "It's all right now, Charlie. You're awake. It's all right."

"It's not all right! I . . . I almost didn't make it . . . Am I really awake?"

"Yes, Charlie. It's all right. I'm right here."

"The old bastard wouldn't let me go. He's stronger than I am . . . time was up. My time was up and he wouldn't let me go. I had to promise I'd remember."

"Remember what?"

"I'm not sure. I don't know." He saw her write something in a notebook. "He showed me something. He pointed . . ."

"At what? He pointed at what?"

"I don't know." He sobbed. "He dragged me over to the dresser . . . pointed at the floor."

"The floor?"

"The floor, the bottom of the dresser . . . I don't know." His voice broke and rattled in his throat.

"You're all right now, Charlie."

"Goddamnit, you don't understand! If I can't remember,

he'll come back . . . come back for me. And the next time he won't let go!" He turned on her, his teary eyes wide with terror.

"What would happen then? What would happen if he didn't let you go and your time ran out?"

"I'd die. I'd go insane. I don't know. I'll be stuck there, with him . . . forever."

"You won't die, Charlie, no matter what he does." She took his hands in hers; his head lolled back against the couch. "It's not real. It's just a . . ."

"What is it?" He saw the look on her face.

"Your throat. There are bruises on your throat."

"It's just a dream? That's what you are going to say, isn't it? Then what about this . . . and this?" He showed her his right wrist, the fresh scratches. "What about this?" With a sarcastic smile, he ran his fingers across his throat, and winced at the pain.

"I don't know. I was right here."

"Did I choke myself? You were right here, did I do this? Or this?"

"I don't think so. But Charlie, it was just a dream."

"Just a dream? I don't think so, Sam. I sure as hell don't think so any more."

"Charlie, you're soaking wet. You've sweat right through your clothes. Get up. Take a shower and I'll wash your things. Come on, get up."

"I have to remember. I have to remember . . . everything."

"I took notes. Everything you said. I have it all down. It's all right. Come on, now. Get up and get in the shower."

She helped him up and guided him, leaning on her, to the bathroom. She peeled the fetid clothes off of him and rolled them into a ball. Then she reached inside the stall and turned on the water, hot. In a few seconds the room was steamy. She pulled and pushed him into the shower and closed the door behind him. He stayed there for a long time. The steaming hot water beat down on him, dimpling the flesh of his arms and shoulders as he stood with his head bowed, supplicant to the plumbing that brought him slowly back to his senses. When he finally came out, he remembered waking up as if it were part of the dream. His clothes were gone. He wiped the mirror with a towel so that he could see himself through the steam. Discolored bruises that looked like fingerprints stood out on his throat. That had not been just a dream, either. He found a hot cup of coffee and a heavy terrycloth robe on the counter by the sink.

The coffee burned his stomach so badly that it doubled him over at first, but it quit burning after a minute or so. It helped to clear his head. Wrapped in the warm, clean robe, he felt almost safe, almost sane. Sam was waiting for him outside the bathroom door, and she led him to the kitchen bar. While he finished his coffee, she made him an omelet, and he realized he was hungry. His stomach felt better when he had eaten. Sam poured another cup of coffee.

"Charlie, I think I was wrong about you."

"What do you mean?"

"I told you that basically there were two possibilities: phenomenon or hysteria."

"Three. You also said I might be crazy."

"That's right, three. The interesting thing, besides the bruises, is what happened to your vital signs during your dream." She sipped her coffee thoughtfully. "After you nodded off, I did some research. I was surprised at how much stuff I found right here in my own little library. Some of these books I had never read before. Anyway, I found that there is a pattern among subjects who seem to be legitimate, people who do astral projections and things like that. There is a pattern in their vital signs."

"And?"

"And your vital signs fit the pattern."

"What does that mean?"

"It means that your dreams may not be just hysterical reactions to stress. They may be something else."

"What?"

"Who knows? We're talking about things that are over my head here. This is stuff they haven't finished writing about yet."

"How about your close personal friend, the psychiatrist you tell everything to, the guy who's tops in his field, the one on all the staffs and faculties?"

"What about him?"

"Well, why don't you bring him in on this? Don't tell me he doesn't know all there is to know about this, too."

"He probably knows as much as anybody. He just doesn't happen to believe in it."

"He doesn't believe in it?"

"Let's just say that he feels about this kind of stuff the same way your friend Wes Braverman feels about physical evidence."

"He thinks it's bullshit?"

"That's about it. He's old school, doesn't believe anything he can't see, hear, or smell. Says he's never come across a case in his years of practice and teaching, and he doesn't accept lab work that may not have been properly controlled."

"The hard-headed type, huh?"

"He's a good man, Charlie, he's . . ."

"I know, 'tops in his field.' "

"That's right. He taught me most of what I know. Why are you so sarcastic about him? You don't even know him."

"Which implies that if I did know him, I'd have grounds to be sarcastic about him."

"It does not imply any such thing."

"My mistake. It sounded like you said, 'You can't dislike him, you don't know him well enough yet.' "

"God, I think I like you better when you're delirious. Why do you resent this man when you've never met him?"

"Why are you so defensive about him?"

"I am not going to argue with you about it. Let's change the subject, okay? Since the good doctor doesn't believe in what I think you have, let's talk about somebody who might be able to help you."

"Agreed. Who?"

"Another friend of mine. His name is Vincent Maitland. He's the man I told you about, the real psychic."

"The guinea pig in the field study?"

"That's right." She was looking through her notebook for Maitland's number.

"And they decided he was on the level?"

"Yes." She dialed the number.

"It's not too late to be calling him?"

"I don't think he'll mind. Hello, Vincent? Vincent, this is Sam Cartwright, how are you? I'm sorry to bother you this late. You're sweet to say so, Vincent. I have a friend I think needs your help. He's a policeman. Yes. Yes. No, not yet. Yes, it is an unusual case. An emergency?" She looked at Charlie. "Yes, I believe it is. You will? Thank you, Vincent, you're a sweetheart. I really appreciate it. Yes, I will. Good night." She hung up the phone and turned to Charlie. "Sunday, around one."

"What time is it now?"

"Quarter-to-nine. Why?"

"I want to try my ex again."

This time she answered.

"It's me. I'm sorry," he said hurriedly. "I've been really busy . . ."

"You sonofabitch. You are so crazy about her, your Little Bit, Daddy's little girl. I wish you could have seen her face. She sat out on the front steps this morning, waiting for her daddy to come for her. Her daddy was coming for her. Big deal. Only you never came, did you? You forgot all about her, didn't you? You were so wrapped up in some big case that you forgot about her, didn't you?"

"I can understand your being upset, and I don't blame you."

"You don't understand anything."

"I really couldn't help it. Let me make up for it. Let me take her for a while tomorrow. It's Saturday and you can sleep late."

"How do I know you'll show up?"

"I have the day off."

There was a moment of silence.

"Okay, Charlie. You can have her tomorrow, but don't you dare disappoint that little girl again."

"I won't."

"And be sure you're here by nine, because I have to be somewhere by ten. And have her back by five."

"I'll be there."

The phone clicked dead and he realized that Sam had left him alone to make his call. He found her in the kitchen.

"I take it you made contact. Is she a bitch?"

"No. She's going to let me have Bit tomorrow. I think I'll take her to the zoo."

He paced around Sam, out into the hall and back.

"Nervous, Charlie?"

"I don't know. It's just that I have to do something."

"What?"

"Something. I'm sure not going back to sleep tonight."

"What can you do tonight?"

"As soon as my clothes are dry, I'm going down to the Crockett Hotel and take another look around the captain's room."

"Tonight?"

"Best time. I still don't think you understand. I swore to the old bastard. He was trying to show me something, and I swore. If I can find whatever it is, maybe he'll leave me alone." He traced the marks on his throat absently as he talked.

"Do you hear what you're saying? Charlie, the man is dead."

"I know that and you know that . . ."

The desk clerk remembered him.

"I'm sorry about the captain. He was a longtime resident here, a fine old gentleman. Uh, is it true that he . . . that his death was . . . self-inflicted? I know it's a terrible thing for me to say, but, in a way, I hope that's what happened. As regrettable as that is, it's better than . . . well, I'd hate to think there might be a killer on the loose. Most of our permanent guests are elderly, and . . ."

"I don't think you have anything to worry about."

"Well, that's good to hear, very reassuring. By the way, do you know if the family intends to pick up his things? The room is paid up until the end of the month, but I would hate to see anything stolen. Not that we have a problem with thefts here at the Crockett, but, well, you never know. You can't be too careful."

"I'm not sure. I'll check on that for you."

"Thank you, I'd appreciate that."

"And if you don't mind, I'd like to take another look at his room."

"Really? Oh, I thought the case was closed."

"Just routine."

"Well, I'm sure it will be all right. I'll get you the key."

Charlie looked at Sam as the elevator carried them up. She held up well with no make-up. It's the tan, he thought. Her hand was on his arm.

"Sam, I appreciate your wanting to come with me. But why don't you wait for me by the elevator?"

"No. If anything is going to happen to you in that room, I

want to be there to watch. You are my most interesting case, Charlie, and I want to observe you firsthand."

He felt like a laboratory rat on a treadmill, but he made no reply. As he stepped off the elevator he remembered Moseley House, and a night a long time ago when he had felt the same way he felt now. Moseley House was an old Victorian-style mansion, that had been abandoned to the mercies of vandals, tramps, and the elements back in his home town. Ghost stories grew up around the place like the weeds and brambles that pushed up through the rotten boards of the front porch. When he was a kid, it was a place where boys went to test their courage. He remembered the night it had been his turn. He remembered the stepping stones and the big oak door, the whispers and taunts of the other boys, crouched outside the wrought iron gate in the safe, dim street light. Girls came to watch, too; they stayed farther back. Five minutes alone in Moseley House on a moonless night. That was the test.

Charlie found himself at the captain's door, and it was as if no time had passed since that night at Moseley House. Behind him he could almost hear the whispering of young boys as he put the key in the lock. He would not run away, not this time.

He eased the door open and reached inside for the light switch. The air inside the room felt cold to his hand. He flipped the switch on, off, on again. The room stayed dark.

Inside the room, neither of them spoke. Without saying so, neither of them wanted to disturb the dead man. Boxes sat on the stripped bed; all the captain's effects, his estate, packed in three cardboard cartons. Not much, Charlie thought, not much to leave behind.

On his hands and knees, Charlie probed the carpet in front of the dresser, on either side. Then, with a shudder, he slid his hand slowly beneath the dresser itself. Nothing on the floor; but on the bottom of the dresser . . . there it was! Something taped to the underside of the dresser. He pulled the tape away. A book. As soon as he had the book in hand, he stood up and started for the door.

"Sam, I've got it. Let's get out of here."

The woman by the window did not answer. She stood without moving, her head bowed.

"What the hell are you looking at, Sam? I have what we came for, let's go!"

"Sam?" He took her arm. "Sam, what is it?"

When she turned toward him, she was not Sam any more. Long black hair spilled like a shadow over her face, hiding her eyes. Charlie stumbled back and felt the dresser at his back. He turned and lunged out the door, away from the stranger in the dead man's room.

"Charlie? Charlie! What's the matter? Wait a minute!"

She chased him down the hall and caught him as the elevator door opened. He rushed inside and pressed into a corner, the book clutched to his chest.

"What's the matter with you?"

"Where did you go, Sam?"

"I didn't go anywhere. What are you talking about? I was standing right there."

"Then why didn't you answer me?"

"Because you didn't say anything. One minute you were digging around under the dresser, the next you're running down the hall like a mad man."

"Like a mad man, huh?"

"I'm sorry, Charlie. Bad choice of words." She studied him carefully. "What happened?"

"It wasn't you any more. I told you I had it, that I was ready to go, and you didn't answer. When I touched you, you looked at me, but it wasn't you any more."

"Who was it?"

"I don't know. Somebody else."

"Charlie, I'll be frank with you. 'Mad man' may have been a bad choice of words, but I worry a lot more about the things you see when you're awake than in your dreams. That's your shrink talking."

Charlie was quiet as the elevator moved to the lobby floor.

"Are you all right now, Charlie?"

"I will be, as soon as we get out of here."

13 | THE JOURNAL

CHARLIE DID NOT EXAMINE THE BOOK UNTIL HE and Sam were back at her house and she had poured each of them a drink.

"Do you have any milk, Sam?"

"Milk?"

"Yeah. It helps my stomach."

"In the refrigerator."

Charlie poured the Scotch into a water glass, and topped it off with milk.

"How bad is it, Charlie?"

"It's all right. The milk coats the stomach lining and the booze unties the knots."

"A reputable doctor told you that?"

"Sure. Drinks it himself."

"Well?"

"Well, what?"

"Good God, Charlie, the book! Let's have a look at the book."

They sat on the couch and Charlie laid the book on the coffee table in front of them. It was the dimestore kind, a cheap little thing with black covers and red binding. In gold-colored block print letters the word *Journal* was stamped across the front.

Charlie opened it to the first page. He and Sam exchanged puzzled glances. The page was filled with letters and numbers, all neatly printed by hand. There seemed to be no order to it, no logical sequence. There were no spaces between letters, and no punctuation.

"It's in some kind of code."

"Look in the back, Charlie. Maybe it comes with a set of instructions."

"Think about that for a second. Why would he go to the trouble of writing the thing in code and then put the instructions in the back?"

"Sorry, I wasn't thinking. Codes and cloaks and daggers are just not my cup of tea."

"Well, codes are mine."

"You're kidding."

"Not at all. My Sunday mornings are built around the New York Times crossword. I jog up to the bookstore on Park Lane. It's my only exercise."

"But do you finish the puzzle?"

"Usually, sooner or later. And cryptography is kind of a hobby of mine. Cryptography or cryptology?"

"Beats me."

"Whichever, breaking codes. There's always some of this stuff in the crossword-puzzle books."

"I'll take your word for it."

"I wonder how much of this there is?"

He thumbed through the pages. Half of them, about fifty, were filled with the queer lines. He found a snapshot stuck behind the last written page as a book mark.

"Who is she?" Sam asked.

He studied the face of the mother with a child. She was very young to be a mother; her dark eyes looked out at him above unsmiling lips, with a hint of irony or contempt at the corners. Long, raven hair and, even then, flawless features.

"Julia Copeland. It's an old picture, but she hasn't changed very much."

"Mrs. Edmund Copeland?"

"That's right, Captain Jonas's daughter. She and her daughter Jessica; I guess the baby in this picture is Jessica, all the family the old man had, as far as I know. His wife died in childbirth. Do you know Julia?"

"Her husband and Daddy were on some of the same committees. I think Julia and Mom served on some board together once. I've met the Edmund Copelands at parties a few times."

"What do you think of them?"

"I don't know them that well. I said parties, not encounter sessions."

"She looks awfully young in this picture, to have a baby."

"If it's hers."

"How old is she now, Sam? Do you know?"

"Fortyish. And that baby could be Jessica, now that I think about it. Jessica's about twenty-five now. I know because she and my sister were debs together."

"Debutantes? My God, I'm impressed. Where is your sister now?"

"In Austin at graduate school. She's working on her doctorate."

"Another shrink in the family?"

"Hardly. Comparative Literature. She's dedicated her life to *Finnegan's Wake.*"

"I can believe that. Have you read it?"

"No, Lawrence was more my type. I was the first girl in my seventh-grade class to read *Lady Chatterley's Lover.*"

"You were reading D.H. Lawrence in the seventh grade?"

"Just the dirty parts."

"I see." He turned to face her, and took her hand. "Before I wade off into the captain's secret code, I'd like to tell you something."

"Does it have anything to do with *Lady Chatterley's Lover?*"

"In a way." They exchanged smiles. "It's just that, when I dreamed earlier . . . it was good to find you here when I woke up. And going down to his room, that was hard for me. I'm glad you went with me. What I mean is, if I were alone at my place tonight, after what's happened, I'd be in a hell of a shape. Instead, I'm here with you, talking about books we've read, and . . . you make me feel better. Thank you."

"That's sweet, Charlie." She leaned toward him, her scent preceding her, and kissed him on the forehead. "And now, master code-breaker, I'll make us some coffee. We may need clear heads tonight."

When she had gone, Charlie wished he had said more. He imagined undressing her, and then turned back to the captain's book.

He knew that one way to unscramble a code was to identify the letter or figure most often repeated and then substitute the letter E for it, E being the most frequently used letter in the English language. Charlie could remember the three or four most frequently used letters in order. Once they were substituted for the letters that appeared most frequently, in descending order in the text, patterns should emerge, words suggesting themselves. He was still at it when Sam returned with two cups of coffee. Cream and sugar; he was flattered that she remembered.

"How is it coming?"

For the third time, he scanned the legal pad on which he had copied the captain's first page, making the indicated substitutions.

"It isn't. This doesn't make a damned bit of sense."

"What now?"

"Beats the hell out of me. Any suggestions?"

"You're the cryptographer or cryptologist, or whatever."

"Right. And the letter S appears most often. That means S should stand for E. But when I substitute them, it still doesn't make any sense."

"Maybe Captain Jonas didn't know about crypticism. Maybe he didn't read the *Times*."

"Yeah, if there is anything I can't stand it's some amateur screwing things up."

"Don't give up, Charlie. I have all the faith in the world in you." She snuggled back into the couch, drew her knees up under her, and drank her coffee.

"All right, I'll try a different approach."

"Attaboy, Charlie. When I was a little girl, I couldn't even figure out my Mom's."

"Your Mom's what?"

"Code. It wasn't even a code, really. She managed the antique store, just for something to do. She worked out a system so that she could write notes to herself on the backs of price tags. That way, she could look at the tag and see how much she had paid for a piece, but a customer couldn't. It was simple after she explained it to me."

"How did it work?"

"It was based on a key phrase. The phrase had to have ten letters, none of them repeated. Then you just assigned a digit to each letter, in order. Her phrase was BLACK HORSE. B equals one, L equals two, see?"

Charlie nodded. "The trick is knowing the key phrase. It could work with letters of the alphabet, too."

"More coffee?"

"Please." He found the legal pad he had used earlier. "Wait a minute. I've been checking some things here. By my count, the captain only used fourteen letters . . . and seven numerals. So we are looking for a fourteen-letter phrase. Hey Sam, you know any fourteen letter non-repeating phrases, offhand?"

"Sorry." She returned with his coffee. The phone rang. "Hello. Yes this is Doctor Cartwright. Yes, I will, Operator. Yes. Yes, Don, what is it?" With the heel of her hand over the mouthpiece, she whispered to Charlie that it was a client. "Have you taken any? How many? You'll have to speak up, I can hardly hear you. Wait a minute, hold on. I'm going upstairs. Just hold a minute." She laid the phone down on the arm of the couch. "Charlie, this is a client from my private practice. When I get upstairs, hang up down here." She yelled down a minute later, and he hung up the phone.

Charlie surveyed the debris scattered over the coffee table, couch, and floor. There were offense reports, photographs, notes, everything he had collected since the first dream. The answer was there somewhere. Think like the captain, he told himself.

He spied the partially covered album jacket on the table, and picked it up. This song is part of it, he thought. It fits somehow. *Rhapsody in Blue.* Not a song, a rhapsody. What's the difference, he wondered. Then he answered his own question. The difference was four letters. "Rhapsody" is eight letters. Plus two for "in", plus four for "Blue" equals fourteen. Fourteen letters, none of them repeated. "You old son of a bitch," he said softly.

At first he went through the old man's book page by page. Then he flipped through the remaining pages, stopping at random to check. The coffee cooled untouched as he tried substituting letters. R equals A, H equals B . . . reverse it. Nothing made sense. "Fourteen letters and seven numerals," he said aloud. "It won't work."

He decided to give it a rest. His head hurt, from the base of his skull to his temples. His neck was stiff, it cracked when he stretched. He went to the kitchen for fresh coffee, then toured the ground floor.

Everything, furnitures, and art, was simple, real, and lovely. Each room was carefully furnished with fine pieces, leaving plenty of room to move freely. Except in the dining room and kitchen, there were bookshelves on every wall. More than a hundred titles on psychology, some by authors whose names he knew. *The Cocaine Papers* and *Confessions of a Lotus Eater* caught his eye. There was a good deal of fiction, too, some of his favorite writers. She had books by most of the "serious" writers he had learned to enjoy, but shamelessly scattered among them were dozens of mass-market formula jobs. She reads any and all of them, he thought. And doesn't care who knows it.

She came down half an hour later, and found him back on the couch, reading a book of Faulkner's short stories.

"Do you like Faulkner, Charlie?" She had changed into a kimono and slippers.

"I try. But can you help me understand why he writes this way sometimes? Here in *The Old Man*, he has sentences a page long. Why is it profound when he does it? If I'd tried that in Lit. 101, it would have just been bad writing."

" 'Genius is knowing all the rules and when to break them.' I read that somewhere."

"I suppose so. Have you read this?"

"I read the parts I understood. The rest, I don't worry about."

"Some of this reminds me of home, Sulphur Springs."

"Sulphur Springs? You know, I'm not surprised that you're a small town boy."

"You spotted me for a hick, huh? What gave me away? I haven't worn a polyester leisure suit or a white belt in years."

"I bet you never did."

"You're right. How did you know?"

"I think that's where you learned your compassion, growing

up in a small town, where you knew everybody. Everybody is somebody, with a family and a life story. It's hard to depersonalize people in Sulphur Springs, isn't it?"

"It used to be." He put Faulkner back on the shelf. "What about your client? Did you resolve his crisis?"

"Postponed it, anyway. Sometimes that's all I can do. He admitted he hadn't actually taken any pills."

"Would you like to talk about it?"

"That's thoughtful of you, Charlie, but it's not necessary. There are too many clients with too many crises to let one throw me. He'll probably be all right. If not, I know I've done my best for him, and that's all I can do."

"I think there's a moral there for me."

"Could be. You have to know when to let go."

"You sound like Wes."

"Charlie, are there any good books about murder?"

"What did you have in mind?"

"I want to know more about what you do, what you have to deal with."

"*In Cold Blood,* by Truman Capote, and *The Onion Field,* by Joseph Wambaugh. You could plow through a dozen textbooks and not get the feel of it you will from either one of those. They're the best things I've ever read about it." He did not ask why.

"Which should I read first?"

"Capote's."

"I'll pick up a copy on my way to work tomorrow." She lit another cigarette and offered him one; he declined again. "Sit down, Charlie, you look tired."

When he joined her on the couch she moved close to him and brushed his hair back off his face. He took off his glasses and rubbed his eyes.

"I expected to find you asleep when I came back down here." Their eyes met.

"I'm afraid to sleep. It's like . . . God, I've never told this to anybody . . . like when I was a kid. Daddy worked nights once for about a year. I was afraid of the dark then for some reason. I had to sleep in the bed with Momma or I'd have nightmares. My brother teased me unmercifully, called me names." He fiddled with his glasses. "What does that mean?"

"Something Oedipal, I imagine."

"Yeah, that's what I thought."

"How old were you then?"

"I was nine or ten, I think. Then my Dad went back on the day shift and he and Momma went back to sleeping together. What does *that* mean?"

"They got tired of your nonsense. I wouldn't worry about it. Are you gay?"

"No."

"Bisexual?"

"Never paid for it in my life."

"You're a funny guy, Officer Gants. Are you really afraid to go to sleep?"

"Yes."

"Is there anything I can do?"

He imagined the kimono falling away from her shoulders under his hands, her breasts rising to his touch. Then remembered all the real and beautiful things in the house, things that had been sought with patience and chosen with care. Solid, genuine things.

"Two things."

"Yes?"

"First: would you stay with me until I'm asleep?" He smiled sheepishly.

She returned his smile warmly, pulled him to her, and nestled his head on her breast. "What else?"

"Tell me why you had lunch with me today? Why am I here with you? Why are you getting involved in all this?"

"I already told you, Charlie. You need me."

"Do you need me?"

"I need to be needed."

"Would you like to go to the zoo tomorrow?" he mumbled drowsily, but he was asleep before she could answer.

14 | THE ZOO

LITTLE BIT RAN LAUGHING DOWN THE TRAIL ahead of him, past the giraffes and toward the monkey cages. Charlie followed her slowly and happily, sauntering along in the warm sunlight, a battered Panama hat pulled low over his eyes. The zoo was full of children, running noisily among the docile animals. It was a bright, lively place, and Charlie felt good.

"Daddy! Daddy, come see the monkeys."

He waved and smiled at his little girl, and finally caught up with her as she jumped and squealed with delight. The monkeys were in top form for the Saturday crowd. The birds were next. She exhausted him with questions about all the kinds of birds, and he made up most of his answers. As he followed her from place to place through the clamoring crowd, the dead captain seemed less and less real.

"Daddy, can I have a snow cone, please?"

"As long as you sit down to eat it."

Bit's face was red from her nose down, and the front of her yellow sundress was dotted with ice and streaked with strawberry syrup by the time she had finished. He washed her hands in a water fountain.

"Little Bit, will you do something for me, please?"

"What?"

"I want you to slow down a little. We have all afternoon to see the rest of the zoo, and I promise we will ride the train, okay?"

"Okay. Is Sam coming?"

"Yes, Bit. Sam will be here around noon, at the front gate. We have time to see something else first."

"Good."

"What would you like to see next?"

"I want to see Charles."

"Who's Charles?"

"He's a friend of mine, like Sam's a friend of yours."

"Well, any friend of yours is a friend of mine, kid. Let's go."

She was gone in a flash, running into the crowd. Charlie groaned to his feet and followed as best he could. He caught sight of the yellow ribbon bouncing in her hair as she darted between a woman and a little boy, veering to the left at a fork in the path. He found her, her face pressed against the chain-link fence that caged the zebras. Her little fingers clutched the squares of the fence as her lips puckered in a wet but soundless whistle.

"See, Daddy, see! That's Charles right there, the pretty one."

All the zebras looked alike to him, but he looked along her stubby pointing finger and chose the one nearest the fence.

"You're right, Bit, he's the best-looking one in the bunch. How did you know his name was Charles?"

" 'Cause I named him that."

"You named him the last time you were here?"

"No, I named him in my book."

"Your book?"

"About the Ark, my book about the Ark. His picture was in it, and I named him Charles."

"That's a good name for him. That's my name."

"I know that."

"Let's start working our way toward the front gate. Sam will be there before long."

"Carry me."

He lifted her over his head and sat her on his shoulders, her feet dangling down on his chest. She took his hat and put it on her head, and rested her chin in his hair. He walked slowly, pointing out things here and there that he knew she would like. When they reached the gate, Sam was there, with a picnic basket at her feet.

"Hello, you two."

"Hello yourself." Charlie lowered Bit to her feet. "Little Bit, Elizabeth, this is Sam. Sam, Elizabeth."

Bit tugged at his arm and whispered up at him behind her hand, "Daddy, Sam's a girl."

"By golly, you're right."

"Sam is a funny name for a girl."

"Charlie's a kind of funny name for a zebra. Don't worry about it."

"You're right honey," Sam said. "Sam is a funny name for a girl. My name is really Samantha, but people call me Sam, like your Daddy calls you Little Bit."

"Oh."

Charlie nudged Bit and she said hello. He lugged the basket and the two girls with funny names followed him to a grassy spot away from the crowds. As Sam unpacked sandwiches and soda, she watched Charlie rough-housing on the ground with his daughter.

"So, you guys, what's this about a zebra named Charles?"

"Bit named him."

"He's the prettiest one in the bunch, isn't he Daddy?"

"You bet."

"And you named him Charles," Sam said.

"She saw him in her picture book about Noah and the Ark."

"Charles is your name, isn't it? That's interesting. What did you name the other one, Elizabeth?"

"The other one?" Charlie eyed Sam suspiciously.

"The other zebra, Charlie. On the Ark there were two of everything. Elizabeth, what name did you give the momma zebra?"

Bit did not answer.

"Elizabeth, what is your mother's name?"

"Sam!" Charlie gave Sam a look that said, "Leave her out of this!"

They ate, watching people pass by. When they were through, Sam repacked what was left and said good-by. Charlie took Bit to ride the little train that ran around the zoo. Before they left, he took her back for a last look at Charles the zebra, promising her they would come and see him again.

He carried her to the car. She was tired, finally, and nuzzled against him, her arms around his neck.

15 THE PSYCHIC

SAM EASED THE DATSUN INTO ONE OF THE NARROW spaces on the parking lot of the Oak Lawn singles complex.

"Is this where your mystic lives?"

"He is a psychic, Charlie, not a mystic. And yes, this is where he lives. Were you expecting something a little more arcane?"

"Of course not. Psychics are people, too. They can live anywhere they like."

Actually, she was right. He associated psychics with mysticism, fortune-telling, and witchcraft. He had imagined an old Victorian house over in Lakewood somewhere. He had imagined Moseley House, remodeled a little. Now that he was here, in the bright daylight, and it was real, he had second thoughts.

"Sam, why don't we just forget this nonsense? I feel silly going into a stranger's home to have my fortune told."

"Vincent is not a stranger. He is a friend of mine, who values his time and has agreed to see us today as a favor to me. And, he is not a fortune-teller. You've come this far, Charlie, let's see what he has to say."

"Yes'm."

Charlie followed her toward the hedge-lined entrance.

"Honestly, Charlie, where is your sensitivity? After the

things you have been through yourself, I would think you might have a little empathy for Vincent. I expected you to take a much more mature attitude toward this whole thing. Unless . . ." She whirled and fixed Charlie with a hard stare that brought him up short. "Unless you've been faking this whole thing somehow, and you're afraid Vincent will find you out. Have you, Charlie? I swear to God, if you've been faking . . ."

"Wait a goddamn minute, Sam. How can you say that? How about the bruises on my throat? My vital signs? You can't think I faked all that. You're the professional, do you think I could trick you?"

"Anything is possible, Charlie."

"Terrific. I really appreciate that. Can you tell me why I would be faking all of this? Do you think I want to convince people I'm nuts so I can be put away somewhere?"

"People do things for crazy reasons. If you're not afraid of being exposed as a fake, why are you so hesitant about meeting Vincent?"

"I don't know, Sam. That's the truth. I just have a strange feeling about it." He looked back across the parking lot toward the street, at the cars passing. He wished he could turn around and walk away, and forget about all this.

"Just relax and go with it, Charlie. You might be pleasantly surprised."

They walked together without saying anything else, through the entrance and up the walk, through a shaded courtyard to Maitland's door. After they rang the bell, they heard a door chain rattle, and the door opened. They were greeted by a slightly plump but attractive brunette in her early twenties.

"Hi. I'm Sam Cartwright, and this is Charlie Gants. Vincent is expecting us."

"Yes. Please come in, and I'll tell him you're here. I'm Melanie."

Melanie showed them into the apartment, a sunny, tastefully furnished place with several hanging baskets, a terrarium, and groupings of expertly arranged seascapes, landscapes, and still lifes. Charlie was secretly disappointed, but he did not say anything. He thought the place looked more like the home of a decorator than a psychic; he had expected something more theatrical.

Sam and Charlie made themselves comfortable on an oversized couch, and Melanie bounded up the carpeted, spiral staircase, the tight blue shorts riding fetchingly over the cheeks of her ample bottom. Charlie noticed.

"Sam, how old is this guy?"

"Forty-five, but he likes coeds."

Somewhere at the top of the stairs, they heard Melanie call out: "Vinnie, someone's here to see you."

Charlie leaned closer to Sam. "Vinnie? What the hell kind of a name is that? He sounds like a bookie."

She answered him with a scolding mother look. He felt she was still a little upset with him, and remembered his surprise at her suspicions. He quietly surveyed the room. Everything looked expensive. The ashtrays were of heavy crystal and looked like Steuben glass. He remembered his ashtrays at home, little plastic ones that came from the Tom Thumb.

"Psychics must make pretty good money." He could not help saying that.

"Vincent is a vice president at one of the larger advertising agencies in Dallas. He does not do this for money, just as a favor for friends. Keep that in mind and don't embarrass me." Sam's half-in-jest warning stung Charlie.

Vincent and Melanie appeared on the staircase. He was a tall, thin man with stooped shoulders. His hair was dark with a lot of grey, combed back on the sides, and down over his collar in the back. His left arm was draped over Melanie's shoulders, and they came down the stairs in step, laughing quietly.

"Sam! How have you been? You look delicious!" He took Sam's hand with a toothy smile too big for his lean face. "I haven't seen you in months. Where have you been hiding?"

Charlie stood when Sam did, and waited to be introduced.

"Vincent, I'm so glad to see you. It has been too long." They kissed. Very show biz, Charlie thought. "Oh, and I want you to meet my friend, Charlie Gants."

Maitland turned to Charlie and smiled. Charlie thought he looked like a lean hungry wolf.

"A pleasure to meet you, Charles. Any friend of Sam's, you know."

"Call me Charlie."

"Whatever you say, Charlie."

Maitland offered his hand and Charlie took it. As soon as they touched, Maitland's smile vanished, and he drew his hand away. He stared at Charlie, as he offered drinks.

"Scotch, if you have it." Charlie looked away from Maitland's eyes.

"And you, Sam?"

"Just some white wine, I think."

Charlie knew that Maitland did not want him there, and that suited him. He did not want to be there, now that he had seen Maitland, touched him. Something was wrong.

Maitland looked at the two women and smiled again. "Melanie, would you mind making the drinks? I'm not having anything just yet."

Melanie bustled off to the kitchen, and Maitland sat on the couch by Sam.

"Tell me, Sam, how's your work with the Police Department going?"

"I'm just getting my feet on the ground, but it's been interesting so far."

Melanie returned with the drinks. When she had served Sam and Charlie, she knelt on the floor at Maitland's knee. Maitland studied Charlie as he drank his Scotch. Charlie felt the man looking through him, and inside him. He squirmed on the couch, avoiding Maitland's eyes. The drink was not helping.

"How long have you been with the department, Charlie?"

"Nine years."

"And how long have you been a detective?"

"I'm not a detective, technically. I'm an investigator."

"What is the difference?"

"Detective is a civil-service rank, same as sergeant. They don't give detective tests any more. They're phasing them out. Investigators are appointed. It's technical, but there is a difference."

"I see."

Charlie tried not to be obvious when he checked his watch. He could not think of a good reason to leave. He saw Maitland patting Melanie's plump leg. He did not look at Sam.

"Sam," Maitland said, "why don't you let Melanie show you our collection of tropical fish? I know you're not a fish person, but we have a fifty-gallon setup in the study that you won't believe."

"Dying to see it, Vincent." Sam and Melanie left them alone.

"Can I freshen your drink, Charlie?"

"Please." Another drink was what he needed. Maybe several more. Maitland brought him his drink and pulled a chair around to face him squarely.

"Charlie, to be perfectly honest, I was not very enthusiastic about having you over today. I'm in the middle of a big ad campaign, and I need my day off to rest up, get the juices flowing again. I agreed to see you strictly as a personal favor to Sam. She and I are very close, if you follow me." Charlie did not know if he followed him or not. "You wouldn't believe it, Charlie, the number of people I have calling me, ever since word of the field study got out. Everything from contacting their dear departed to finding lost jewelry to stock market tips. It's incredible."

Charlie had not touched his fresh drink. He was watching Maitland, and he felt that he could not relax.

"Then, when we shook hands just now, I came very close to asking the two of you to leave. Something is definitely going on with you, but I have no idea what, not yet. I've decided that I will try to help you understand."

Maitland picked up a thin brown cigarette from the silver case on the coffee table. As he lit it, Charlie took advantage of the pause to gulp down as much Scotch as he could. Then Maitland was staring into his eyes again, exhaling smoke through his nose in a long thin stream.

"A man died. Was he your father?"

"No." Charlie answered, taken back. "My father died less than a year ago, but he's not . . . it's someone else."

"This man died violently."

Charlie said nothing. He wondered how much Sam had told Maitland.

"It was a suicide." Maitland's eyes closed, and his head cocked at an angle. "No. It seemed to be suicide. The man was murdered. He was murdered by someone he knew very well."

"Who?"

"Someone he knew. He was expecting someone . . . I can't see any more than that. He was sitting on his bed and . . . he was shot." Maitland's eyes opened and he stared at Charlie. "Tell me about your dreams."

"Dreams?"

"Yes. You must tell me everything, or there is no point in any of this."

"I guess Sam told you."

"She has told me nothing."

Charlie told him everything, and Maitland listened in rapt attention until he was through.

"You have left nothing out?"

"That's all of it."

"Then there is very little more that I can say." He leaned forward and laid his hand on Charlie's shoulder. Their faces were inches apart, and Maitland whispered, "You are the object of a powerful force. I am sure of that. Its source or its purpose I cannot say. Take my warning, Charlie: you are in physical danger, I think, but there is more. You are a lightning rod. I have never been in the presence of so powerful a force. Never."

The whispered warning struck a chord of terror in Charlie, deep in the banished, savage part of him. He saw a flicker of it reflected in Maitland's eyes.

"What can I do?"

"Nothing." Maitland rose to his feet, and Charlie stood, too. "You cannot resist it. You must not resist it. The mind is a fragile, delicately balanced crystal piece, Charlie, hung by a thread. If you fight it, the forces may shatter that delicate piece. If it pushes you too far, if you see too much . . ." He did not finish, but Charlie saw the sad, frightened light in the older man's eyes, like a dying campfire in the primal mist. And then, as if a curtain had fallen, it was over. Maitland turned away from Charlie, and called aloud, "Melanie?"

As Melanie and Sam came back into the room, Maitland whispered one more thing, so that Charlie could hear: "Don't come back here. Please don't come back." Then, to Melanie: "Charlie tells me they must be going."

"So soon?"

"I'm afraid so. They have things to do."

"That's right," Charlie added. "We have to go."

The women exchanged goodbys and made plans for getting

together for lunch someday. Charlie and Maitland shook hands. Then Charlie found himself outside, walking to Sam's car.

"What did Vincent say, Charlie?"

"Tell me the truth, Sam. How much had you already told him about this case?"

"Nothing. You were there when I called him. I haven't spoken to him since. What did he say?"

"I'll tell you in the car."

16 | THE CAPTAIN'S TABLE

"FOURTH AND A LONG ONE, AND TIME IS RUNNING out for the Dallas Cowboys."

"That's right, Bob. It's now or never for the 'Pokes.' "

"It's only the first game of the preseason, Jim, and Tom Landry told us in the pregame interviews that winning was not the main thing on his mind today . . . ."

"That's right, Bob. There's no question about it. Tom has a lot of new talent that he wants to look at. The Cowboys, like all the other teams in the NFL are looking ahead to those roster cuts, when they have to make those tough decisions about who stays and who goes."

". . . but I think we all know Tom well enough to know that he'd really like to put this one in the win column. He's a real competitor, folks, not to mention Danny White. Yes, sir, I don't think it would be presumptuous of me to say that I think Tom and Danny are using their last time out right now to try to come up with a way to move that ball down close enough to give Septien a shot at a winning field goal. After all, even in the first preseason game, winning is the name of the game."

"I don't think there's any question about it, Bob. Winning is the name of the game."

The time out was over. As the credits rolled and the play-by-play man thanked his spotters and statisticians, as he reminded sports fans everywhere of the great job his director and producers and cameramen had done, the Cowboys broke their huddle.

"Well, this is it, folks. It all comes down to this play!"

"That's right, Bob. The Cowboys are in a short yardage set. You'll usually see them run out of this formation, but time is very, very short. They may not have time for another play."

It was a play-action pass, but somebody did not pick up a safety blitz, and Danny White was sacked. The ball went over on downs. Lots of crowd noise. The play-by-play man and the color commentator were screaming, both jazzed on the simultaneous thrill of victory and agony of defeat. They were up for their game. Sportscasters have to make the cut, too.

"Charlie, can I get you a beer or something?"

"Huh? Oh, no thanks. I have a little headache coming on." She snapped off the television and sat down beside him.

"What is it, Charlie? Are you still upset about what Vincent said?"

"I wouldn't say upset." He got up and paced. "I think I would say terrified. Yeah, it would be a lot more accurate to say I was terrified."

He paced in silence, from one end of the room to the other, around and around the couch, then back and forth again.

"At the risk of playing Pollyanna, I'd like to point out the bright side."

"The what?"

"The bright side. The up side, Daddy used to call it."

"You are joking."

"No, I'm not. Sit down here beside me and let's look at it rationally." She sat with her feet tucked under her, so that she was taller than Charlie. He slouched forward, his elbows on his knees. "The things Vincent told you were frightening, I admit. But at least he confirmed that something is happening. It's not just your imagination. Think about it, Charlie. I didn't begin to believe you were on the level until there was some confirmation. I saw your vital signs, the scratches and bruises. Except for that, all the rest of it happened in one place, your mind."

"You seem to be forgetting one thing."

"What's that?"

"The journal."

"Yes, that's true." She paused thoughtfully for a moment and then added. "Now you have the journal and you have Vincent's confirmation. You have some evidence."

"And some advice: don't fight it, try not to see too much or I'll lose my mind, and never go back to Vincent's."

"He told you all he could."

"I'll never forget the look on his face. He was scared to death of me."

He massaged the back of his neck at the base of his skull, where the headache had finally settled in earnest. Sam took over and did a better job of it.

"Sam, I'm sorry I ever got you involved in this. I swear, I just wish the old man would leave me alone."

"I don't want to upset you, Charlie, but I have a hunch he won't let you rest until you find whatever he wants you to find. And I'm involved because I want to be."

"I don't know where I'd be without you." He laughed sarcastically. "Actually, I do have a pretty good idea. I'd be on the 'rubber gun' squad."

"The what?"

"It's where they put cops who snap. They hide you back in the files somewhere, where you can't tear up anything."

"You haven't snapped, Charlie Gants, and you're not going to. I'm here to see to that. I'll admit, I had my doubts at first, but I really think you're holding up pretty well."

"Because of you. You listened to me and you're here when I need you. I hope you'll always be here for me. Sam, I think I . . ."

She pressed a finger to his lips. "Before you say anything else, I think I need to play shrink for a minute here. You've been under terrific stress, and I'm glad I'm able to help. But you need to take the big steps one at a time. Get the business with the captain behind you before you make any heavy emotional commitments. When things get back to normal, you may feel differently."

"How about you, Sam? How do you feel?"

"As I said, Charlie, one thing at a time. What you need right now is a nice dinner in a swank restaurant. It will help you relax."

"It would suit me fine if I just picked up a pizza."

"Okay, Officer Gants, the truth. What I need is a nice dinner in a swank restaurant. That's not too much to ask, is it?"

"I guess not."

She used the phone on the end table beside her.

"Hershel, how are you? This is Dr. Cartwright. For two. Yes, eight o'clock would be nice. Thank you. We'll eat at eight, Charlie. What would you like to do until then?"

He did not answer.

"Would you like to go upstairs with me?" She eyed him almost clinically. "I'm propositioning you."

"But you just said . . ."

"I'm not talking Romeo and Juliet, Charlie, I'm talking about sex. Not love, sex. Think of it as therapy."

He returned her smile. She took his hand and led him up the stairs.

It was almost seven when he felt her stir beside him. He watched her as she turned toward him, the movement exposing her right breast above the crisp clean sheets. Usually, he thought women looked better dressed than undressed. Sam was the exception. As good as she looked in her clothes, her body exceeded its promise. She was exquisite. Preoccupied with the contour of her breast as it rose and fell, he did not see her eyes slowly open.

"See something you like, guy?"

She laughed at the look on his face. "You looked so solemn. Even when you were making love to me you looked solemn. Sex isn't spiritual, Charlie, it's fun!"

"With you, it's both." He reached for her and she rolled away.

"No time for that now, you sex fiend. Our reservations are for eight, sharp."

He lay back on both arms and watched her disappear into the bathroom.

"Sam, how expensive is this place?"

"If you have to ask . . ."

"That's what I was afraid of."

"It'll be my treat."

"Do you want me to feel emasculated at this point in our relationship?"

"Okay, we'll go dutch."

Sam ordered while Charlie worried over the menu. There were no prices.

"Have you decided, Charlie?"

"It all looks so good." Sam ordered for him.

"The whole idea is for you to relax. If you're going to sit there aggravating your pre-ulcerous stomach all night worrying about the bill, it's just a waste of good food and atmosphere."

"Could you just give me some idea what a dinner for two will run in this place?"

"This one will run about two or three hundred dollars before I'm through."

"Do you have any idea what my take-home is?"

"Of course not."

"Well, let me explain it this way: if I had my paycheck with me, I could just about deduct my rent and leave the rest on the table. The waiter would be a little miffed about the cheap tip, but I don't expect to be a regular here, anyway."

"Charlie, I told you it was my treat. If it will make you feel better, I'll slip my credit card to you under the table and you can sign for it. Sign it 'Sam' and nobody will be the wiser."

"Thanks. That would be almost as good as your letting me drive your Z car all the way over here."

"Look, I can't help it if my folks left me some money, any more than you can help it if yours didn't. You have to get over this money fetish, Charlie. I swear, you have a lot to learn."

"All right, all right, don't get upset about it."

"Fine, let's just relax and enjoy ourselves."

"Fine."

"You look real nice in Daddy's suit."

"Thank you."

The steward brought the wine list and offered it to Charlie. He studied it elaborately, nonchalantly, and ordered a bottle of Chateau-Thierry.

"Charlie, you are incorrigible. We are not on a budget. They have an excellent wine celler here. Why did you order that one?"

He blushed. "It was the only one I could pronounce."

She threw back her head and laughed, a hearty, honest laugh. Her laugh made Charlie feel good again. He forgot about money and the captain and everything except her. And, he really began to enjoy himself.

They talked and laughed and drank the wine before the food came. Sam ordered a second bottle. Charlie thought the food was excellent, steak smothered in an exotic sauce.

They had finished eating and were laughing and smoking Sam's Nat Shermans when Charlie saw the dead captain, sitting alone at a table across the room, his back to Charlie. Sam saw the horror in Charlie's face before he could speak.

"What is it, Charlie? What's wrong?"

"Nothing. Really, it's nothing. I thought I saw somebody I knew, but I didn't. Nothing's wrong."

Wait a minute, he told himself. Get a grip on yourself. You're not dreaming now. All this is really happening. The captain is dead, Charlie boy. He only crawls around in your head, he doesn't mingle with real people in restaurants. I mean, can't you just see the rotten old bastard trying to get past the maitre d'?

"Am I boring you all of a sudden?"

"What?"

"I've been talking to you, Charlie. Got something more interesting at another table?"

"Sam, please tell me I'm going crazy."

"What are you saying?"

"At the table over there. Look and tell me what you see."

"What am I looking for?"

"Well?"

"Nothing. I don't know, Charlie, just people eating dinner. What am I supposed to see?"

He looked again. Nothing. The captain's chair was empty. He buried his face in his hands.

"Who is it, Charlie? Who did you see?" She grabbed his wrist. "You thought you saw the captain, didn't you?"

"Sam, I swear to God he was there. I tell you, it was him!"

He put his hands on hers. "Or else I really am losing my mind."

When he looked back, the captain was in his chair again.

"I won't let you out of my sight this time, by God!" Charlie lurched to his feet, knocking over the ice bucket stand. The half-bottle of wine rolled across the floor, spewing patrons with expensive Beaujolais.

"No, Charlie, no!" Sam screamed.

Charlie strode across the room. He grabbed the captain's shoulder and spun him around. "Leave me alone! Leave me alone, you goddamned old sonofabitch!" Every head turned at the sound of his voice, like the cry of a wounded beast at bay.

Charlie glared down at the crinkled pink face, with its thin white mustache. The poor little man's food spread over his chin and spattered down the front of his shirt as he sputtered helplessly in the grip of the madman. Charlie held him and glared, not speaking, until he felt Sam's hand on his arm. Then he knew what he had done. He looked around at all the people who were watching him closely. Even when he saw the look on Sam's face he did not say anything. He released the little man and stumbled out of the restaurant.

She found him in the parking lot, his hands in his pockets, staring at the ground. He was crying. When her car came around, he got in and she drove away. They said nothing until they got out of the car in front of her house.

"Everything's all right at the restaurant, Charlie. I bought the little man's dinner and explained to him that you are not well."

"You told him I was crazy."

"Actually, I said you were a Viet Nam vet, suffering from a delayed stress syndrome. What did you want me to tell him, that you're haunted?"

"I'm sorry I embarrassed you, Sam. I know that is one of your places and I made an ass of myself. I'm sorry."

"Being sorry has nothing to do with it. Don't expect any sympathy from me right now. I'm not going to hold your hand and reinforce that kind of bizarre behavior."

He looked at his watch. "Sorry, Doctor. I believe my hour is up." He turned toward his own car.

"Come back here, Charlie. You're in no condition to drive, much less to spend the night alone."

"Who's talking now, the woman or the shrink?"

"Somebody who cares about you, Charlie." There was a trace of a smile as she led him inside.

17 | THE CODE

CHARLIE FOUND HIMSELF LOOKING DOWN A NAR-
row street, a street where he had once lived and run barefoot as
a child. It was a late spring evening. Along either side of the
street, large oak and elm trees shaded the white frame houses.
He walked slowly along the bumpy asphalt under the awning of
trees, not knowing or caring why he was there. It was good to
be home again.

He knew that he was not alone. A woman appeared at his
side.

"Hello, son."

"Momma?" He looked into her gentle face with a mixture of
joy and disbelief. "Momma!" It was her, it really was. He
hugged her, savoring her faint lilac scent. "I've missed you,
Momma."

She stepped back to look him over, and brushed his hair back
from his forehead the way she always did. "Come on, Charlie.
Come home."

She took him by the hand and led as she had so many times
down the street toward home. He followed with a sense of
warmth and ease, past homes of old friends. There was the
Cantrell house, the Parks's place, the house where Aunt

Maudie, whose real name was Mrs. Bastrop, used to live. She'd paid him with cookies and lemonade for doing her chores and errands. Time had changed nothing since he had been a boy, except that not a single light showed in a single house in the darkness just after dusk. And there was no sound from any of the houses.

As they passed a house on the right side of the road, Charlie saw someone sitting in a large porch swing. He could see that it was a woman with long, dark hair, but her face was hidden in the shadows. She watched him as he walked by, and the swing moved slowly to and fro as she rocked.

"Who is she, Momma?"

His mother did not answer. Charlie looked back at the woman in the swing. Her full white dress almost seemed to glow in the dark, and the double row of her white teeth showed in a Cheshire cat grin. He saw the silhouette of a man in the open doorway behind her.

And then they were home. The house was just as he remembered it, a place of memories that were suddenly alive again.

"Come on, son. We have to go in now." His mother led him across the yard to the foot of the steps.

Charlie heard the porch swing groan, and turned to see the woman in the white dress disappear into the dark house.

"Not yet, Momma. Not yet." Charlie slipped loose from her hand and walked past the houses, like mausoleums, toward the house with the porch swing. When he reached the porch, the girl was gone, and the front door was closed. The man was gone, too. The swing still rocked gently in the black, moonless, spring night.

Charlie made his way to the side of the house, and pressed his face to a window, trying to see inside. Without turning to look, he suddenly felt someone at his back. His heart leaped, and he screamed in wordless terror as unseen hands reached out for him. Run! Run! He ran headlong into the night, a silent terror at his heels.

Sam shook him violently and called his name a dozen times. When his eyes finally opened, he found himself in her bed. Every light was on and she was holding him tightly, shaking him as she called his name. He stopped struggling and lay back, exhausted. His chest heaved as if he had run a marathon. Sam brushed his hair up off his forehead.

"Charlie, everything's all right. I'm right here."

"Oh, Sam. Goddamn . . ."

"The captain again?"

"Not this time. This time . . . I'm not sure. Momma was there."

He put his arm around Sam and drew her close. "I don't want to tell you about it right now."

"Why not?"

"If you tell a dream before breakfast, it will come true."

She smiled at the superstition. "All right, if you're going to be that way about it, I'll get up and make us something."

"Coffee'll do. A cup of coffee is as good as anything."

She pulled on a robe and padded off downstairs to the kitchen. Without bothering to dress, Charlie followed her as far as the den. While the coffee was brewing, he stood, staring blankly at the captain's book. He took the hot black coffee from her with an apologetic smile, and they sat on the couch.

"Tell the truth, Sam. Your interest in me is purely professional, isn't it?"

"As a matter of fact, you're right. At least, it was at first."

"What?"

"It's true. Obviously, it's gone a little beyond that now. I don't make a practice of bringing my case studies home to bed with me."

"I'm a case study? You keep saying that."

"Charlie, don't pout."

"You don't make a practice of going to bed with case studies. Have you ever done it before?"

"Yes." She watched him, saw the hurt on his face. "Don't ask me a question if you can't handle the answer. I'm not going to lie to you. I haven't the time or energy for games." She lit one of her brown cigarettes. "I went to bed with you because I wanted to and because I thought it would be good for you. Is there anything wrong with that? Has anything changed because you were not the first?" He shrugged. "Tell me about the dream."

"It was my mother this time. I was back on the street in front of my house, the one I grew up in. My mother still lives there, but the house has been redone. In the dream, it was just like it was when I was a kid. It was dusk, getting dark, but none of the other houses had any lights on. Momma's was the only one. She wanted me to come inside with her, but there was someone else. There was a woman on the porch of a house that wasn't there when I was a kid. A man, too. They seemed to be watching me, waiting for me. I wanted to see their faces. But when I went back, they were gone. And then somebody tried to get me and I ran."

"What do you think it means, Charlie?"

"You're the shrink, I'm the case study. You tell me."

"You wanted to go home, as we all do, at one time or another. Home is the safest place, but you feel you can't be really safe until you find whatever it is the captain wants you to find. You couldn't tell who the people were on the porch?"

"No, it was too dark. I could only see that the woman had long dark hair. And she was wearing a white dress."

"How do you feel about your mother?"

"What do you mean?"

"We talked about her once before. You said you went through a phase when you had to sleep with her or you would have nightmares."

"So?"

"And that this was a time when your father was away, working the night shift. Your mother was the one who made you feel safe and secure. I asked you then if you thought you were homosexual or bisexual, and you joked about it. Joking is a way to hide serious feelings. Sometimes it's a defense mechanism. Answer me truthfully this time. Are you homosexual?"

"That's a hell of a thing to ask me after I've just made love to you."

"Bisexual?"

He did not answer.

"Have you ever had homosexual thoughts or instincts? Ever been curious? Has a homosexual ever propositioned you?"

"Sam, you just covered a lot of territory there. I think everybody has some homosexual feelings at times. That doesn't make everybody homosexual." He drank his coffee, staring into his cup. "I was propositioned once. I was a kid. The guy came up to me. Afterwards he apologized. Apparently, he looked at me and thought I was gay. What does that mean?"

"I think it means that you have a problem with it. Your mother was your dominant figure during your formative years, and your father was more distant. That's a common background for homosexuality. And you are exactly right, Charlie. In every man there is a trace of the female. The same is true about women. That's nothing to be concerned about. It doesn't make you homosexual. But, if you have guilt about it, if you overcompensate for it, you may make problems for yourself."

"Do you think I do that?"

"Yes. I think that's why you became a policeman. The badge, the gun, how masculine can you be? But if you secretly feel that you're not really masculine enough, you may feel that you're a fraud. It could make you a little neurotic. Your own suffering makes you more sensitive to the suffering of others, which makes you even less suited as a cop, which reinforces your notion that you are not man enough for the job. It's a vicious, self-perpetuating cycle." She stubbed her cigarette out. "I'm not surprised that your stomach hurts."

"I wasn't good in bed, was I? That's what tipped you off, isn't it?"

"You were good, Charlie, but you were anxious, solemn. It was your anxiety that I picked up on." She put her arm around his shoulder. "I'm right, aren't I?"

He didn't answer. He put his coffee cup on the table beside the captain's journal. He picked up the book and thumbed through the pages, watching the coded entries pass by meaninglessly. "The answers I need are in this book, Sam. If only I could break the old man's code."

She stood up. He did not look up. He found his legal pad and went back to work on the journal. Once he heard her putting things away in the kitchen.

Again he went through the process of substituting letters, using the song title every way he could imagine, with no luck. He was not aware of how much time had passed when he heard her behind him.

"Charlie, what if the numbers don't stand for numbers? What if they stand for letters, too?"

"Then we have twenty-one letters. We need twenty-six."

"Not if he only used consonants. Leave out the five vowels and you have twenty-one letters in the alphabet."

"Why would he leave out the vowels?"

"Who knows? To make the code tougher. You said he was a strange man."

"Okay, let's see. There are seven numbers used. Zero, one, three, four, five, six, seven. Two then five consecutive." He arranged the numbers in ascending order, in combination with the song title, and assigned letters, excluding vowels. That did not work. It did not help to reverse the order, either.

"A phone number, Charlie."

He turned around then, and was surprised to see her dressed for work. "What did you say?"

"Your seven numbers. What's the first seven-digit number you think of? Your phone number. It came to me in the shower. I guess I'm in an analytical mood this morning." She looked at him gently, and he looked away.

"Yeah," he said, "each number stands for a consonant. The phone number tells you in what order, which consonant each number stands for. All we have to do is figure out which phone number the old man used."

"Not we, Charlie. You may be on vacation, but I'm still a working girl. Lock up when you leave, and call me when you figure it out."

For the first time, Charlie noticed the sunlight that embroidered the drawn curtains. "What time is it?"

"Seven-fifteen. Time for me to go. Look, I know you're obsessed with this, and I understand how you feel, but let me give you a little professional advice. Put that stuff down for a while. Shave and shower, relax a little. You'll do better. When you get it all worked out, call me." He promised he would. "And think about what I said last night."

She left, and he remembered that he was naked when he stood up to walk her to the door to say good-by. She waved and was gone. Information gave him the number of the Crockett Hotel. It did not work. Seven digits with none repeated, but it made no sense.

She was right about the shower. He was in no hurry now. They had the key, it was only a matter of time. And he knew what the jumbled consonants would spell when he sorted them out: JL CPLND, Julia Copeland, the face in the picture.

18 | THE SIDEWALK CAFE

SHE RAN THE LAST BLOCK TO THANKSGIVING Square, where Charlie waited. The little park was full of people eating lunch, escaping from their offices to eat in the fresh air. A construction crew from the skyscraper in progress across the street lined the wall along the sidewalk, eyeing all the women who passed. Some of them whistled and yelled as Sam hurried by.

"Well?" She was breathless.

"Well, I got a couple of Reubens from the sandwich shop downstairs at the bank. That all right with you?"

"Charlie! What did you find out? Did you solve it?" She took her sandwich and sat beside him.

"You were right. It was a phone number. The tough part for me was figuring out which phone number. The first thing I thought of was his number at the hotel. I mean, if you were going to use a phone number in a code, your number would be the logical choice, right? Especially if there were no digits repeated. That should have been it."

"And?"

"It wasn't. Then I remembered who we are dealing with here. The captain only had one real home in his whole life . . .

Homicide. Six-seven-oh-five-one-four-three. It fit and it made sense. It took me I don't know how long to translate the whole thing. Then I had to break down all those consonants into words. I called you as soon as I finished." Charlie looked at his sandwich and put it aside. "The captain thought he had solved the Slasher murders. At least, he had a theory. It's bizarre, Sam, but he suspected Julia Copeland."

"His own daughter?"

"Yeah, and he had some evidence to back it up, too. Circumstantial stuff, but that's how it usually starts out. See, he was in a position, right before the department turned him out, to see everything that was being done on the Slasher case. A detective over here turns up a little something, one over there comes up with something else. In itself, each little bit means nothing. But if a man were in a position to put them with other little bits, they might mean a lot. Especially if that man knew more than was in any report, if he knew something or somebody we didn't know about at all. We were looking for a man. The way those boys were worked over, the force used, the victim's records; everything pointed toward a man. But there were things here and there, little things, that went the other way."

"Maybe it was a woman. But, Charlie, his own daughter?"

He drew a sheaf of yellow pages from his jacket pocket. "Take a look at this."

The top page appeared to Sam to be a random grouping of letters: T S HRD FR M T THNK M DGHTR CPBL F MDR. BT BCS F TH TRRBL THNGS THT HPPND WHN SH WS JST FFTN ND BCS F WHT DCTRS ND PRSTS HV TLD M, CN THNK NTHNG LSS. TH FCTS F TH SLSHR KLLNGS SPPRT M BLFS. GD HLP M.

"This doesn't make sense, Charlie. I . . . wait a minute," she said pointing to the page. "This looks like 'daughter' and this . . ."

"Maybe this will help." Charlie said, pulling a sheet from the bottom of the stack and laying it on top for her to see. "It took me a while, but this is it."

Sam read aloud, "It is hard for me to think my daughter capable of murder. But because of the terrible things that happened when she was just fifteen and because of what doctors and priests have told me, (I) can think nothing less. The facts of the Slasher killings support my beliefs. God help me."

Sam shook her head. "What happened when she was fifteen?"

"I have no idea, Sam. That's all he says about it, just that something terrible happened. Apparently, it was so terrible that he consulted doctors and priests about it. And whatever they told him supported his suspicions, or at least didn't put them to rest."

"Charlie, this is incredible, but how does it tie in with the captain's death? If he was despondent about all this, that might explain suicide. How does it fit in with your idea that he was murdered?"

"Read the last page."

Charlie slipped the translated page from the stack for her to read.

"Followed her. (I) know the truth at last. Looking at her sweet innocent face in the picture it seems impossible she could commit murder, but it is true. (I) am going to tell Julia tonight. Somehow together we can . . ."

"To have a murder you need a suspect, somebody with a motive. The captain told Julia what he knew. That was her motive. We know the old man well enough to know he would never hide something like this, not even to protect her. He probably gave her the option of turning herself in, getting professional help. The way I see it, she went to see him. Probably knocked on his door as he was writing that last line, that's why it ends in mid-sentence. And here's what he used to mark his place."

She took the picture and looked at it as if she had never seen it before. Julia, little more than a child herself, with her baby held stiffly in her arms. She was beautiful, with her guileless eyes. She was not smiling.

They said nothing for a long time, sitting quietly in the sunlit park as people moved around them. Then Sam realized that she had to get back to work.

"What now, Charlie? What happens now?"

"I'm not sure. This isn't anything I can go to the department with. They think I'm crazy, anyway. This wouldn't get me very far, accusing Mrs. Edmund Copeland of multiple murders and patricide."

"What will you do?"

"I'm going to show Wes what I have and see what he thinks, then just go from there."

"Charlie, I've been thinking."

"Really?"

"If you're right . . . , I mean, if we are right, the captain and you and I, then Julia Copeland is a very dangerous woman."

"That would be an understatement."

"Be careful, Charlie. Just be careful."

She rose to leave, and Charlie expected her to kiss him, but she did not. When she was gone, he went to call Wes.

The clerk who answered the phone in Homicide told him that Wes had gotten a call from a woman and had left to meet her for coffee. They were not at the Farmer's Grill or at either of two other cafes Charlie checked, places frequented by cops. Maybe it's somebody he doesn't want to be seen with, Charlie thought. A conquest-in-the-making that he is keeping to himself.

Charlie drove to the Quadrangle on a hunch. Nothing was farther from Wes' taste, but he had mentioned it once or twice. There was a little sidewalk cafe where shoppers rested from their explorations of the quaint and tasteful shops that clustered around Theater Three, where Charlie had once enjoyed an excellent Cole Porter revue. He spotted the city car angled inconspicuously into a corner stall and parked nearby. He followed the walkway that wound around to the cafe.

He saw Wes sitting at a table with his back to the wall, as usual. The woman who sat opposite him across the small round table under the colorful umbrella had her back to Charlie. Her wide-brimmed straw hat trembled in the light breeze, and the ruffles of her summery print dress danced brightly. Wes saw Charlie, and looked surprised at first. He said something to the woman, then waved Charlie over with a wink and a big smile.

"Well, tell me, partner, what's it like, not having to work for a living?"

Charlie did not answer. He looked down at the lovely face behind the fashionably large, tinted glasses.

"Charlie, you know Jessica Copeland."

"Yes. How do you do?"

She smiled and offered her hand. "I'm well. But how are you?"

"Fine. I hope I'm not interrupting anything."

"Of course not." She assured him. "Are you really all right? I'm sorry that Edmund had you suspended."

"It's not that bad. I'm not suspended, actually. They're still paying me."

"Charlie's just on vacation, that's all. Have a seat, partner."

Charlie sat in the chair Wes offered. "Wes, the office said you were meeting someone for coffee, and I just stopped by here on a hunch. I didn't mean to barge in on you."

"Don't give it a thought, partner. I'm glad you're here, as a matter of fact. We were just talking about you."

"Really?"

"Yep. Jessica asked me what kind of a guy you were, and I told her you were all right, just a little crazy."

"I appreciate that, Wes."

"Seriously, Mr. Gants, I know how Mother is. She can be unreasonable, and I was afraid she overreacted, without giving you a chance to explain yourself. Do you have any new information about grandfather's death?"

"I don't have any real evidence. Like I told your mother, I just have a feeling about it. Since I've been on the case, I feel that I have learned a lot about the captain, and I just don't believe things happened the way the department says. I wanted to ask your mother some questions, that's all. Please believe me, I didn't mean to upset her. I should have realized how she would react."

"My mother is easily upset. In fact, she can be irrational. I know that better than anyone."

There was an awkward pause. Charlie looked at Wes.

"But she said you had dreams about grandfather, Mr. Gants."

"I'm afraid I've been living the case a little too much, that's all."

"You're not psychic, are you?"

"Hardly. I don't want to keep anything from you, I just don't have anything solid yet. And I'm afraid I've been ordered to stop looking for anything."

"That may be for the best. I am glad you're not suspended. Please accept my apologies for Mother."

"That's very nice of you, but it's not necessary."

"Look at the time. As pleasant as I find your company, gentlemen, I'm afraid I must go. A photographer is waiting."

The two policemen stood as she rose and shook Charlie's hand again.

"If I can be of any help, please call me, Mr. Gants."

"Charlie. And thank you, I will."

"I hope so, Charlie. Bye-bye, Wes."

She walked away in a swirl of color and sunlight, leaving the two men watching as she disappeared around a corner.

"Wes, she's a knockout."

"And young enough to be your daughter. Sit down and tell me what's on your mind."

They settled on the little chairs as a waiter brought fresh coffee.

"Did you really tell her that I was a little crazy?"

"You are, aren't you? Or do you have a good explanation for all this dream crap?"

"It's hard to explain, Wes. I'm not sure I understand it myself. Sam says . . ."

"Sam? The lady shrink?"

"Yeah."

"Well, by God, I'm glad to hear you've got enough sense to get some help. Whether you need it or not, it wouldn't hurt to have her on hand in case you wind up before a departmental trial board."

"Trial board? Do you know something I don't?"

"Don't get excited. I'm just talking in general. As far as I know, you're okay for the time being. But I don't think it's any secret that if you pull another stunt like you pulled at the Copeland's house, you are going to be in a world of trouble. A trial board might be just the first step down a long road for you."

"You think they'd fire me if I stirred up the Copelands again?"

"Damned right, and I wouldn't blame 'em. Those are heavy

hitters you're messing around with, boy. And for no reason. If you had some new evidence or something substantial, it would be different."

"Well, I think I may have something now. I didn't have it when I went to see Mrs. Copeland."

"What?"

"I found the captain's journal. It was in code, but I finally figured it out this morning." He took the yellow pages out of his pocket. "I didn't want to say anything in front of Jessica."

"Partner, when in hell are you going to learn? Leave this goddamned deal alone while you still have a job."

"Before you say anything else, take a look at this and tell me if you think I ought to leave it alone."

Braverman studied the yellow pages carefully, stopping from time to time to look up at Charlie. When he finished reading them, he folded the pages and laid them on the table. He leaned back, eyed Charlie carefully, and shook his head.

"Well, that's something, all right. Damnedest thing I believe I've ever seen. You say it was in code?"

"Yeah, I've had it since last Friday. I just figured it out this morning."

"Where'd you get this, Charlie?"

"I don't think you want to know. No point in setting you up to take any heat over that. What do you think?"

"Well . . . it's something, I'll give you that. I don't think you'd want to go to the department with it, not the way you stand around there right now."

"There's something else. Look at this." Charlie handed him the photograph. "That was what he used to mark his place. It was stuck between the pages, right there at the last. That is the picture the captain was looking at when he wrote that last part. That's the 'sweet innocent' face."

"Jesus H. Christ, partner. You hand me a snapshot of the Madonna with child and tell me we're gonna sell a jury on the idea that she's not only a psychopathic killer, but that she also gunned down her old daddy to keep him quiet. Jesus H., I can't look at this and believe that myself."

"Wes, what is the terrible thing that happened when she was fifteen?"

146

"I don't know. Whatever it was, it was before my time. And the captain never had much to say about his family."

"She looks awful young in that picture. Not much more than a kid herself."

Braverman smiled. "Yeah, but she sure did start fillin' out early."

"What do we do now, Wes?"

"You go home and try to stay out of trouble, partner. If word gets out that you're still snooping around on this, we might both wind up looking for jobs."

Charlie watched the older man as he studied the photograph carefully, thoughtfully. He felt good about having another ally, especially since it was Wes. He knew from working with him that Wes would know what to do.

"There's one thing I know as sure as my name is John Wesley Braverman: whether she's a killer or not, that little lady right there has plenty of influence. Before we tell anybody anything, we'd better be double damned sure that we're right and that we can prove it. If you go off half-cocked and you don't have anything to back you up except some weird-assed diary that a senile old man wrote in some off-the-wall secret language, you're gonna be the one that ends up behind bars. We've gotta remember that the old cap'n could write anything that came into his head. This stuff is interesting, all right, but it don't prove a damned thing."

"I know that, Wes. That's why I wanted to talk to you. I want to make sure we're right before we stick our necks out."

"Well, like I said, you just go home and stay out of trouble. I'll check around and see what I can come up with."

When Charlie left the cafe, he felt better than he had in days. He had Wes in his corner now, and at last he knew what the captain had been trying to tell him. Maybe now the old bastard would let him get a good night's sleep.

Driving home, he remembered what Sam had said. If they were right, Julia Copeland was a dangerous woman. He checked; he did not think he was being followed.

19 | THE VICTIM'S VICTIM

CHARLIE SLEPT LATE THE NEXT DAY, TUESDAY. HE awoke with nowhere to go and nothing to do except wait to hear from Wes. He called Sam, but she was out of the office.

He did his wash, tiptoing barefoot across the sizzling pavement to the damp coolness of the laundry room beside the pool. It was another blue-sky oven of a day, and the pool area was deserted.

He called Sam again. Her secretary said she had returned his call and missed him. Finally, as he brought in the last of his clean, dry clothes, she called again. He asked her to dinner, but she had plans. He called his ex-wife to see if he could take Bit out for dinner that evening, but got no answer. Then he realized that Bit had been his second choice, and he felt guilty. He did not like the idea of his little girl playing second fiddle to anyone.

From his rear patio, Charlie could see a slice of Greenville Avenue, and he stood watching the outbound flow of traffic thicken into rush hour, with a drink in his hand. North Central Expressway would be even worse.

"Well," he said aloud, "there's always the club."

Club Sixty-Six was a private club for cops and their friends, run by the Dallas Police Association. They named it that because a signal sixty-six was code for an officer's end of tour of duty.

Charlie left his car on the lot next door and made his way through the solid metal door, up the steep, narrow stairs toward the club. It was already noisy, with men shouting. He noticed as he went that the garish red carpet on the stairs had been replaced with brown. Upstairs, he saw that the whole bar had been redone since his last visit. The four booths that had separated the barstools from the dance floor were gone, replaced with a bank of video games. Half a dozen young officers, fresh from work, were playing the games. They were making all the noise.

At a long table near the door, two men, a little older than Charlie, sat on either side of a pitcher of beer. One of them, a bald man with a paunch, waved at Charlie.

"Hey, Charlie, grab a glass and pull up a chair."

Charlie waved and went to the bar. Ruby, the manager, was in her office, so he reached behind the bar and took a glass. As he passed the electronic games on his way to the table, he saw that none of the game players noticed him. They were too intent on their machines. Each of the electronic boxes blared its own loud music and sound effects.

The bald man poured Charlie a beer and shook his head. "Ain't it hell? Those boys play those damned machines all night long. It's like trying to have a quiet beer on the midway at the state fair."

"I didn't even know they had put those games in," Charlie said.

"Well, I sure as hell didn't vote for it."

The man across the table, an Intelligence Unit investigator with blond hair and a face that seemed young, at first glance, laughed.

"Say what you want, Ruby told me those games bring in more money than the drinks do, except on Friday and Saturday nights."

"It's still a hell of a note."

"You're just getting old and cranky, partner," the blond man laughed again.

"I haven't been up here since they fixed the place up," Charlie said. "It looks nice."

"Yeah, I noticed you haven't been around. You find a better place to do your drinking?"

"You know, Charlie," the bald one said, "he's kinda highbrow. He don't want to be seen in here too regular, it might screw up his image. I ain't seen him up here on a Friday or Saturday when the place was full."

"You might, if you'd have a decent jazz band once in a while, instead of all that shitkicker music."

They went on that way through several more pitchers of beer, arguing good-naturedly about music, bemoaning the way rookies were nowadays, and occasionally cursing the chief of police and the city manager. As policemen do, they remembered when they were rookies, and told each other stories of old partners, old cases, and ex-wives and sweethearts.

Finally, Charlie said he had to go. When Ruby brought his tab, he put on his glasses.

"By God, Charlie, you're getting old," the bald man said.

"Wearing those don't make you old," the blond one answered. "If I have to spend another day staring at the microfilm machine, I'll be in the market for some cheaters myself."

"Microfilm?"

"Yeah, we got a deal working on a real old killing. We think it might tie in to some people running a little syndicate here now. I've been looking through some of the old records, and they're all on microfilm. That stuff can drive you blind, man."

Records. There are records of everything, Charlie thought, especially terrible things.

On his way home, Charlie stopped at the Central Patrol Division. It was half-past-nine, and the desk man was alone in the Investigative Unit.

"What's up, Charlie?"

"I need to use your machine for a minute."

"Help yourself. It's been down most of the day, though."

Charlie sat at the computer terminal in the back of the room. He looked over his shoulder and saw the desk man on the phone. He pressed the CLEAR button and saw the lights labeled SYSTEM AVAILABLE and SYSTEM READY blink alive, like two red eyes. He was in luck, the machine was up.

A typed list of commonly used formats was taped on the desk

beside the keyboard. He found the one he wanted and pressed the keys, each character flashing upon the screen as he typed it:

DMV/ID.1210.COPELAND,JULIA.W.F.

He knew the evening watch investigators would be coming in soon to check out at the end of their tour. He did not have much time. He checked to make sure he had typed the format correctly. "Department of Motor Vehicles, slash, Identify, period, his radio call number, her name, white female, date of birth unknown." That was what he was looking for.

The desk man was still on the phone when Charlie pressed the ENTER button. The characters flickered, and a message appeared at the bottom left corner of the screen: QUED FOR LIDR. Now he waited, while his inquiry was fed into a data bank in Austin, the capital. Whatever happened when she was fifteen would not be in the computer but, if his luck held and there were not too many Julia Copelands with Texas drivers' licenses, the machine would tell him her date of birth. That would make his search much easier.

The loud machine-gun stutter of the printer startled him. The noisy printer advanced a roll of perforated paper. He tore off the three-inch wide piece that held his answer. He read it hurriedly:

SEARCH ON COPELAND, JULIA
COPELAND, JULIA M.
WHITE F 030243 5 07 125 BLACK BROWN
101017 MEANDERING MEADOW DALLAS 75230
DL 0127382 OPER 030285
CURRENT STATUS
CLEAR
022779 ACC MOTOR WITH MOTOR DALLAS
END MESG

He wanted to run wanted and records checks next, on her married and maiden names, but his time had run out. He could make up an excuse to be at the terminal, that was not unusual. But he did not want to be found with Julia's name on the screen. He heard voices in the hall outside, the investigators coming, as he rose and walked out past the desk man.

"Find what you were looking for?"

"Nah, they must have given me the wrong license number. It's no big deal. Thanks."

"See you around."

Charlie eased out the door and turned right, away from the approaching voices. He found his car and pulled away, sure he had not been seen by anyone but the desk man, who had not shown much interest in him. Born in 1943, he thought, as he drove north on Central Expressway. So she was fifteen in 1958. That was where he would start, first thing in the morning.

Wednesday dawned clear and warm, with the promise of another in an unbroken chain of days with temperatures over one hundred. Charlie left his car at a pay lot across the street from the *Dallas Times Herald*. Inside, he took the stairs to the basement, where the newspaper files were kept. The "morgue." A clerk produced three spools of microfilm and showed him to a viewer.

He knew it would take time; that was the best part of it. He had too much time. Starting with Julia's fifteenth birthday, March 2, 1958, he pored over the papers, day by day, a page at a time. He was into September when he stopped. His eyes burned and his neck ached. He found nothing so far except nostalgia. It was almost two. When he finished the reel that ended with the September 15th sports section, he stood up. He was hungry. Across the street and around the corner from the newspaper was an eatery he knew, a lunch bar that shared the ground floor of an office building with a drugstore. It was across the street from One Main Place, a glass-and-concrete box thirty stories high.

October tenth turned out to be the day. The headline read: COP'S DAUGHTER ATTACKED, SUSPECT SLAIN. Charlie paid for a photostatic copy of the story. There was a picture of a young girl being escorted into Parkland Hospital's emergency room. Charlie recognized the flawless features of her face and the long dark hair. "Sweet and innocent," he remembered the captain's words. He also recognized the burly young patrolman who held her arm gently in his big hand. Sergeant Burden, a patrolman then. Burden could tell me all about this, he thought. On the other hand, maybe Edmund Copeland didn't make the call that got me taken off the case. Maybe Julia called

Burden, and that was all it took. He filed that away for future reference.

The newspaper story was discreet to the point of vagueness. While her father, a detective, had been away from home working on a case on his own time, she had been attacked by a young white teenager who broke into her home. He was not identified. At some point during the rape, she had managed to stab him fatally. That was all, except that the pretty young face in the picture looked out at him with stunned, withdrawn eyes. Charlie reread the article. This was the terrible thing, then. She had been raped and she had killed the rapist. She was fifteen when it happened, twenty-four years ago, almost to the day. Was that the basis for her father's suspicion?

He went outside. He walked the three blocks south to Commerce Street, where the Hop-A-Bus ran. It was a bilious pink shuttle with rabbit ears on top that ran back and forth from near the Triple Underpass on the west to Central Expressway on the east, the length of the downtown district. After waiting a few minutes, he decided to walk the dozen or so blocks to the Municipal Building.

As always, downtown Dallas was in the throes of construction. Squat, old brick buildings were being demolished left and right to make way for ever taller and sleeker skyscrapers. Some of the old buildings were the best of Dallas's meager Art Deco legacy, but they were doomed along with the rest. Charlie crossed from one side of Commerce to the other and back again as he walked east, to avoid whole blocks where the sidewalk was boarded off beside building sites where he could hear heavy machinery at work. Dallas was becoming a city of chrome and concrete, but there were still a few of the kinds of places he liked. He passed the Commerce Street newsstand, where he bought the *New York Times* occasionally, and tip sheets for betting on pro football. The newsstand owner had once been jailed for selling *Tropic of Cancer* in paperback, while a "classier" bookstore up the street displayed the hardback version in its windows. Next door was Sol's Turk Bar, a dark, Runyonesque grill where loud, good-natured waitresses dispensed sandwiches, pizza, and beer in an ambiance of down-home hospitality.

On his left, Charlie looked up at the refurbished gargoyles

and Gothic trim of the newly reopened Adolphus Hotel, one of the city's oldest. It was even older than the Crockett. Across Akard, where it met Commerce, he noticed all that was left of the equally legendary Baker Hotel, a vacant lot, the future home of the phone company's expanding office complex.

At Harwood Street, he saw Burden, Braverman, and two or three others from Homicide across the street and a block over at Main. They were on their way to the Plaza Hotel for coffee. They did not see him. When his light changed, he jogged across Harwood, angling down the block toward the front steps of the Municipal Building, a five-story strong-house with pseudo-Grecian columns and two dozen broad granite steps leading up to iron doors.

He hurried past the information desk, through an unmarked door, and down a narrow flight of stairs. He reached the basement, which housed Building Security, the Records and Reports sections and the jail elevators. Turning left, he walked twenty feet down a hall, past the stairs that led to the police locker room in the subbasement, and again left into the door of the Physical Evidence Unit. A young black man with close-cropped hair stood at the long counter. He looked up as Charlie came in.

"May I help you, sir?"

"Is Sergeant Carson in?"

"Yes, sir, just a minute."

Charlie guessed that the young man was a police recruit, working here until the next academy class started. Charlie remembered when he had worked and waited at the counter and in the files, when all of the Identification Section had shared the big room by the elevators. Crime Scene Search was the part he liked best, where they kept photographs of old and bloody horrors. Now it was called Physical Evidence, and had an office of its own.

Sergeant Carson emerged from a row of file cabinets. He was sixty or more, and almost stoop shouldered from his years in the files. He had tutored Charlie, as he had dozens of other new cops before and after. He smiled when he saw Charlie.

"Detective Gants. It's good to see you. I was just telling Paul here about you and some of the other boys I've helped train.

Paul, this is Charlie Gants. He works Homicide. Charlie, this is Paul Du Pree. No relation to the football player."

Charlie shook the young man's hand. "When does your recruit class start, Paul?"

"In three weeks."

"I hope you're in shape. I hear they do a lot of running out there these days."

"No problem. I've been working out every day."

"Charlie, I've told him just about everything I know. Why don't you give him the benefit of your experience."

"All I can tell you is get the hell out while you can." Charlie meant it, but the other two laughed, and he laughed with them.

"What can I do for you, Charlie?" Carson said.

"Well, I know it's a long shot, but I thought you might tell me where to look for crime-scene pictures on a killing that happened twenty-five years ago."

"Good lord, Charlie, you don't want much, do you?" The old man scratched his head. "I'll tell you, if by some strange coincidence we still had 'em, they'd be boxed up back there in storage. How bad do you need 'em?"

"Not bad enough to tie up any of your people. I know you're busy. It's just a wild hare of mine. Would it be all right if I looked through that stuff myself?"

"I guess so. If you find anything you need, don't forget to sign it out. If you don't have anything better to do, I don't see why not."

The long, narrow room at the rear of the office was stacked from floor to ceiling with cardboard cartons, each one dated by hand. Each box seemed to average two or three months of pictures. The carton with the dates Charlie wanted was at the back, near the bottom of the stack. It was old and battered. He dug it out and fished through the manila envelopes that were marked with offense numbers and dates. There were several with October dates, old yellowed black-and-whites of bodies in various stages of destruction and decomposition. At last he found the one he wanted. A note attached to the slim bundle of photographs said that the body in the pictures was that of a rapist, that the rape victim had killed him in self-defense, and that she had, in turn, been no-billed by the Dallas County Grand Jury. Charlie's stomach knotted when he saw the first picture. The boy was not stabbed, he was slaughtered. His throat lay open to the spine, and his shirt was in shreds, his body crisscrossed with deep, gaping gashes that poured out his blood, in which he lay. One picture showed the weapon used, a pearl-handled straight razor with the initials T.G.J. on the handle.

Charlie remembered what Sam had said, "If we are right, Julia Copeland is a dangerous woman." He slipped one photo of the dead boy into his pocket and returned the rest to the carton. Then he replaced the cartons and walked out of the long, narrow room and closed the door behind him.

"Find what you were looking for?" Carson asked.

"No, I gave up on it. All I got was dirty."

"It's the thought that counts, Charlie."

"Right. Thanks, I'll see you later." As he left, Charlie patted Paul Du Pree on the back and said, "Good luck at the Academy."

"Thanks." The young man smiled broadly, adding, "Thank you, sir."

Deep in thought, Charlie walked back to his car. He got in and rolled down the windows, but there was no breeze to soften the stifling heat. It shimmered in waves off the concrete all around him, and the reflected sun off the cars and buildings blinded him. He reached under his seat and pulled out his file, the manila envelope in which he kept everything he had put together about the captain and the Slasher murders. He spread the pictures on the seat beside him. Three sets were in color, the Slasher victims. The lone black-and-white lay to one side. He studied each of them. The wounds did not match exactly in any two, except that every boy's throat was cut. That was the first thing he did, he decided; cut their throats so they couldn't scream. Otherwise, the wounds appeared to be made randomly, consistent only in their vicious deepness. The boys themselves were more similar than their wounds. The only difference was that the boys in the color shots had longer hair. They had the same incredulous stare, their mouths agape, tongues lolling out. We thought it had to be a man because the wounds were so deep, Charlie thought.

How does Burden fit in all this, he wondered. He unfolded his copy of the news story and smoothed it out beside the photographs. If Burden got the call and was there right after it happened, he knew everything. Then Wes must know, too. Wes, the friend of the family. In twenty-five years, Burden would have said something; or was that how he got to be the captain's boy, by not talking? The more he thought about it, the more Charlie could see a conspiracy taking shape around him. Wes knew more than he would admit. If anything is going to be done, I'll have to do it myself, Charlie decided. Then he put the pictures away and thought it all through again. Paranoia, he told himself, you'd better watch out for the paranoia. Next thing, you'll suspect Sam. It is strange, though, her with her silk blouses and her house in Highland Park, interested in Charlie Gants. She said she was a social friend of the Copelands, didn't she? And she only got interested in me after I told her about the dreams . . . .

He drove to a pay phone and called Sam because he needed to hear her voice. She had just gotten home from work, and he invited himself over. He had to tell someone what he had found.

"This is the terrible thing that happened." He showed her the copy of the newspaper story and the black-and-white photograph. She studied them carefully. "And here are the Slasher victims. You've seen them before."

He paced circles around her as she examined his evidence: pictures, offense reports and supplements, the captain's journal and his translation, notes—everything he had accumulated that he thought might be useful.

"I think the old man might have been right. Isn't this enough to go to the department with?"

"Ordinarily it would be. But do you recognize the policeman in the picture, at the hospital with Julia?"

"Sergeant Burden?"

"Patrolman Burden then."

"What does that mean?"

"I'm not sure. All I know is that I don't know who to trust any more. It was Burden who sent me home, said I needed a rest. He claimed Edmund Copeland pressured the Chief. For all I know, Burden may have done it on his own." He continued to pace the floor. "I'm not even sure of Wes any more. You're the only one I can talk to." He remembered shamefully that he had even doubted her.

From the pile of papers and photographs spread across her coffee table, Sam picked up the snapshot of Julia holding the baby Jessica. "You know, Charlie, this picture of Julia looks as if it were taken about the same time as the one in the newspaper."

Charlie sat beside her and held the news photo up beside the snapshot. The similarities went beyond the look of withdrawal in the eyes, a look that varied only slightly in degree. The beauty that would never desert her was apparent in both pubescent faces. The girl with her baby was still a girl, and the trauma that showed in the news photo was there, less naked, but still there.

"My God, Sam. I should have made the connection as soon as I read the story."

"Of course. That would explain a lot of things."

"She had a baby by him. Jessica is the daughter of the boy who raped her mother."

"That kind of history makes Julia an even more likely candidate as the slasher, Charlie."

"We need to know for sure. If I could get to a terminal again, I could pull up her date of birth, but I don't want to push my luck. I don't want Burden to know I'm still working on this. I could get Jessica's birth certificate. That would give us the date, and I'd like to know who it says is the father. I can call Austin tomorrow and get that by phone."

They sat together on the couch for a time, each of them silent and thoughtful.

"Sam?"

"Yes, Charlie?"

"Maybe she has stopped. It was in the press that the police think the captain was the Slasher. If she doesn't kill again, she's home free."

"You're assuming that she can stop. The fact that she made her father's death look like suicide means she has some control, some capacity for premeditation. But maybe she can't stop. It depends on what made her start, after all these years."

"Do you have any ideas?"

"It could be almost anything. She thought something or

someone threatened her, or Jessica; a man, something to do with her father. Any emotional stress might have set her off." Sam sipped her coffee. "Whatever started it, the death of her father made it worse. Even if she did kill him, it was an awesome shock. And then you came along."

"Me?"

"Look at it from her perspective, Charlie. However she felt about it, she was finally rid of her father. The relationship was over at last. Then you show up, with your dreams, talking about getting messages from him. As she must have seen it, you were digging up her father's grave, dragging him back into her life. Imagine how she felt. How do you think Julia sees you now, Charlie?"

"What do you mean?"

"You are a threat. If she killed her father because he suspected her, where does that leave you? What if she sees you as an extension of him, his agent of retribution? Charlie, it may very well be that the only person you've convinced that you are in touch with a dead man is the woman who murdered him." Sam glanced at the pictures again. "She waited a year after the first murder, only a few weeks after the second. If she kills again, it could be any day. She's due."

"Then that settles it."

"Settles what?"

"She works at night, picking up boys around bars between ten and two. So, starting at sundown tomorrow, I'm going to set up on her house. If she goes anywhere after dark, I'm going to be right behind her."

"Charlie, you weren't listening. You may be her next target. Stay as far away from her as you can."

"If she's coming after me, I want to know where she is. I don't want to wait around for her to come up behind me. Besides . . . ."

"Besides what?"

"I haven't made much headway as the captain's avenging angel. I may not be able to nail her for these . . . . ," he pointed at the photographs of the three dead boys, "but I'd hate to think that I was responsible for her killing another one."

"You're serious, aren't you, Charlie?" He nodded. "All right, then. Pick me up here tomorrow evening on your way out there."

"You're not going with me."

"Why not?"

"For the reasons you just gave me, and you'd get in my way. Besides, I already have enough on my conscience without letting something happen to you."

20 | THE STAKEOUT

HE THANKED THE CLERK IN AUSTIN AND HUNG UP the phone. According to the birth certificate, the baby was born to an unwed Julia Milton Jonas, nine months and seventeen days after the rape. Julia was sixteen at the time. The father was listed as deceased, no name, and the baby Jessica was given the surname Jonas. Oddly enough, Charlie was not surprised, although he had assumed it would be otherwise. If Milton were a family name, why not name her Jessica Milton? Why not make up a name? Why not do any number of things to avoid making the situation so obvious? For a man like the captain, abortion would have been out of the question, but why make it worse than it had to be?

He thought he knew why. Captain Jonas was not just a moral man, a man with a sense of justice and guilt. He was pathological. Putting himself in the old man's place, Charlie knew what guilt there must have been; his for not having protected her, for failing to make the world safe for her, for being away when she needed him. He knew the captain saw her guilt, too; the woman's ever-present guilt. He would not permit a lie, not even an innocent deception, on the birth certificate. There would be no harmless subterfuge to lessen the pain. They had sinned, all of them, and God had sent the child as a sign, a symbol of their guilt.

"No," Charlie said aloud, alone in his apartment, "I don't suppose the two of you were very close, Julia." Not when the captain made the child an icon that grew between them. A scarlet letter would have been kinder punishment than the captain's heartless sanctimoniousness for the sin forced upon her, against her will, by a swaggering young punk. Her name and the story behind it must have been the little girl's secret, the thing that made her different.

"Heaven help me, old man, I think I'm getting to know you . . . . too well."

It was dark when he pulled up in front of Sam's house. He saw her at the window and was glad she had insisted on going with him. He felt safer with her, saner and surer. He needed her. On another level, he knew he was no match for her and felt at ease giving in to her.

He watched her swing down the walk with her long, sure strides, in her white skirted suit and strapless high-heeled shoes that clicked with every step. She opened the car door and climbed in with an eager smile.

"Ready, Holmes?" She giggled.

"Not quite, Dr. Watson. First, I want to give you a couple of pointers. It's about your clothes."

"What about them?"

"Well, the next time you go sleuthing, wear something dark and inconspicuous, that's the first thing. Second, a pantsuit is better than a skirt slit up the side. We want to blend into the background, not turn heads."

"Anything else?"

"Yes, your shoes. Wear something more practical next time, something you can walk in, run in if you have to."

"I don't intend to chase anyone."

"I don't either. But, before the night is over, somebody may be chasing *us*. Besides, you may have to be on your feet for a long time at a stretch. You need shoes that are comfortable."

"It looks like I did everything wrong. It will only take a minute to change."

"No time for that. It's almost dark and I want to set up on the house early."

He eased away from the curb and drove east on the tree-lined street to Preston Road, then north past Northwest Highway, where the lights of two swank high-rise apartment buildings sparkled on their right in the early darkness. Charlie turned west on Royal Lane and crossed the Dallas North Tollway where the rear guard of the evening rush straggled home. Several blocks later he swung north on a street that wound its way through woods and creek bottoms where opulent homes stood on enormous lots, hidden from view by high walls.

When he rounded the last broad curve and the Copeland house came into view, he tapped Sam's shoulder and pointed it out to her.

"It's one of the finest places out here," he said, "as big and plush as anything I've seen."

"I have no doubt. Edmund Copeland is a very rich man."

Charlie drove past the house, then turned and came back, approaching it from the west. He turned off his lights and eased to a stop at the curb, downshifting the gears and using the hand break. His VW rolled to a stop just short of the crest of a low rise.

"Now what, Charlie?"

"Now we wait for a while."

"Well, since I'm taking notes on how to become a super sleuth, explain why we just drove by the house. Seems like we should have stopped before we drove past it."

"I did a drive-by so I could make sure she was there. Also, if she decides to go somewhere, she'd most likely head east toward Royal. This way we'll be behind her."

"I say, Holmes, how do you do it?"

"Elementary, my dear Watson."

"Looks like we're in the perfect spot."

"Hardly. My old Volkswagen is just a little out of place in this neighborhood. If someone doesn't call the real cops on us, it's only a matter of time before the neighborhood security patrol makes its rounds and finds us. And I don't want to have to explain to any rent-a-cop who I am and what I'm doing."

"So?"

"So, we'll chance it until it's dark enough and then move up to that empty lot across from the house. I think it's wooded enough to cover us. Meanwhile, if anybody comes nosing around, we'll pretend we've got car trouble."

As they sat in the growing darkness, Charlie heard familiar evening sounds, made by the nearby creek-bottom denizens enjoying their last refuge. He remembered summer evenings on the front porch beside his silent father, his mother shelling peas on the steps, where it was cooler than inside. She sat with a pail of peas at her left hand and with fluid motions that enthralled him, snapped and shelled them, letting them fall into the curve of her apron between her knees, dropping the shells into another pail on her right as she reached for more. It was a study in efficiency, unconsciously acted out by a woman at leisure from her other chores. Now and then a breeze brushed over her and Charlie smelled the loamy freshness of the garden peas mingled with the scent of lilac. An occasional car would moan and rattle by, its tires humming and crackling unhurriedly over scattered bits of gravel, a sound felt as much as heard. He remembered waving to every car that passed and to every person who walked by, whether or not he knew them. He almost heard the locomotive on the track a mile from his mother's house. The engineer played a sad song on the steam whistle, clarion clear as he crossed the highway, then thinning to a plaintive cry and finally dying out, leaving Charlie behind with a bittersweet emptiness. His whole world had centered on a town square ringed by rolling woodlands and farms where cattle grazed and crops grew, far from the heart of life, the city, where thousands waned and won and loved and lost.

Beyond the old sounds, and underscoring them, Charlie heard another familiar noise, the ballistic whine of city traffic, drivers clenched like fists behind their steering wheels, sealed and oblivious to the world around them as they all raced somewhere. Now the emptiness he felt was only bitter.

"How dark must it get, Charlie?"

"Huh?"

"Isn't it dark enough, yet?"

"Yeah, I think so. How do you like cop work so far?"

"A little boring, to tell you the truth. I thought police work was exciting."

"You never heard that from me. It's like what they say about

164

flying: hundreds and hundreds of hours of routine, punctuated by seconds of panic."

Charlie eased the car down the hill and found a trail that led into the wooded lot. He pulled around a clump of brush beside a stand of scrub oak trees near the center of the lot, almost directly across the street from the Copeland house. When he parked, he was not happy with the spot, but he stayed and cut his engine.

"Charlie, can you see anything? All I can see is bushes."

"I can see enough to tell when anyone leaves. That's all that's necessary. Just remember, the more we see of them, the more they see of us."

"But, I want to see, too."

"Maybe tomorrow night you'll have the good seat."

He heard her sigh loudly.

"Charlie, can we at least turn on the radio?"

"Too risky. Sound travels at night. Somebody might hear. Besides, it would run my battery down."

She stretched and turned and punched the seat. Then she fumbled with the seat release and laid the seat back as far as it would go. Sam was quiet for a while and Charlie thought she was sleeping. He watched all that he could see through the brush, now and then moving his head to one side and back to change his sight picture, so that he could keep the darkened drive in focus.

"Charlie?"

"I thought you were asleep."

"I can't sleep in a car. And there's something else."

"What?"

"I have to go."

"Sam, we just got here."

"No, you don't understand. I have to go. You know . . . . the ladies room?"

"That's another thing. A good detective always takes care of that before he gets to his assignment."

"I'll remember that next time. What about now?"

He smiled and pointed toward the bushes at the rear of the car.

She shook her head, "I'll wait, thank you."

She turned away on her hip, her head against the door, and

folded her arms at her waist. Charlie turned back to watch the cars. Minutes later she was snoring.

She sat up drowsily when he stopped for the traffic light on Preston Road and Northwest Highway.

"What is it, Charlie? What's going on?"

"We're calling it a night, Dr. Watson."

"What time is it?" She yawned.

"A little after ten."

"I thought you were going to stay until one."

"Looked as though she had settled in for the night. Besides, I was afraid your snoring would give us away."

"I don't snore!"

"No, and you can't sleep in a car, either."

The next night Charlie and Sam waited half an hour later and drove directly to their hiding place on the wooded lot. A man in a dark suit appeared at the side door of the Copeland house shortly after nine. He carried what looked like two suitcases, one under each arm. He opened the trunk of the car nearest the house, a black Mercedes sedan with dark-tainted windows. After he placed the cases in the trunk, he closed the lid and waited beside the car. He was too large to be Copeland. Charlie guessed that it was Copeland's driver. A short time later the side door opened again and another man strode out. Charlie was sure that the man was Edmund Copeland. The big man opened the door for Copeland, who got in without looking back. Charlie thought he could see a woman's figure at the door of the house before it closed and the Mercedes drove away. After that, everything was quiet. Charlie finally gave up and took Sam home a few minutes after midnight.

As soon as they had settled in at their post on the third night, Charlie saw that there were only two cars in the driveway, a red Alfa Romeo and the black Cadillac that reminded him of a funeral limousine.

"I guess Edmund is still out of town."

He had pulled Sam's car in at an angle this time, so they both could see the Copeland's drive. Sam had offered Charlie her car and he had been glad to accept it. It looked more at home in the neighborhood, and it had a lot more life to it than his VW.

"What did you bring in the bag, Sam?"

"Coffee and sandwiches."

"You're going to drink coffee tonight?"

"I think I'm going to need it. Working all day and staying out with you half the night is beginning to take its toll." She glanced sheepishly toward the bushes. "And if I have to go, I will, that's all."

They sat in the silence of the car under the dark awning of trees for a while. Finally, Sam yawned and stretched her arms over the seat.

"Charlie, this is really a boring job. How do you stand it?"

"It takes getting used to. Besides, we don't do it all the time. You may not believe this, but stake-outs have gotten a lot of officers hurt or killed."

"Were they bored to death?"

"No, after so long it's hard to maintain concentration. That's usually when something happens that you're not expecting. Anyway, we won't have to worry about that much longer."

"Why?"

"Tonight is the last night we're going to do this. I think we're just wasting our time. Even if I'm right about her, she might not do it again for weeks, months, maybe never."

The rest of the evening went by very slowly. At nine-thirty Jessica Copeland left in the Alfa. By midnight all the upstairs lights were out.

"Looks like she's in for the night."

"Come on, Charlie, thirty more minutes. Something's just got to happen. I hate to think I've spent three uncomfortable nights for nothing."

It was twelve-thirty-five when Charlie cranked the Datsun to life.

"Well, as I used to say at the drive-in movie, 'hang up the speaker and let's go home.' "

This time Sam did not protest. Charlie cut the wheels to the right as he let the car roll down a rise, then slipped it in gear and pulled onto the street, headed east.

"Wait a minute, Charlie!"

"What is it?"

"She's coming out!"

In the rear-view mirror, he saw the lights of a car as it backed around the front of the Copeland mansion and then turned toward the street. He took his foot off the gas pedal and eased the gear shift into first, using his transmission to slow down. In the mirror, he saw the headlights sweep across the street as the car came toward him. Then as he rounded the curve, he lost sight of them. Charlie shifted and gunned the car to lengthen the gap between them and the car behind. When he saw a driveway ahead on his right, he screeched to a stop and whipped the Datsun backward into the tree-lined opening, as he cut the lights. There was a closed gate, but luckily it was set just far enough off the road so that the nose of the Datsun was hidden. Charlie pulled Sam down against his chest and slid down as low as he could just as the car went past.

"Was it her?"

"Yeah, it had to be."

"You're going to follow her, aren't you?"

"Give her a couple of seconds to get some distance."

He waited until he thought it was safe, then pulled out of the driveway, turned on his headlights and gunned the car, hoping he had not given her too much time. He thought he saw her moving fast on Royal Lane, going east, when he reached the intersection. He turned that way and pulled within two blocks of the tail lights he had seen as they approached the tollway. He was still going east on Royal Lane when he drew close enough to be sure it was the Cadillac that he was following. It went south on Central Expressway, weaving smoothly through the light traffic at a constant sixty-five miles per hour.

"Sam, she drives like she's got a place to go and a time to be there."

Charlie kept her in sight without crowding her, always keeping traffic between them. He saw her signal to exit and reached the ramp in time to see that she turned south on Fitzhugh.

"Where is she going, Charlie? What's down this way?"

"East Dallas."

"My God, Charlie, you were right."

The Cadillac continued south on Fitzhugh, past the street where the first victims lived, all the way down to Columbia Avenue. It caught the green light and turned on Columbia. The light turned red and caught Charlie with cars ahead of him. When he finally rounded the corner, the black car was nowhere in sight.

"Damnit!" Charlie punched the dashboard.

He went on toward Carroll Avenue, slowing to look both ways on each side street, looking in every parking lot and stall.

"Sam, these clubs all close at two, and it's almost one now. If she sticks to her pattern, it doesn't give us much time."

He stopped for the light at Carroll Avenue and looked into the parking lot of the 7-Eleven directly across the street. There were clubs in every direction, country-and-western lounges, Mexican bars, strip joints, pool halls and all-night coffee shops. When the light changed, Charlie swung left on Carroll, then right into the parking lot in front of the Times Square, a big, brightly lit pool hall above a coffee shop. There were dozens of cars in the big L-shaped lot, but not one black Cadillac. He made a U-turn and went west on Main, past a fenced lot of used cars, to an old hamburger stand that was closed. He pulled in there and went through its parking lot into the one behind, and drove past the It'll Do, a landmark East Dallas lounge.

Time is running out for somebody, he thought, as he left the It'll Do behind and turned right onto Elm Street, back toward Carroll. And there it was! The black Cadillac, the funeral car gleaming under the street lights. Charlie leaped out and tried the driver's door. It was locked, and there was no sign of Julia. When he got back into the Datsun, Sam felt his excitement.

"She's not far," he said.

He squealed the tires as he shot around the corner and careened to a halt in front of the 7-Eleven.

"You stay here, Sam. This time I mean it. Stay right here. If anybody bothers you, go inside and call the cops."

"How will you find her?"

"Bar to bar." He checked his watch. "It's five after one and the bars will start running everyone out a few minutes before two. I've got about forty-five minutes."

"Charlie, wouldn't it be simpler to wait for her to bring the kid back to her car?"

"Yeah, and I'd do it that way if I were sure she'd come back to her car before she does it. But what if she just takes him outside in the dark parking lot or an alley? What if they leave in his car?"

"Be careful."

He stood up beside the car, then ducked back inside.

"Sam, lock the doors. I left the keys. Slide under the wheel in case you need to move. But, stay here unless something happens, you hear me?"

"I hear, Charlie."

He turned and jogged away. The It'll Do was the best bet and would take longer to search because of its size. But he took them in order and started with the corner bar where the black car was parked. The next place was a tiny dump and he saw it all from the front door. He hurried to the It'll Do next. Once inside, he stood near the door to let his eyes adjust to the darkness. If she is here, he thought, she could cut my throat and be gone before I realized what happened. The crowd was large and Charlie practically felt his way across the dance floor. He saw a woman leave the ladies room and asked if anyone was in there. She said no, and something else that he didn't hear as she walked away laughing. When he was sure Julia was not in the club, he held his watch near a neon beer sign to read the time. It was one-thirty.

He spent less and less time in each bar after that, trotting from one to the other west along the south side of Elm to Peak. Then he crossed the street and worked his way back along the north side toward Carroll, where he had started. It was a quarter to two, and he had had no luck. He made his way back to the 7-Eleven, to the waiting Datsun. Sam was not there.

The manager in the 7-Eleven remembered Sam, said he didn't see many women that nice down here. He remembered the other woman, too. Tall, with long black hair. A real knockout.

"She was on the phone when the little car out there pulled up. Oh yeah, you were the one with the other lady, huh? Anyway, the black-haired lady bought some smokes and walked out. I got busy with another customer, but I did see them both go off in that direction." The manager pointed across the street.

Charlie ran across Carroll to the two-story building opposite the 7-Eleven. Sam had been gone more than half an hour, and he knew it was hopeless. She could be anywhere.

There were two doors in the front of the building. Charlie

looked through the filthy glass of the one on the left and saw a stairway that led up into darkness. The other door was painted with the name of a bar. The building was dark. A notice stapled to each of the doors announced that it had been condemned by the Dallas Health Department. The doors were bolted shut.

Beyond the building he saw a parking lot and a Chinese take-out restaurant, closed at night. Charlie angled across the parking lot toward the diner, looking into every shadow, hoping desperately to find some trace of Sam, some trail she had left.

He was nearing the diner when a headlight flashed behind him. He spun around, but the lot was empty. The light flashed again, and then several times in rapid succession. He looked up and saw light filtering through the cracks of the painted windows on the second floor of the condemned building. As he watched, the steady, pale light disappeared in another series of flashes. In the pulsating light, he saw a door facing the lot. He hit it on a dead run, and the rotten wood splintered before him. He landed at the foot of a flight of stairs and rolled over into a crouch, his gun drawn, listening. He heard muffled voices from the floor above him and a rhythmic grinding that kept time with the flashing lights. The grinding light fluttered, stopped, then spurted and fluttered again, like a palpitating heart.

I'm too late, he thought, I'm too goddamned late. He took the rickety steps two at a time, with careful strides, making himself stop after each step to listen. Slowly, he told himself. You're no good to Sam if you charge into a trap.

At the top of the stairs, a light pulsed through a crack at the bottom of an unseen door, brighter than before. Charlie groped for the knob. He found it and turned in his hand. He heard sounds like bodies falling on the floor, again and again, each thump accented by a flurry of the grinding lights. He took a deep breath to steady himself, but his stomach clenched even tighter and his chest ached with the rush of adrenalin. He gave the knob another quarter turn and felt the bolt clear.

He rocked back for leverage and started forward, but the sound of a high-pitched, jabbering voice pulled him up short. Louder and louder and more frenzied, like a pagan chant, the voice rose to a fever pitch, matched by louder thumping. The blinking lights came faster and faster, and Charlie threw himself through the door.

From the dark landing, Charlie broke through the door into a world of blinding light. He stopped two steps inside the room, his pistol thrust blindly in front of him, his left arm across his face. The thumping stopped, and he heard screams and feet scurrying around him. The grinding light stopped then, and Charlie drew his arm away. He could see the floor at his feet and lights in a semicircle in front of him at staggered heights. There were people. He could make out their silhouettes as they edged back into the shadows beyond the lights. The room was silent now. He saw a figure coming toward him, a woman, her features dark, bathed in an aura of light.

Charlie raised his arm again to shade his eyes, and lowered his revolver.

"Is that you?"

She came steadily on and, when it was too late, he knew it was not Sam. It was Julia.

Her hand lashed out of the blinding light and Charlie fell back, away from the razor he could not see. He stumbled against a ragged cot and fell backward onto it. Julia stood over him, her finger jabbing down at him. Her finger, not a razor. He looked at his own empty hand. His gun was gone.

"What is the meaning of this?" She trembled with suppressed rage, her words spat out between clenched teeth. "Do you have any idea who these people are?"

From the cot, Charlie could see much more of the room as the effects of the lights lessened. He saw a flophouse ward; filthy mattresses on rusty frames and reeking derelicts squatting against a wall. And beautiful women with exotic faces and bizarre costumes, heavy gold bracelets and lamé gowns.

"Mother?"

Jessica Copeland pushed her way into the circle of lights. She was one of the beautiful women who did not belong here. Sam came in behind her. Charlie was relieved beyond words to see her, but a look of fading hope in her eyes worried him.

"Sam, are you all right?"

When he said her name he saw the hopeful look fade completely.

"You!" Julia turned on Sam. "You're part of this! He must be the client you mentioned!"

"As a matter of fact, he is, Julia. I believe I can explain . . . ."

"Don't bother!"

Jessica hugged her mother to her and turned away from Charlie, leaving Sam standing in the light beside him.

"Jessica . . . ," Sam began.

"Not now, Sam. You've done enough." She led Julia away, toward the exit.

Sam did not look at Charlie as he rose from the cot and looked beneath it. He found his revolver there and holstered it. He went to Sam, who showed him her back.

"Sam?"

"Wait for me in the car, Charlie."

He started toward the front and saw a lean, bearded man clutching an expensive looking camera to his chest. Various pieces of photographic equipment lay scattered about the rear of the room. The bearded man eyed Charlie suspiciously and edged closer to a taller man on his right. The two of them broke into a fast-paced conversation under their breaths. Charlie could not hear what they were saying, but he was certain it was not in English. He remembered that the front door was locked and stopped at the doorway. Jessica, still with her arm about her mother, eyed him coldly.

"I hope you haven't ruined things for me."

One of the derelicts walked past him toward the stairs, jangling a chain of keys on his fingers.

"Come on, man, I'll let you out."

Charlie followed the key man out and went to Sam's car. It was locked and he sat on the fender to wait for her. He saw the tall man come out with Julia. He held her arm as he escorted her across the street toward her car. Sam came out after them and ran to catch up with Julia. Sam said something to Julia, but Julia did not answer. The tall man spoke curtly to Sam, and she stopped in the middle of the street. She paused a moment, then came toward Charlie.

He looked away as Sam stalked nearer. Charlie saw the black Cadillac turn north onto Carroll, its tires squealing as it sped away. The tall man crossed the street to the building and disappeared inside.

Charlie bowed his head and stared at the ground between his

feet. He felt Sam's eyes on him and waited for her to speak. But she said nothing. With her eyes never leaving him, she reached down beside him and yanked a sheet of paper from beneath the windshield wiper on the driver's side. She folded it and stuffed it into the pocket of his shirt, which she patted sarcastically.

Still without a word, she unlocked the car and got in. The engine roared and Charlie slid off the fender, not knowing if he was supposed to go with her or not. She rolled the window down.

"Are you coming with me?"

He got in and they raced off toward Thornton Freeway, opposite the way that they had come. She swung through downtown, then north on Central, driving as fast as he had ever gone. He waited until she had finally slowed to seventy before he said anything.

"Sam, I'm sorry about what happened, but I don't understand why you are so upset with me. Don't you understand how I felt? I thought you were being killed. I imagined all sorts of things."

"Charlie, read the note."

"What?"

"In your pocket. Read the note, Charlie."

It read: "Wait here. Be right back. I'm all right. Explain later."

"I didn't see it, Sam."

"I know, Charlie, I know you didn't. And I know you had good intentions. In my head, I know that you were brave to try to rescue me. But right now, I am still so upset with you that all I want to do is get away from you until I can work through it. I don't want to hurt you with anything I say."

When they reached her house, Charlie said, "Sam, I'm sorry I screwed things up for you. But I still don't understand everything that happened tonight."

"Let me help you with that. First, Julia went to East Dallas to watch her daughter work with Henri LaMarque, one of the most famous fashion photographers in the world. He is here working with local talent, all the way from Paris. All the weird stuff you saw back there were just his props."

"Why the hell did he have to pick the middle of the night to come to East Dallas and take his damned pictures anyway?"

"It's his style, Charlie, his technique. He is famous for contrast in his work and he works on a tight schedule."

. "He's not the same idiot that nearly got those three women killed last year in the Middle East somewhere is he?"

"He was doing some fashion work using the street fighting in Beirut as a background, Charlie. No one was hurt and believe me the models were well paid. Not only that, it's quite an honor to be chosen by him."

Sam looked away, out of the window of the car, and tried to control her anger.

"Second, you have concocted a theory about Julia the slasher, and you had me believing it. In all fairness, you may be right. The problem is that you screwed up in your execution. You let yourself get so emotionally involved that you were careless, and you overlooked the one clue that could have prevented this whole debacle tonight."

"Your note."

"That's right, Charlie. You were hardly out of sight when Julia came out of the store and saw me. We talked, and I made up a story about looking for a client. When she insisted that I go with her to the session for a look, I even came up with a reason to leave a note. I said I was helping the client's wife look for him, and the note was for her. All you had to do was to read the note and wait for me. That's all. God only knows what your midnight raid has done to Jessica's career. Or mine, for that matter. Jesus, Charlie, I have never been so embarrassed in my life. I'm really tired. Don't call me tomorrow. I'll get in touch with you."

That hurt him more than anything else she had said. As he left for home in his car, the knot in his stomach tightened again, and he felt as if he were trapped in a falling elevator. He knew it would fall all night, and crash at eight in the morning, when the Internal Affairs Division opened its doors. Julia Copeland would be their first customer.

At the stop sign at the end of Sam's block, he opened the glove box and took his revolver off his belt. He studied the gun for a moment then tossed it inside and slammed the door. "Statistics and circumstance," he whispered, and drove on.

21 | THE NIGHT VISITOR

HE AWOKE TO THE UNNATURAL QUIET OF HIS room. Whatever had awakened him was still now, and he lay without moving, listening. He felt another presence in the room and he remembered the night of the first dream. This feeling was almost the same. He could see nothing without moving his head. He thought he must not move. The only sound was the rustle of the drapes at the open front window. The open window. Where was his pistol? In the glove box in the car, parked almost a block away in the crowded parking lot.

Out of the corner of his eye, at the far edge of his vision, he saw a glint of light, the light from outside sparkling on something. Another silent movement. He sensed a quick form bearing down on him and rolled away, off the bed. He fell onto the floor. A strange wordless whisper, a fierce breathless whisper rose behind him as he dived out the open window and landed in a heap in the flower bed.

He ran across the parking lot to his car. His own breathing was deafening. He did not look back. The car was locked. He glanced back toward his apartment and saw nothing, just his open window. No sounds from inside. He lifted one of the big white rocks that bordered the lavish flower bed; the shattering of the window on the driver's side of his car was surprisingly loud in the quiet of the parking lot. He ripped open the door and fumbled the glove box open. The cool, hard butt of the revolver felt good in his hand.

As he retraced his steps to his apartment, he thought of his car window and hoped it had not been another dream. Crouching outside the open window, he could see nothing inside. The window screen crunched beneath him. He eased himself head-first through the window and stopped halfway. Realizing how vulnerable he was, he hoped it had been a dream, and went on.

Inside, he could hear nothing except the usual night sounds. He pressed his back against the wall until he could see, then inched along the wall until his outstretched hand found the light switch. The sudden brightness almost blinded him. Squinting hard, he saw nothing amiss. He made his way carefully to the kitchen, then the bathroom, turning on every light as he went. The place was empty. Everything was as he had left it.

With a sigh of relief and exhaustion, he slumped on the bed and laid his revolver beside him. It was a dream; he must have left the window open, he sometimes did. He lay back upon his pillows and immediately recoiled as he felt fingers rising up around his throat! He leaped up, his heart pounding wildly, and saw nothing. Just the foam stuffing of his pillow spilled over his bed. He almost screamed, and laughed at himself instead. The damned pillow is busted. Then he looked more closely and saw that the pillow had been slashed with a stroke from side to side; there was a long incision where his throat had been. He did scream now. He screamed and grabbed his gun and spun around. He was alone.

When he stopped screaming, he picked up the phone. He dialed Sam's number and got a busy signal, then another on his second try. His third call was to the operator. She reported no conversation on the line, some problem with the instrument.

Charlie landed running as his car lurched to a halt in gear, crossing the curb, and died. Her house was dark. He punched the doorbell and hammered on the door with his fists, then stepped back and looked up at her bedroom window. No light came on. He pounded the door again, and was off the porch on his way to the back when he heard the door open against the chain.

"Who is it?" She sounded sleepy and cross.

"Sam! Are you all right?" He leaped back upon the porch and shoved his head between the door and the jamb above the chain. "Are you all right?"

"Charlie?" When she saw his face, she jumped back at first, then covered her face with her hands. "I don't believe it. I do not believe that this is happening." When she uncovered her eyes and he was still there, she said, "Charlie, why are you doing this to me?"

"Please, Sam, I have to talk to you."

She studied his face more closely, and unlatched the chain and let him in. He followed her into the den, where she sat on the edge of a chair with her arms drawn around her, leaning forward.

"Tell me about it, Charlie. What have you done now?"

He took a deep breath and organized what he would say in his mind. He wanted very much to sound sane.

"I went straight home and went to sleep. Then, a little while ago, something woke me up. I thought I heard something, but . . . ."

"But you weren't sure whether it was real or a dream, were you?"

"Sam, I know how you feel, and I don't blame you, but just hear me out." She rubbed the backs of her hands across her eyes and hugged herself again. "So, like I said, something woke me up. There was somebody there. Whoever it was tried to kill me, Sam, tried to kill me with a straight razor!"

"I haven't had any sleep, Charlie, and I have to go to work in a few hours. Are you trying to tell me that Julia Copeland broke into your apartment and tried to kill you? Are you positive it wasn't another dream? How can you be sure? I don't see a scratch on you."

"By God, Sam, you were right about me. I'm not thinking very clearly. I should have brought my evidence with me. If I hadn't been in such a hurry to get over here and make sure you were all right, I might have thought to bring the pillow. Then I could show you the goddamned gash. Maybe you'd believe me then."

She shifted in the chair and stared off into the middle distance. "Could we put this on hold until tomorrow, Charlie? I'll call you."

"Not from here. Your phone is out of order."

"Oh, for Christ's sake, Charlie, I took my phone off the hook so I could get some sleep."

"In case I called, you mean?"

"Yes, damnit!"

Charlie turned on his heel and went to the door. She followed him.

"Charlie, I don't mean to come down on you so hard. I tried to tell you earlier that I need a little distance, a little time. Let me get through a day at work tomorrow, if I still have a job. I'll call you and we'll talk, okay?"

His voice failed him as his throat tightened. He cleared his throat and said, "Okay. But promise me one thing. Promise me you'll put your phone on the hook just in case."

"Charlie . . . . all right. If that's what you need, I will do it. I'll tell you what, let's make a contract. Promise you won't call unless it is a real emergency, and I'll get back to you tomorrow."

"I promise."

"Charlie, listen to me. I do want to help you. But, if at all possible, let's try to wait until business hours tomorrow. I think I'll be more myself."

He nodded without trying to say anything more, and walked out the door. He heard her close the door behind him just as he realized that he had left the lights on on his car in his hurry to see about her. "I swear, God," he prayed aloud, "if my battery is dead, that's the last fucking straw."

The ignition groaned and finally the engine cranked. He slammed his door, backed off the curb into the street, and left. He looked back, hoping to see Sam in a window, watching him drive away. The house was dark. He realized as he drove that he had nowhere to go. Not back to his place, certainly.

The door opened a little and Wes's face appeared, sleepy and alarmed.

"Charlie?"

"Yeah, it's me, Wes."

"Hold on a second."

The door closed and Charlie heard the chain being taken off. It opened again and Wes, pistol in hand, invited him in. He stumbled to the middle of the room and stopped, at a loss.

"You look like you need a drink," Wes said.

Wes laid his pistol on the bar and produced a bottle of bourbon and two glasses. Charlie took his drink and finished it in a gulp.

"Don't tell me, partner. You've had a lovers' quarrel." Wes grinned.

"Wes, somebody tried to kill me tonight."

"Do what? Where?"

"At my place."

"Who was it? Did you get a look at him?"

"It was too dark."

"Hold on a minute, partner. I'm still asleep. Let me pour you another one." Charlie drank the second bourbon more slowly, holding the cool tumbler in both hands. He stared past Wes, trying to make some sense of everything. "You just sit here and nurse that one, partner. I'll go hop in the shower and wake myself up."

Safe now, Charlie tried to push Sam out of his mind. He thought about how much he would tell Wes. He would tell him about the pillow. He wanted somebody who would believe him to know about that. It had to have been Julia. If she had left well enough alone after that scene tonight, when he looked like such a fool, if she had just lain low, he would not have been nearly so sure. But she could not do that, she had to come after him. Whatever doubts he might have had before, now he was certain. But he would not tell Wes. Not yet. He still felt that Wes was holding something back, that he knew more than he would admit.

He finished his drink and started to pour another, but the bourbon was making his stomach hurt. He went behind the bar and looked underneath. Wes should have some Scotch somewhere. It won't hurt to tell Wes about barging in on the photo session, he thought. That will be all over the department by noon. He opened a sliding door in the back of the bar, and his hand brushed against a calendar that hung from a nail below the phone. Something on the calendar caught his eye: "Jonas.

Crockett Hotel. 2:00 P.M." It was scrawled in Wes' hand in the little square for Wednesday, the twelfth. Charlie found the Scotch and started to pour a drink. The twelfth? He looked at the calendar again. That can't be right. That was almost two weeks before the captain died. Wes never mentioned meeting him there. In fact, he said he had heard the captain was living there.

Charlie did not feel safe any more. He sat the Scotch down beside Wes's pistol on the bar.

"All right now! I'm back among the living." Wes stood in the doorway. He was dressed, his hair still wet from the shower. He brought his glass to the bar and refilled it. He picked up the Scotch and pointed the bottle to Charlie. "You gonna stand there empty or reload, partner?"

"I've had enough."

"Bullshit. Have one more, it'll settle you down." Wes poured Charlie's glass full. "That's more like it. Now, Charlie, you go sit down on the couch over there and make yourself comfortable."

Charlie looked down at Wes's gun, and almost grabbed it. But he stopped himself, and moved to the couch. As he sat down, he pressed his left elbow against the butt of his own revolver, tucked in his belt under his shirt. Wes leaned on the bar.

"Now, partner, you have my undivided attention. Take it from the top, just like we tell the citizens to do."

"I had a rough night and I went right to sleep. I don't know how long I slept. What time is it now?"

"A little after four."

"I slept longer than I thought. This all happened about an hour ago, I guess, maybe a little more. I got the hell out of there, and I don't want to go back tonight. This is the only place I had to go."

"Take it easy, Charlie."

"I woke up and somebody was there, but it was too dark. I couldn't see who it was. Whoever it was tried to kill me."

"No offense, partner, but are you sure this wasn't one of your dreams?"

"It was not a dream."

"Well, the way you've been carrying on, talking to dead people and everything . . . ."

"Wes, I know the difference between dream and reality."

"That's what keeps you from being crazy. As long as you're sure."

"My slashed pillow is real enough."

"What?"

"My pillow was slashed, Wes. Like it was done with a razor."

Wes said nothing. Their eyes met, and Charlie looked in vain for some sign. A razor, just like the one she used on the kid who raped her. You must know about that. We both do. Now what, partner?

Wes's hand suddenly swept across the bar, and Charlie reached for his gun, knowing he would not be in time. His hand closed on the butt as he saw Wes grab the phone. Charlie could hear the echo of the ring he had not heard. He had been so intent on Wes that he had not heard the phone ring.

"Yeah? Where?" Wes turned his back toward Charlie, his voice low.

Charlie eased his gun back into his belt and lay back on the couch. Goddamn, goddamn, he thought.

"When? Yeah, I know. I'll take care of it."

Wes turned toward him, his face a tight gray mask, as he swept his pistol off the bar. Charlie tensed again.

"Let's go, Charlie."

"Where?"

"Parkland Hospital. That was the office." He stuck his pistol into his waistband.

"What's up?"

"They think they've shot the real Slasher."

22 | THE MORGUE

PARKLAND EMERGENCY ROOM WAS BUSY. THE parking lot was cluttered with ambulances. Braverman found a space at the curb and flashed his badge at the attendant. Inside, there was organized pandemonium. The wounded and injured lay about on guernies or sat huddled in chairs, waiting to be seen. The nurse at Triage sent them down a corridor to a door guarded by a patrolman.

"How does it look?" Braverman showed his badge again.

"Beats me. They're in there."

Gants and Braverman opened the door and stepped inside. A nurse was returning a machine on wheels to its place in the corner. A tired intern met them at the foot of the trauma table. Behind him a body lay beneath a bloodstained sheet.

"D.O.A., officer. We'll have details for you when things quiet down a little." He left the room at a brisk slouch, followed by the nurse.

Braverman motioned for the patrolman to wait outside. He shut the door.

Gants cleared his throat and said nothing. He knew who they would find beneath the sheet, and he was ashamed of a feeling of smug vindication. He thought he would wait until business hours to call Sarr and tell her that he had been right all along. He had never felt more sane. He felt the familiar chill as he reached for the bloody linen. But something he saw in Braverman's face stopped him. He waited, and thought he saw a tremor in Braverman's hand as he lay it for a moment upon the hidden face. Finally, Braverman took the sheet in hand and slowly drew it down. First, Gants saw the long black hair. Julia looked younger now. And then he understood, little by little, until he saw it all, until he could not deny it anymore, and the sweet taste of vindication turned to bile.

"Jessica!" It's a mistake, he cried silently. It's supposed to be Julia!

Braverman stood over the dead girl, his head bowed, hands loose at his sides. "Charlie, go and check on the victim." His voice was soft and flat.

The victim was still in surgery. Gants found a patrolman writing his report, his clipboard resting on an unoccupied gurney in the hall.

"She picked him up coming out of an after-hours pool hall down on Beacon. Took him in a little red sports car to a park down off of East Grand. They got out of the car and he went to kiss her and she pulled a razor on him. The kid's lucky. She went for his throat, but he got his hand up in time. Got a hell of a gash across his forearm, and he lost a lot of blood. He tried to run, but he said she was on him like a cat. She got him again down across the back of one shoulder. Doctor said it was deep, messed up some ligaments. Anyway, this Park Police unit came by on his rounds about then and caught her at it. He yelled at her to drop the razor, but instead of dropping it, she came at the officer with it. He backed up flat against his own car before he started shooting. Got her twice in the chest."

"Yeah, I just came from there."

"She didn't give him any choice but to shoot."

"Sounds like it."

"Charlie?" It was Sergeant Burden. He looked surprised. "What are you doing here?"

"I was at Wes's when he got the call."

"Oh. Well, what's the deal?"

"Let's go down to the Police Room. I need to talk to you."

The Police Room was closet-sized, with a desk and a phone.

It lay just off the Emergency Room entrance. They found it unoccupied, and Gants closed the door behind them.

"It's Jessica Copeland, the captain's granddaughter."

"What? Who is? What are you talking about?"

"The Slasher suspect, Sarge. The one the park cop shot. It was Jessica Copeland."

"You're not serious."

Gants nodded.

"Oh, sweet Jesus! No!"

"She was pronounced dead on arrival. I just came from there. The m.o. and everything fits. Just like the others."

The fat sergeant paced in the little room, shaking his head. As he fumbled in his pocket for a handkerchief, he asked, "How about the victim? He going to make it?"

"I think so. He's still in surgery."

"Good. We're okay with the press. We never said the case was officially closed." He wiped his gleaming forehead. "Where's Wes?"

Before Gants could answer, the door opened and Braverman walked in. His eyes were puffy and red. When Gants saw Braverman's face, he remembered that his partner had been a friend of the dead girl, a friend of the family. He wished he had tried to console him in the trauma room.

"Sergeant Burden, did Charlie tell you who it is?"

"Yeah. The world is crazy."

"Somebody has to tell Julia before the reporters get it."

"I'll tell her, Wes. Have you and Charlie taken the statements?"

"None to take. She's dead and the kid's still in surgery. The late night unit has the Park Police officer down at the office. Somebody can come back out here in about three or four hours to talk to the boy. He won't be out from under the gas before then."

"Any press here yet?"

"None so far," Braverman said. "I'm sure they're thick out at the scene. It's just a matter of time until somebody runs a registration on her car."

Burden dialed the phone as he talked. "Okay, I'll call Captain Sharp at home. He can notify the Duty Chief and get somebody from Public Information out here to talk to the reporters."

"Sarge, Charlie and I are going to my place. There's nothing to be done here, and I'm due to go to work in a few hours."

Burden nodded, then put a hand on Gants's arm. "Charlie, if you're ready to come back to work, why don't you and Wes call this a workday and take the rest of the day off. Come in at your regular time Sunday afternoon."

Charlie nodded and they left.

In the parking lot outside Braverman's apartment, Gants said, "I think I'll just go on home and get some sleep. I'll see you tomorrow afternoon, Wes."

"Okay, I'll see you tomorrow, Charlie." But, before Charlie got to his car, Wes changed his mind. "Wait a minute, Charlie. Come on up for one more drink. I want to talk to you."

Wes poured them a drink apiece, and Charlie settled onto the couch, exhausted. Wes leaned on the arm of a chair.

"Charlie, you have a pretty good idea of what kind of man the captain was. You know what I thought of him. Well, one day a couple of weeks before he died he called me up to his room there at the hotel. He said he had a top secret job for me. He told me about his idea that Julia was the Slasher, all that stuff he put in that book you found. I never knew he was keeping a diary. I'm surprised my name wasn't in it. I thought maybe you weren't telling me. Anyway, he wanted me to check her out, see what I could find. And he swore me to secrecy. I gave him my word, Charlie, that I would never tell anybody but him about what I was doing. That's why I couldn't tell you what I knew. My word is about all I've got left."

"Why you? Why not Burden?"

"Birdie is loyal, but he's not smart. Cap knew Birdie would tip his hand. He didn't want Julia to know he suspected her unless he was sure."

"What was the terrible thing that happened to Julia?"

"She was raped when she was fifteen."

"And that made her a suspect?"

"There was more to it than that. The kid who did it was a white boy about seventeen. He hung around too long afterward, and Julia used the captain's razor on him. Cap said she cut him up real bad, just like the Slasher. So you see, there was some method in his madness."

"And the rapist was Jessica's father?"

"Yeah. Cap naturally wouldn't allow an abortion, and he wouldn't let Julia put her up for adoption. He said it was God's will. But after she was born, he was never around much, and that made it all worse."

Charlie sipped his drink thoughtfully.

"Charlie, I'm guessing that you already know a lot of this. I think you're testing me, to see if I'll hold anything back. I don't blame you." He looked down at his drink. "I felt real bad about not telling you, but I couldn't go back on my word. Besides, you've been acting strange lately, and I never knew what you'd do next."

"Neither did I, sometimes."

"I don't hold with all your dream crap, partner, but I have to admit that you figured things out pretty good."

"Not well enough. I was sure it was Julia, just like the captain. We were both wrong."

"No, I knew it wasn't her. I checked her out, and she had an alibi every time she needed one. If I could have convinced Cap Jonas of that, he might be alive today."

"Do you mean you think Julia killed him? Or Jessica, to protect her mother?"

"I can't prove anything one way or another, Charlie. But, like I always tell you, a good detective knows to suspect the obvious. I think the old man convinced himself that his daughter was a killer, no matter what I said. I think he felt like it was his fault, and he killed himself over it."

"But he believed he'd go to hell if he did that."

"And maybe he figured that was what he deserved. You know he believed in justice, no matter who got hurt. Even if it was him."

"But why would Jessica do things like that?"

"Beats the hell out of me." Wes's voice cracked. "She was always the sweetest, prettiest kid I ever knew. Maybe it passed down from her mother, in the blood, or in the way she was raised. That's something you need to ask your friend Sam the next time you see her."

They finished their drinks in thoughtful silence.

"Wes, I need to get home and get some rest."

"I hope everything is straight between us now."

"It is, partner. I'll see you tomorrow."

"It'll be good to have you back."

Sitting in his car in the parking lot, in the bright circle of a street light, Charlie took the photograph from the captain's journal. For the first time, he looked at the other face in the picture, the "sweet innocent" face of little baby Jessica.

23 | THE CONTRACT

BY TWO O'CLOCK SATURDAY AFTERNOON, CHARLIE was up, stretching and yawning in the kitchen while he waited for his coffee water to boil. His body seemed to be coming back to life in stages. His left hand was numb because he had slept with it under him, and his back was stiff and sore.

Sam was on his mind when he poured the coffee. He wanted to call her, but he thought he shouldn't. Tough it out, he told himself. She said she would call. The kitchen was where he chose to make his stand, and he settled there in one of his two chairs, sitting in his boxer shorts with his legs crossed, waiting for the phone to ring. When his first cup of coffee was gone, he put on water for another, and walked a lap around his living room, stretching and bending and craning his neck. His joints popped and crackled as he made his round, and he felt old. He left his second cup on the table to cool while he stuck his head out the front door. He looked left and right up and down the row of little porches. Not a newspaper in sight.

On his way to the shower, he swung by the table and snagged his coffee. A hot shower would make him feel younger, maybe tougher too. Three or four times while he was in the shower he thought he heard the phone ringing. The first time, he threw open the stall door and ran out, leaving the water running. The other times, he just turned the water down and listened.

He did feel better afterwards, warmed up and looser. After he had dried his hair with a towel, he pulled a clean pair of shorts on and whistled as he moved around the little place, tidying up. Cleaning up the scattered pieces of foam pillow stuffing was the job he saved for last, because he could hardly stand to look at it. The ragged little clumps were everywhere, and he had to reach beneath his sleeper couch to gather up the last of them. The job was almost done when he noticed the phone. It was off the hook, just enough to open the line so that he could not get any calls. It looked fine at a glance, but from this close, he could see that the receiver was not all the way down on the buttons. That must have happened last night when I tried to call Sam, he thought. I slammed it down pretty hard. He set it right, and expected it to ring immediately. She may be dialing right now. Maybe she's been trying to get me all day. It did not ring.

When he had done all there was to do in his apartment, he checked the kitchen clock. It was 3:10, and no call yet. On the other hand, she may have been calling all day and couldn't get through. She probably had. Probably worried sick about him.

He sat on the made-up couch and pulled the phone into his lap. But when he had punched three of Sam's digits, he changed his mind and called Elizabeth Gants instead.

"You're not playing second fiddle this time, Bit." He muttered to himself.

His ex-wife was civil, if not pleasant, and put Bit on the line.

"Hi, Little Bit."

"Daddy. Hi, Daddy."

"How did you know it was me?"

" 'Cause you're the only one that ever calls me Little Bit."

"That's because you're my Little Bit, and nobody else's."

"Daddy, are you busy today?"

"What do you mean?"

"Whenever you don't call me very much, Momma says you're busy. Are you busy now?"

"Not right now, Baby. I have plenty of time to talk to you. What have you been doing?"

"Playing."

"Terrific. What else?"

"Just stuff. Can we go see Charles again?"

Charles? "Oh, Charles the Zebra, no relation. Sure we can."

"Can Sammy go, too?"

"Who's Sammy?"

"Sammy, Samantha, Daddy."

"Oh, I'm sure she can. I'll ask her the next time I talk to her. Tell me stuff, Little Bit."

"What kind of stuff?"

"Any kind you like. I just like to hear about stuff."

He settled back on the couch, and she told him about her dolls and pets and friends and everybody else in her world. He did not understand quite a bit of it. She had gone on for fifteen or twenty minutes when her mother came on the line and told Charlie that they had to go someplace. Bit smacked him a kiss over the telephone line, and she told her mother that she wanted to hang up the phone herself.

"I love you, Bit," Charlie said. "Now hang up the phone."

"I love you, Daddy. You hang up."

"You hang up first."

"You hang up, Daddy."

"All right, Bit. Let's count." They both counted to three and hung up at the same time. When he was through talking with his Little Bit, he didn't care if Sam ever called. But before long, he cared again.

"She probably tried to call while I was on the phone. And this morning, when it was off the hook." He was talking out loud. "Besides, Bit asked me to invite her to the zoo."

As he punched her numbers, he mumbled, "It's silly to sit around like a schoolgirl waiting for somebody to call first. It doesn't matter who calls first."

Sam answered.

"It's me, Charlie."

"Charlie! Where have you been? I called you all morning. I was worried about you."

He almost apologized, out of habit, but decided to lie instead.

"Yeah, I had to take the damned thing off the hook so I could get some sleep. It's been like a madhouse around here with all the calls."

"Charlie, I heard about what happened after you left my place last night. Why didn't you call?"

"I didn't want to bother you. It wasn't anything that couldn't wait until you got to the office."

"Well, never mind that now. I had two reasons for calling you. First, I wanted to make sure you were all right, of course. Second, I wanted to see if I could interest you in a home-cooked dinner."

"Oh, well . . . . that's nice of you, Sam."

"Is that a yes?"

"Look, Sam, I've been thinking about what you said last night. If you need time and distance, I understand. Whatever's best for the relationship." He dropped that word in for effect, but it did not seem to have any.

"Charlie, please say you'll come."

"I don't know, Sam. I'd hate to do anything that would jeopardize our rela . . . ."

"Look, Charlie, the least you can do is accept a peace offering graciously."

"All right, Sam, I'd love to."

"Good. Seven o'clock. Bye."

The phone buzzed in his ear after she was gone, and he held it for a minute before he hung it up.

Charlie dressed in khaki slacks and a pullover shirt, and went out for a walk. As he walked, he thought about Sam and remembered things she had said. She had said some nice things, about his being compassionate and sensitive, and even attractive. Other things were worrisome, like when they talked about suicide and his sleeping with his mother. He put the worrisome things aside. He walked out of his complex and down the street, aimlessly, deep in thought.

He remembered another thing she had said, the time that he had almost said he loved her, the only time he had ever made love to her. She had said, "One thing at a time . . . get the captain behind you before you start making any commitments." The captain was behind him now, he was sure of that. He did not admit even to himself, even on his lonely walk, how near the abyss the old man had driven him. Without Sam . . . he did not let himself think about that, either.

Charlie stopped when he found himself at Greenville Avenue, and started back. Something troubled him about his and Sam's relationship. That worried him. He was not sure what it meant, really, except that it could mean almost anything. He was not very clear what it meant for Sam and him, and he resolved to settle that with her at dinner. But the thing that worried him the most was this: the only constant in his feeling toward her was inconsistency. She made him feel very bad at times, and very good at other times. He found that curious, because he reasoned that if two people were honest with each other and they were the same people always, then they should feel almost the same toward each other most of the time. With Sam, his feelings changed back and forth, sometimes several times a day. He had tried to be honest with her, but with all that had been going on lately, it was hard to be sure. Was she honest with him? He could not be sure about that, either. Sometimes he thought she wasn't; other times, too much so. He did suspect that she would make him feel bad or good as it suited her. He decided that theirs was a relationship of parts, good and bad. As much as he hated to admit the bad parts, he did not like to think about living without the good ones again. It is less than I had hoped for, he thought, and less than I had imagined. But as long as I see it for what it is . . . .

He rang Sam's bell promptly at seven, and the door swung open for him. She met him smiling, and hugged him closely. Her hostess gown was silk, and the scent was as he remembered.

"Oh, Charlie, I'm glad you came. Come in."

A tall glass of Scotch stood waiting on the coffee table, and he made himself comfortable on the couch while she went to the kitchen.

"I had no idea a home-cooked dinner would be so formal, Sam," he yelled. She must not have heard him.

He waited for her to come back, and looked around the room as if he thought it might have changed. A set of books on one of the shelves caught his eye, and he was squatting in front of them when he heard voices from the kitchen. He thought: she's hired someone to serve us and clean up afterward, so we can have more time together. But as he pivoted toward the voices, he saw that he was wrong. The tall man walking in Sam's wake was not hired.

"Canapes, Charlie? I made them myself."

He declined, and stood up to meet the man.

"Doctor Branville, this is Charlie Gants, the man you've heard so much about." She wore a broader, tighter smile than Charlie had seen before. "Charlie, I'm so proud of you, I told Doctor Branville all about you. He's remarkable, doctor. Absolutely remarkable."

"Charlie, it is very good to meet you, after hearing so many splendid things."

The doctor was decked out in tweeds and smelled of his pipe. His smile sliced back and forth across his beard as he talked.

"Let's sit down, gentlemen, and make ourselves comfortable."

They milled about and all wound up on the couch, with Sam between the men.

"Charlie, it was very gracious of you to come, after the way I behaved last night. I was a bear with him, doctor. Wasn't I, Charlie?"

"If you say so."

The doctor laughed at that, which is to say, he laughed at Charlie's confusion and dread, it seemed to Charlie.

"I've been exploring new vistas, consulting with the police, and I had quite a lot to work through. Charlie has made it all possible. That's why I felt so bad that you caught the brunt of it, Charlie. You forgive me, don't you?"

"Yes."

"Enough of that, Samantha," the doctor broke in. "I want to hear Charlie's perspective on the Slasher murders, especially last night's chain of events. Remarkable!" The doctor leaned across Sam toward Charlie, all but ignoring her. His eyebrows rose slightly in expectation.

"I don't know what I could tell you about it."

"Nonsense, Charlie. From what Samantha tells me, you were the catalyst that brought the whole thing to a head. An *idiot savant,* as it were. Remarkable!"

"I don't know. I don't think so."

"Relax, Charlie." Sam hugged him again. "Drink your drink and loosen up. Doctor Branville is a great friend of mine, and the top man in his field. He's very interested in you. The two of you will have a great deal to talk about when you get to know each other."

"I can't stay." Charlie edged away from her, toward the door.

"What? Don't be silly."

"No, really. I just stopped by to tell you. It's my ex-wife. She's had a death in the family out of state, and I have to go get my little girl."

Sam released her grip on Charlie's arm to gesture for the doctor when she said, "The most darling little girl you've ever seen! I went with them to the zoo once, and she named one of the zebras Charles, after her father. She is darling, and very, very bright."

Charlie got to his feet before she could grab him again, and moved toward the door.

"Charlie, must you leave? Absolutely?"

"Yes. I'm afraid so."

"But that ruins everything. I wanted the three of us to have a nice dinner and then drinks after, and really get to know each other."

"If he can't stay, he can't stay, that's all." The doctor stood. He was much taller than Charlie. "I would have preferred making an evening of it, but I suppose it can't be helped. If you would give me a moment before you leave, Charlie, there's something I would like you to . . ."

"I have to go now."

"Charlie, at least let the doctor finish, let him tell you what it is."

Charlie looked straight into his eyes and said, as evenly as he could, "I believe I know what it is." And then, "I have to go."

"Charlie, please."

"All right, Sam, you're right. I want to see it."

"It's nothing very much, really, a simple contract," the doctor said. "Won't take a minute to sign."

"What is it for?"

"Research, of course. Really, Charlie, you do know that the doctor heads a research institute."

"Yes, hysteria, parapsychology. Hasn't Samantha told you anything?"

"I think she has. I think she has mentioned you, in fact. What does it mean if I sign the contract?"

"That you are bound to us as a research subject, and we to you as a facility. Nothing more."

"What would you research about me?"

"Dreams, vital signs, body functions, everything."

"And, if I become a subject for you, what would I do then?"

"The same things you have been doing right along unofficially. The contract only makes it official."

"I see. Well, I think it should be official, or not at all. It seems fairer that way."

"What?"

"It was a pleasure meeting you, doctor. Goodby."

"Samantha, I don't understand," the doctor said.

Charlie knew he would cry when he faced Sam. He tried not to, and only nodded when he took her hand. He could not say anything more at all. His throat and jaws ached from holding back the weeping, and the heart was gone out of him. He was mortally hurt, and he did not want her to see.

She followed him to the door and called out, "Call me, Charlie, we'll talk," as he went down the sidewalk to his car.

He held himself straight until he was away from her house, and then he pulled over to the curb and stopped. He put his head on the steering wheel and cried. His hands lay limp on the floor beside his feet.

Later, with no idea how much time had passed, he pulled himself up again and drove home.

24 | THE PARTNERS

CHARLIE WENT BACK TO WORK SUNDAY AT THREE. Wes was not there. He had called in sick, which was not like him at all. When Charlie called his apartment, he got a busy signal.

There really was not much to do. Wes had supplemented most of the cases that were due, and the rest had been parceled out to other investigators. There were some newly assigned cases, but nothing urgent. Charlie made a few phone calls to witnesses, and just before five he went up to the jail to talk to a prisoner. He was through by six. One of the other investigators asked if he would like to get a bite to eat, but Charlie passed it up. He did not feel like making conversation.

By eight, Charlie was restless. He walked over to the police garage and checked out a car, with no idea of going any place in particular. He drove around for a while, and found himself in Wes's neighborhood. Wes's car was parked in his stall, and Charlie started to go up and see him. Then he thought better of it, and drove away.

Sam's house was dark, and her car was gone.

He stopped at Keller's for a burger, and the same car hop brought him beer in a Coke cup. She asked about Wes. When he finished, he drove back downtown and went up to the office. He thought about calling Little Bit, but it was too late by then.

He left at eleven and went straight home. He had two Scotches and fell asleep with his clothes on.

Monday was another clear, brain-baking, hot day, the fortieth in a row. Charlie thought about Jessica's funeral. It was at four. Burden asked if he wanted to go, but Charlie did not think it would be a good idea, so Burden went alone. Wes was out sick again.

Late that night, the phone woke him. He did not answer it at first, because he thought it might be Sam. But it rang and rang, ten, eleven times, and he knew it was not her. He answered it.

"Hey, partner!" It was Wes. "Where were you? That damned phone must have rung a hundred times."

"What is it, Wes?"

"Didn't see you at the funeral, Charlie boy."

"I didn't go."

"Guess that explains it. I saw old Birdie, but I didn't see you."

"Wes, are you drunk?"

"Naw, but it ain't from lack of trying. That's what I called you about."

"What?"

"I need some help drinking all this beer. I want you to come down here and give me a hand."

"Wes, it's one o'clock in the morning. They're gonna throw you out and close the place in an hour. I think you'd better just go on home, if you can drive."

"Oh, I can drive, don't worry about that." There was a long pause. "I ain't sure where I left my car, but if I ever find that sombitch, I can damned sure drive. I just hate to think about you missing out on all the ass-kicking we're fixing to have down here."

"What?"

"Ass-kicking! That's what I said. I'm in the mood to kick some ass, and I've even got a couple of 'em picked out. It won't be long now. That reminds me of a joke, but I can't remember all of it."

"Where are you?"

"I'm down here on Samuell Boulevard. Right here next to

the jukebox, which none of these cheap sombitches will put no quarters into, which is why it ain't playing."

"Do you know the name of the place?"

"Why, certainly. It's, uh . . ." Charlie heard him yelling at someone. "It's old Dirty Gurdie's place. Hell, you know ol' Gurt. You know where it is. It's right . . . you know where it is."

"Wes."

"That's me."

"Wes, you just wait right there. I'll be down there in a minute. Don't start anything. Just wait for me. Okay?"

"Attaboy, Charlie. I knew you wouldn't want to miss a good ass-kicking."

"Wes, stop talking about kicking ass or somebody'll take you up on it. Shut up and wait for me. I'll be there in a minute."

Dirty Gurdie's was a sleazy dive on the north end of Samuell, not far from East Grand. Bikers hung out there. Charlie had never been inside except on duty, answering gangfight calls.

When he stepped inside, the first thing he saw was Gurdie herself, at the bar. Her curly black wig was perched askew, atop her fat, broken face. She was grinning dumbly at a little man in shop khakis, who stood across the bar from her, and Charlie could see gaps where her front teeth had been. When she laughed at the little man's joke, her voice was loud and gutteral. It broke into a smoker's cough, spraying the man and the bar as she hacked and spat and pounded the bar with a meaty fist. As his eyes became acclimated to the bar's dark and smoky interior, Charlie could make out the lettering on the dingy T-shirt that strained across her gelatinous chest. In big letters across the top it said: I AM A VIRGIN. Fine print at the bottom, above her exposed, overhanging belly, added: This is a very old T-shirt.

"Oh, Lord," thought Charlie. "Lord, Lord."

He found Wes at a pool table in the back, shooting with a biker who was tall and had arms like fence posts. His filthy black hair fell down past his shoulders, and his beard was greasy.

"Hey, Charlie! How you doing, buddy? I want you to meet

my friend here. Charlie, this is, uh . . . What did you say your name was, pal?"

The biker eyed them both meanly. "I didn't say, Pop."

"Right. Well, anyway, Charlie. I wanted you to meet him. Bad-ass, ain't he?"

"Come on, Wes, it's about closing time. Why don't we go get something to eat?"

"Terrific idea, Charlie. I'll be right with you, as soon as I finish this game. I believe it's my shot."

Wes, usually a skillful pool player, was obviously off his game. He shot much too hard and the cue ball left the table, flying across the room and bouncing off the cinderblock wall. The biker retrieved it.

"I know what's the matter," Wes announced, as the biker lined up his next shot. "It's too quiet in here. We need a little pool-playing music. Here, Charlie, liven this dump up a little bit." He handed Charlie a fistful of change, spilling most of it on the floor.

Charlie did not argue. He dropped four quarters in the slot, and pushed several buttons at random. It doesn't matter which ones, he thought. They all sounded the same to Charlie.

The biker sank three balls in a row, as some maudlin country song began to wail. Somebody was singing off key about a lost love, accompanied by a steel guitar.

"There now, Charlie, that's more like it."

The biker missed his next shot, and Wes did an elaborate drunken pantomime of sighting down his stick and measuring all the angles.

"Goddamnit, Pops, quit screwing around and shoot. You ain't made a shot all night."

Wes did not make this one, either. He shot much too hard, and the cue ball careened around the table before coming to rest, leaving the biker an easy shot to sink the eight ball and win. He made the shot, and Wes stood silent by the table, leaning on his stick.

"Okay, Wes, that's the game. Let's go."

"I'm ready."

"Wait just a goddamn minute, you two." The big biker leaned across the pool table on both hands. "You ain't goin' nowhere, Pops, until you settle up. You lost five games in a row. At twenty dollars apiece, that comes to a hundred dollars you owe me."

"Why," Wes said, smiling, "you must be mistaken. I was told that betting on pool games is against the law."

Two more bikers who had been sitting at a nearby table stood up. One of them said, "Law or no law, you made the bet, old man. We was witnesses."

The two men who had just stood up were positioned so that they had Wes and Charlie more or less trapped against the table, with the big man on the other side. Charlie looked at Wes.

"Wes, did you bet?"

"Yeah, I did. I would have won, too, but he always shot so that I had a real bad leave. He was just lucky."

"It ain't the leave, man. It's the stroke. You just ain't got no stroke."

With a thoroughly warm and disarming smile that Charlie knew was a danger signal, Wes said, "No stroke, huh?"

"That's right, man. Now pay up." He nodded at one of the men from the table, who drew a knife from under his leather vest and opened it.

"Well, that seems fair," Wes said. "But first, tell me one thing. How is this for stroke?"

Wes's voice gave nothing away, except to Charlie, who heard the lethal flattening, the tiny edge on it, and he was about to speak when Wes's cue suddenly left the floor, describing a perfect arc beneath the naked bulb that lit the table.

It was a rare and magic thing, a perfect swing, kinetic energy accelerating from the balls of Wes's feet, up through his body, to his arms, out to the barrel of the stick, connecting with a gratifying, solid thump against the big biker's chin. It was the kind of pure swing and perfect, solid hit that Babe Ruth only managed sixty times in the best year of his life. The poor bastard didn't go down, he disappeared.

The second man rushed Wes, his knife held low. With a neat pivot, Wes reversed his swing and the stick caught the man in the face. He dropped the knife and went to his knees.

The third one came at Charlie. He fell back to avoid a round-house punch, and reached behind him onto the table for a ball. He rolled off the table as the man came at him again, and slipped another punch. They squared off, the last biker looking as if he had lost interest. Charlie feinted with his left, then delivered a stiff, snappy right, hitting the man above his left eye, his fist wrapped tightly around the pool ball. The man staggered back and fell to the floor. The fight was over.

"Here now! Y'all stop that, or I'll call the cops." Gurdie yelled from the bar. "I don't allow no fightin' in here."

"Yes, ma'am," Wes called back to her, smiling and bowing from the waist. "We were just leaving."

Outside, Charlie asked him, "Don't you remember where you left your car?"

Wes was drunker than Charlie had realized, drunker than he had ever seen him. He did not answer, just stood, swaying uneasily, and shook his head. Charlie drove him home.

All the way home, Wes talked about the Navy and cried.

"I'd be a chief by now, Charlie. A goddamn chief petty officer. C.P.O. John Wesley Braverman, U.S.N." He sniffled and sobbed. "And I would be stationed in Japan. Did I ever tell you about the women in Japan? Goddamn little yellow devils, they know what they're for. They know how to make a man happy. Don't give you no trouble, either. They bathe you, Charlie, can you imagine? I mean they give you a bath."

It was like that all the way home, and continued while Charlie wrestled him up the stairs and onto the couch.

Charlie checked around his waist and did not find a gun. He pulled Wes's cowboy boots off and looked inside them. There was no gun. He had never known Wes to go out unarmed. He had never known Wes to go to a place like Gurdie's. Wes's idea of socializing centered on meeting women. When he went drinking, he liked to go some place where there were pretty women. He preferred hotel bars and lounges.

Charlie made coffee. He thought Wes was asleep, but he lurched up to a sitting position when Charlie sat down on the coffee table.

"Hey, partner," he slurred, "what's going on?"

"Nothing much. How do you feel?"

"Like a million bucks. And you?"

"I'm fine, Wes."

"Good, let's go drinking."

"You've already been drinking. Want some coffee?"

"God, no. How 'bout some whiskey?"

"No thank you."

"Well, you won't mind if I do." Wes staggered to his feet and stumbled to the bar. "Sure you won't have one?"

"No, thank you. I'm driving."

Wes poured bourbon onto a glass, spilling some. "I'm not." He made it back to the couch, spilling more.

"Wes, I'm a little worried about you. Are you all right?"

"You bet."

"I've never known you to get drunk, much less to work at it this hard. Is there anything you want to tell me?"

Wes fixed him with bloodshot eyes, and tears started. He shook his head.

"I know you were fond of Jessica, Wes. The funeral today must have been hard on you. If there's anything . . . ." He stopped when he saw Wes shaking his head, his eyes squeezed tightly shut.

Wes cleared his throat. When he was able to speak, his voice was thick with pain. "You're a good man and a good partner, Charlie, and I appreciate it. But there's nothing . . . I just get like this sometimes. I don't usually let anybody see me this way, that's all."

"Will you be all right here by yourself, Wes? I can stay if you want me to."

"Nah, Charlie, I'm okay. You go on home and I'll see you tomorrow. I'll see you at work tomorrow."

"Are you sure?"

"You bet." Wes smiled, with his heartbroken face.

Charlie rose to leave. At the door, he turned and looked back at Wes. "I'll come by and get you, okay?"

"Charlie," Wes said, holding his drink up as if making a toast, "I should have stayed in the goddamn Navy."

25 | THE FLOWER GIRL

CHARLIE LET THE PHONE RING AGAIN AND AGAIN. Finally, Wes answered, unintelligibly.

"Wes, this is Charlie. Can you hear me?"

"Mmnh."

"It's half-past one, Wes. You are due back at work at three. I'm calling to see if you need a ride in." Charlie heard a sharp cough, followed by another, then a fit of coughing. "Wes?"

"Oooh, goddamn, partner. Goddamn."

"Why don't you call in sick today. Roll over and go back to sleep. I'll see you tomorrow." Wes did not answer, and Charlie hung up.

He turned on the hot water tap in the bathroom sink and let it run to get hot. Because his apartment was quiet and empty, he decided to play a little music while he shaved. As he walked across to the phonograph, he thought how empty his apartment seemed, and he thought about Sam. Before her, he had liked the time he spent alone here.

Rhapsody in Blue was still on the turntable. He had not played the phonograph since the night the captain died. It seemed a long, long time ago. Why not? It's just a piece of music now. His phone rang, and he answered, expecting to hear Sam's voice. It was Wes.

"Partner, I think I'd be better off going to work today, if you don't mind picking me up."

"I'd be glad to."

"I appreciate it. I don't think I can stand any more leisure time."

"I'm shaving now. I'll be by about two-fifteen."

"I'll be ready."

Charlie lathered his face and mowed a path down the left side of his jaw with a well-worn disposable razor. He dipped the blade in the sink, then remembered to close the drain, and turned off the tap. When he looked in the mirror again, something had happened. Instead of a disposable, his hand in the mirror held a sleek straight razor, the kind an old-fashioned man would use. Its honed, hungry edge sparkled in the light. Horror lit the eyes of his reflection. He leaned closer to the mirror, and a long deep gash opened across his cheek, from jaw to eye socket, like a second mouth. He tried to scream but could not, and saw blood gurgling from the gaping slit across his throat. Mute and paralyzed, he watched the face in the mirror as the flesh fell away in shreds.

With a splash, the razor fell into the soapy water. He closed his eyes and covered his face with both hands. He brailled his face, his fingertips gently testing the skin for wounds. When they found none, he slowly opened his eyes and forced himself to look in the mirror again. It was his face, with patches of dried shaving cream and bulging, frightened eyes. Nothing more. He pushed the plunger knob and watched the water swirl away, leaving nothing behind but the innocuous plastic disposable razor. He leaned against the door facing, breathing hard, and was aware of the music again. He turned and ran across the living room to the record player, and ripped the spinning record straight off the spool, breaking the tone arm in the process. He hurled the record against the wall with such force a piece broke off. He backed away, staring at the bits of plastic on the floor, and stumbled backward onto the couch.

He sat there for several minutes, his head in his hands, until he was breathing normally again. Then he got to his feet and walked purposefully back into the bathroom, where he hurriedly shaved and showered. He dressed quickly and started out the door, then turned back to look at the room again. A lot has happened, he told himself. It will take a little time. That's all, just a little time.

Driving over to Wes's apartment, Charlie told himself again that it would take time. Don't panic. Stay calm, he told himself. You are all you've got this time. There's nobody else.

Wes looked bad. He was pale and still a little shaky when he got in the car. Charlie was glad Wes had called him, and glad he had gone. At least he had Wes; they were partners again.

At the Homicide office, Wes picked up a set of keys and handed them to Charlie. "Here, partner," he said, "as soon as we get our paperwork together, I want you to take me someplace where I can get a good meal."

"You want me to drive? You've never let me drive a city car before, not since we've been together."

"I've never felt like this since we've been together, either. As a matter of fact, I don't believe I've ever been hung over so bad. I'd have to get better to die."

Wes sat in a chair, balancing his head carefully, while Charlie collected their cases and gathered up his accordion file and some extra supplement forms.

"Come on, Wes. Let's get out of here."

"I'm ready. Find me a dinner that is bland and starchy, partner. I need something to soak up all the poison."

"Hold on there, men." Burden called from the door of his office.

"Don't stop us now, Sarge. We're on our way to save my life." Wes turned his whole body to look back at Burden, as if turning his head alone would hurt too much.

"Y'all will have to eat a little later, I'm afraid. There's something you need to do first."

"No, Birdie, no."

"What is it, Sarge?"

"It's Julia Copeland. She called this morning and left word she wants to see you first thing, as soon as you come in. First thing, she said."

"What's it about?" Wes sounded genuinely concerned.

"Something about Jessica and Captain Jonas, but she

wouldn't go into any detail on the phone. I told Captain Sharp she called, and he is plenty worried."

"Why?"

"Because it was his theory that got leaked to the press about the captain's secret life. He's the one that thought Cap Jonas was the Slasher. He's scared to death Julia is gonna sic Edmund's lawyers on him. Personally, I'd like to see her sue his little ass off, but I don't think she's even thinking about that right now. I'm supposed to call Sharp at home as soon as you report back to me, so you get on out there, and give me a call as soon as you finish talking to her. Then you go feed your hangover."

"The way I feel, it may be too late by then."

"What about me?" Charlie asked.

"You go with Wes."

"Is that a good idea, Sarge?"

"She asked to see you, too, Charlie. She may feel like she owes you an apology."

Julia opened the door herself. Her face was drawn and pale, but she was still beautiful, in a ghostly way. She showed the two policemen in and led them down the long hall, the same one where Charlie had walked with Jessica the first time he came there. Charlie noticed that all of the pictures of Jessica had been removed. As they walked along, he realized that everything had been taken down. The walls were bare. As they passed open doors, Charlie saw that all the furniture in the room was covered. Their steps on the terrazzo floor echoed in the big empty house. Halfway down the hall, Julia stopped, and showed them into the study.

"Please be seated. Would you like coffee, or tea?"

"Coffee's fine," Wes said. "Black."

"Coffee for me, too." Charlie added, "Cream and sugar if it's no trouble."

She left and returned in a few minutes carrying a silver tray.

"I'm afraid we must serve ourselves," she said. "The staff has been let go."

"You fired all of your servants?" Wes asked.

"Edmund did. Yesterday, after the funeral. Even his favorite, the chauffeur. He was less abrupt with me. I have until the end of the month to be out."

"Why, that sonofabitch!"

Julia smiled drily at Wes's outrage. "Edmund is sensitive to scandal. He values his image. He has gone to New York on business, and he won't be back until I'm gone. Ours was an arrangement of mutual benefit; and now, it has been dissolved."

"What will you do?"

"Travel, I suppose. Dallas is all I have known, and I could never be happy here again."

Charlie sipped his coffee and listened as they talked. Wes told Julia about his time in the Orient with the Navy, and she seemed interested. Charlie noticed that, as they talked, she looked at him from time to time. He said nothing, and soon finished his coffee. He held his cup and saucer in his lap for a time, and then set them down on the tray. He noticed when he did this that the tray seemed to swim a bit at first, until he forced himself to see it clearly. He also noticed a numbness in his lips.

"Julia . . . Mrs. Copeland, Sergeant Burden said that you asked us to come out here as soon as we got to work. Is there something we can do for you?"

She put her cup and saucer upon the tray, and drew herself up straight in the big wingback chair where she sat facing the two men, who sat at either end of the divan. The tray sat on a coffee table between them.

"Yes, there is. Especially you, Mister Braverman. I understand that you were there when Jessica was . . . when she died. I want to know what happened. I want you to tell me everything."

Charlie sensed something wrong with his partner. Wes was always in control, but his voice cracked when he spoke now of the dead girl.

"Mrs. Copeland, I don't think it would be a good idea to go into a lot of detail. You've suffered enough, and it won't change anything."

She is in control, Charlie thought. She fixed Wes with a cold, deliberate stare, and he shifted uncomfortably on the couch.

"Your concern for my suffering is touching, but I insist. I want to know."

Wes swallowed hard but did not answer.

A ripple of lightheadedness washed over Charlie, a strange swell of motion. She was looking at him now.

"Mister Braverman, I mean to know every detail of the incident. That is why your superiors have sent you here."

Wes cleared his throat twice before he could get the words out. "There was not much pain. She died . . . . instantly."

"That is some comfort."

Their voices echoed in Charlie's head, and played across his field of vision; now he could see their words. He watched in mute awe as every sound they made appeared, in vivid colors. Wes's voice made fat blue globs that waffled in the air and slowly settled to the carpet. Julia made red diaphanous waves, like windblown scarves. They wrapped themselves around her, and then faded away. She was looking at him again. He tried to smile at her, but his mouth drooped wetly, unresponsive.

"Tell me, Mister Braverman, did she die in your arms, or couldn't you allow yourself that luxury? It must have been difficult, with all your fellow officers there."

With childlike fascination, Charlie noticed that each movement of Julia's head as she spoke created a trailing image. Wes was not so interesting. He did not move at all.

"Answer me, Mister Braverman. Did you take her in your arms? Did she gasp her last words in your ear? How touching that must have been!"

Her words had changed from scarves to lasers, striking out at Wes like darts.

"I wasn't there. I saw her at the hospital, later." Wes did not make blue globs this time, just a black, sobbing dribble that puddled on the floor. "Julia, I don't know what the hell you're getting at, but this is not helping anything. If you want to talk, we can do it later alone."

"We are alone."

It was true. Charlie was not in his body any more. He had gone away to see Little Bit. He told her that he would take her to the zoo, but Sam would not go with them any more. She said she didn't care, as long as he was there, and Charlie felt better. He came back to his body in time to hear Julia say:

"I put something in his coffee, something I found among

Jessica's effects. Did you know she used drugs, Mr. Braverman? You must have. You shared all her little secrets, didn't you?"

"I don't understand," Wes said.

Charlie did not understand either.

"I also found *this* among her things."

Julia produced a slim, leatherbound book from beneath a cushion at her side, and held it up for Wes to see. Then she dropped it on the coffee table in front of him.

"This should make things clear. Hardly literature, but I found it most interesting."

Wes picked up the book and opened it to a page at random. His face paled, and he muttered, "A diary. Just like the old man."

"Won't you read for us, Mister Braverman?"

Wes did not move or speak. She took the book from his hands and opened it to one of the three pages she had marked with snapshots of Jessica:

" 'He is different from all the others, different from the men Mother told me about, different from Edmund, different from the boys I know, different, different, different. I love him. I really do. Last night he made love to me. He loved that I was a virgin, and he was gentle and wonderful. I never dreamed it would be like that. I know I was wrong. It was evil. He should be punished, but I could never hurt Wes. I love him. I am confused.' "

Julia looked at Wes as she turned to the second marked page, and lay that snapshot beside the first on the coffee table. Wes looked down at his hands, and Charlie could see that he was crying.

" 'I feel wonderful!' " Julia read. " 'I'm not confused any more, and it's wonderful! Wes and I quarreled last night. It was funny how a sad thing can bring a happy thing. We fought because he would not tell Mother about us and didn't want me to tell her, either. I was very angry at him, and I decided he had to be punished. I love him, but I saw that he had to be punished. I knew how to do it, the way Mother did it to the boy who hurt her. I was going to punish Wes that way, when something funny happened, something good. There was this boy I had never seen before, a dirty, greasy boy. He said things to me and thought he was smart, so I punished him, instead. Now I'm not confused any more, and I feel wonderful! It balances everything out. Wes and I made up.' "

Julia looked at Charlie before she read the third page. He was looking above her head, watching the last of her words crackle and sputter in the air. "You and your stupid meddling, babbling about my father. If you had left us alone . . . ." Her voice did not rise a note. It was soft and flat, with an almost imperceptible edge. She turned to Wes, her face coloring for the first time. "And you, you beast, you . . . man. You ruined her. You took her, the way I was taken. You . . . fucked her!" She spat the word out as if it were a clot of blood from her throat. "If I had known she would come to this, I would have taken a coat hanger to her while she was still in my womb." As her rage built up inside of her, her voice softened even more, until this last was a whisper.

Her soft tone meant nothing to Charlie. To him, her words had become fireballs that burst and showered them all with sizzling sparks. He held out his hand to catch one, and giggled when it did not burn.

"Mister Braverman, my daughter was an innocent child. She never hurt anyone until you ruined her."

"Me?" Wes's voice was louder now. "You're the one who taught her to hate men. You made her see every man as the man who raped you, the man you butchered, the man you punished. You say you loved her, but she knew how you really felt. She could see it in your eyes, that you remembered your past every time you looked at her." He leaned forward, and looked as if he might lunge across the table at the woman. "She didn't learn about razors from me!"

"You knew she killed those three boys, and you did nothing. You did not try to get help for her, you did not stop her. You did nothing."

"She was worth a thousand of those punks. And what help? Was I supposed to take her to some quack doctor? They would have put her away somewhere and made a vegetable of her. I've seen it before. Is that what you'd want?"

"And my father? Did she kill him, too, or did he kill himself because he found out what she had become?"

"She had nothing to do with that. She didn't know about it until later, when Charlie started stirring things up."

"You killed him, didn't you, Mister Braverman?"

"I had to." Wes stood up. He looked at them both, and looked as if he might run out of the room. Then the look on his face changed. He was suddenly calm, as if he had made a very important decision. When he spoke again, his voice was steady, and he was in control. "He was going to turn her in. It's funny in a way. He suspected you. I told him you had alibis, but he wouldn't let it go. Wouldn't take my word for it, had to see for himself. Jessie took your car the night she killed the Estep boy. Cap thought he was following you. When he went into that motel and found what she had left of that punk, he saw that it was Jessica who did it. Even he was stunned. So stunned, in fact, that he just let her walk away from the scene of the murder without saying a word." Wes looked at Charlie who was watching his words. "He went back to his room at the hotel and called me. He was going to turn her in, but I told him to wait until I got there. I fixed up Charlie here as my alibi. He was waiting in the car while I went to talk to a snitch. Only I went out the back and down the alley to the Crockett, then up the service elevator. Killing the old man was easy. I was surprised how easy it was. I knew where he kept the pistol the department gave him. When he reached for the phone to call you, I shot him. All the people on that floor are so damned old, I had plenty of time to get out and down the service elevator before they came around. Then back up the alley and in the back door in time for Charlie to tell me we had a call at the Crockett. My partner here never suspected a thing. He always waits in the car when I talk to snitches. You have to protect your sources. You're only as good as your sources."

Julia did not seem to be listening to him any more. There was a distant look in her eyes. "I only told Jessica what happened to me," she said. "I told her the truth about the boy, what he did to me and what I did to him. She had to know what men are. She had to know the pain she had caused me."

"She caused you? She had nothing to do with it, you crazy bitch! She had nothing to say about it."

"She was part of it, part of him, the part I couldn't forget. If I could have cut out the part that was him . . . ."

"But you couldn't, and you hated her for it."

"I loved her."

"So did I, Julia. I really loved her, and I wanted to protect her. I would have done anything for her. I did . . ."

His words were black and heavy, like the ominous clouds of Charlie's childhood, the ones that spawned the killer tornadoes. Charlie remembered the dank safety of the storm shelter, and the deathly, windless stillness before a storm. That same stillness was there now, in the room. It was not fun any more, seeing things that no one else could see. He was stranded out here in the open, and could not run for shelter. He tried to go away again, but it was too late. His body would not let him go this time. He was trapped.

"You loved her, Mister Braverman, and you protected her. And now she is dead, shot like a rabid dog." Now her soft words crackled, jagging down out of the black clouds. The storm was close and coming.

Ignoring the woman for a minute, Wes paced a circle around the couch, and stopped in front of Charlie. "And how much of this is getting through to you, partner?" He looked into Charlie's eyes and shook his head. "What am I going to do with you?" He reached gently inside Charlie's open jacket and drew out his revolver. "You won't be needing this."

Wes kept his eye on the woman as he walked to the windows, where the drapes were closed. He peered through them at the sunlight outside, then turned back to face Charlie and the woman. "It happened this way: Charlie and I came out here to see you and you went crazy. You blamed Charlie for messing with you and your family. You figure that was what stirred Jessica up and got her killed. You got Charlie's gun, and he was shot in the struggle. I had to kill you in self-defense. When the stuff you put in his coffee shows up on the autopsy, that will explain why Charlie has been acting so strange lately; he's been using drugs."

Julia ignored him. She sat, stately and aloof, in her wingback chair. Her head nodded slightly, as if in agreement, as she stared at the book on the coffee table, and the photographs of Jessica.

Wes stood over Charlie. "Try to understand, partner. I loved her. It doesn't sound like much, I know, but I'd never felt that way before. I knew it was hopeless. I knew from the start that it was going to turn out bad. But I couldn't give her up. No matter how bad it was, I couldn't live without her. I was like a junkie or something. No price was too high to keep her. I thought I could take care of her, keep her from hurting anybody else. Maybe I could have, too, if you hadn't stirred things up with all your crazy talk about the captain. Julia was right about that, you know. If you hadn't come around with all that business about your dreams, Jessica might still be alive. When you came to my place that night and told me about your slashed pillow, I knew it was her. And I knew, if she got worked up enough to come after you, she wouldn't stop. She'd have to go after somebody else. So, it really was your fault, in a way." Charlie looked up at him mindlessly, slavering. "I'll make it as easy on you as I can."

Charlie saw compassion in his partner's face. He felt like the horse in a B western. His leg was broken and he was about to be shot by the cowboy hero, reluctantly. Goodby, old Paint, he thought, and remembered Elizabeth. His Little Bit.

A zipper opened loudly. And closed. And opened again. Charlie saw the look on Wes's face change from compassion to surprise. Wes dropped Charlie's gun and spun around unsteadily. Charlie saw that the zipper was not a zipper at all. It was a razor in Julia's hand. Wes's back was in shreds. The razor blurred in her windmilling hand as she struck at Wes's face. He tried helplessly, silently, to scream. Charlie wondered at that, no sound from all those mouths. Wes reached out with his left hand as if to catch the blade. He drew his gun clumsily with his right, but it fell out of his hand onto the floor beside Charlie's. Wes crumpled to his hands and knees and tried to crawl away. She hovered over him as he trailed gore across the carpet toward the windows, hurting him but keeping him alive.

To Charlie, the flood of red was floral. Every new wound sprouted a bouquet. He watched the woman bobbing up and down over Wes, cutting the flowers like a mad wood sprite. There were flowers in her hair, on her hands, everywhere. It was beautiful. The storm had passed, and the garden was in bloom.

Charlie sat watching the flower girl at work when he noticed an old man watching her, too. The gardener, he thought. The sight of the old man reminded Charlie of something he was supposed to do. But what?

The old man said, "Charlie, can you hear me?"

"Yes, sir."

"Do you know who I am, Charlie?"

"You're the gardener."

"No, Charlie, I am the captain."

"Captain Jonas?"

"That's right, Charlie. Listen to me very carefully and do as I say. You must leave this house. You must go quickly."

It was all right now, watching the flower girl at work. Charlie did not want to leave now.

"But the flower girl . . ."

"I'll see to her, Charlie. That is the one thing left for me to do. You mustn't bother her. Do as I say and no harm will come to you. Leave, Charlie. Go quietly."

Charlie looked back at the flower girl. Odd, the more flowers she cuts, the more there seem to be. He turned to ask the gardener why, but he was gone.

Must leave, he thought, and not bother the flower girl. Somehow he knew he must obey the gardener. The captain. He tried to stand, but he fell back on the divan. Important, Charlie remembered. Important to be quiet. Don't disturb her. He struggled to his feet, finally. Where was he? Which way was the way out? He lumbered across to the hallway door. Must be quiet. Shhhh. Down the long hallway he saw several doors. Which one?

He heard the crash and saw the broken vase at his feet, beside the overturned little table. The pieces of the vase were flower petals. He turned and saw the flower girl. She stopped what she was doing, and looked over her shoulder at him. And then she came after him, waving her flower-draped arms and screaming.

He tried to run, but felt as if he were in waist-deep water. Behind him, the flower girl was running fast. She was close behind him when he stumbled through a door and slammed it shut behind him, just as she threw her weight against it. He heard her screaming and felt her beating on the door. He put his back to the door and held it closed. His legs would not hold him any more, and he slid down with his back against the door and sat on the cool tile floor. It was a bathroom.

There was a mirror, and he could see a strange man in it. It was him sitting on the floor, holding the door shut. Above the man's head in the mirror, he saw fingers with flowers on them crawling like snakes between the door and the jamb. Then the whole hand was through the crack, and the crack was a little wider. The hand had flowers all over it. It looked for the man in the mirror like a snake, turning this way and that. Then it found the man, and Charlie felt the hand in his hair, jerking his head up and back against the door, stretching his throat up and back. He heard the flower girl, her face pressed against the crack of the door screaming.

He heard another voice, the voice of the gardener, the captain. It was gentle, and he could hardly hear at first. It was outside the door, mixed with the woman's screaming. Then the screaming stopped. He heard the woman on the other side of the door crying, crying, crying. The hand let go of his hair and his head lobbed forward onto his chest. The woman was crying, crying like a baby now. The captain's voice, the gardener's voice, was gentle, soothing her. Then silence. He waited in the quiet for a long time, trying to hear anything except his own breathing. At last, there were voices again, muffled voices beyond the door. He could not make out the words, but the captain's voice was calm and reassuring; the woman was weeping softly in the quiet of the big house.

When he felt stronger, Charlie tried to get up. He put his hands, palms down, on the floor to push himself up, and he felt something warm and sticky there. Flowers, he thought, looking at his hands. Wet, sticky flowers? It was blood. It was all blood, oozing in under the door and spreading across the tiles. He held his breath and bit his fist to keep from screaming, and he heard her voice beyond the door, echoing more and more faintly.

"I love you too, Daddy. I love you, Daddy. I love you . . ."

And then silence.

EPILOGUE

BIRDS SANG. THEY CHIRPED AND TWITTERED, AND
flitted back and forth overhead. The people on the patio outside
the long, low building could look out over the big lawn, across a
pond, to a place on the other side where a jogging trail disappeared into the shadows of a stand of trees that ran across a low
rise and down the other side, out of sight. On this side of the
rise, a big willow stood with bowed head beside the trail.

There were a lot of people on the patio, standing in a semicircle. Their heads were bowed, too, except for one. Sergeant Burden was there, sweating and forlorn. Captain Sharp was there,
with the chief of detectives. Even the Big Chief was there, with
his driver. Charlie's ex-wife was there, with a man in a three-
piece suit and rimless glasses, just like at Charlie's funeral, the
one in his dream. All these people and more were there with
their heads bowed, looking down at Charlie. Elizabeth was
there, too, holding her mother's hand. Her head was not bowed.
She was looking up at the birds.

There was a photographer who was careful to take pictures of
everything the Big Chief did. He was the police photographer.
The others were from the newspapers. There were television
people there, too, with Minicams. Sam was there. All these

people almost filled the patio, which was in back of the long building, between it and the pond.

Charlie looked up at all the people standing around him, looking down at him, and realized that this must be his funeral. He had been feeling sane occasionally the last few days, which is to say, he had times when he thought that he was seeing and hearing the same things as everyone else around him. Now he figured that had been his last little spark before the end, little bursts of sanity before he died. He regretted not having used his sane moments to write something down, to let people know how he felt. He would have left a note if he had known he was going to die.

But then it wasn't his funeral at all. He looked up at a hawk circling high overhead, and, when he looked back down, it was someone else's funeral. He, Charlie, was standing in a crowd now, along with all the other people, looking down at someone else. It was his father's funeral, and they were standing on the low hill in the cemetary by the little church in Sulphur Springs, a hawk circling effortlessly above them. The Big Chief of the Dallas Police Department was saying a eulogy for his father:

" 'The Police Commendation Bar, awarded to Investigator Charles T. Gants. For exceptionally meritorious services and outstanding contributions to the police profession, without regard for personal welfare or safety, of such magnitude as to bring honor and recognition to himself and the Department. Awarded by the Meritorious Conduct Board, Dallas Police Department.' Congratulations, Charlie."

The Chief bent down and put the certificate into Charlie's hands. Then he pinned a metal ribbon onto the lapel of Charlie's bathrobe. The ribbon was red, with two vertical blue lines. Charlie looked at the certificate lying in his lap, and he did not notice that the Big Chief had offered his hand. Finally, he did notice, and took the Chief's hand in his. The police photographer took a picture, and so did all the others. The Chief smiled broadly, and made sure they got all the pictures they wanted. Charlie did not do anything.

The Big Chief said he would like to say a few words, and everybody listened. He stood beside Charlie's wheelchair and talked. Charlie did not pay any attention. He reached inside his bathrobe and pulled two letters out of the pocket in his pajamas. One was from the pension Board. It said that he did not qualify for disability pension because he could not prove that he lost his mind in the line of duty, or words to that effect. It said he could appeal if he wanted to. The other letter was from his mother, written in her hand on little lined sheets. It said:

"Dear Son,

You know I would like to be there when you get the medal, but it is hard on me, making the trip. Just like you know I would come to see you more often, but the trip is hard on me, and I have to impose on your Uncle Fred to drive me over. I pray for you every day, Son, and I want you to think about what I said, about moving back home. That way, I could see about you and I wouldn't worry so much about you or have to bother your Uncle Fred to drive me, or have to make that trip every time to see you. I love you, Son, and I want you to come home where I can see after you. You know you always have a home here. Take care of yourself, and write to me. It would mean so much to me to hear from you.

Momma

P.S.
Stop talking about the captain. Tell them whatever they want to hear, so they will let you go."

The Chief was answering questions now. To one of the reporters he said, "No, no question at all. Based on our investigations and Jessica's diary, we are satisfied that she was the East Dallas Slasher, and that Wes Braverman murdered Captain Jonas to protect her. We suspect that Braverman was able to sidetrack us whenever we got close to finding out anything, and he may have kept us from solving the case earlier. We are checking on that now. Julia had a history of instability, and we believe that the death of her daughter was just too much for her. She found the diary, and killed Braverman for revenge. Then she took her own life. It is all very sad, like a Greek tragedy."

When there were no more questions, the Chief thanked them all and they left, straggling out across the big lawn away from the pond, toward the parking lot. All of them left except Sam, who stood behind him, and his ex-wife and the man with the rimless glasses. They stood off to one side, with Elizabeth between them. One of the reporters stayed, too, and he asked Sam something.

"No, I am no longer a consultant with the police department," Sam answered. "I am on the staff here at the Branville Research Institute now." The reporter asked something else. "Yes, it is true that Charlie unknowingly ingested a hallucinogenic drug called phencyclidine, or "angel dust" as it is commonly referred to, that day at the Copeland mansion. But the effects of the drug itself were short-lived, and were not a serious problem. Charlie is being treated here at the Institute for a more serious, deep-rooted emotional disturbance that revealed itself in the weeks after Captain Jonas's death. We are guardedly optimistic about his chances for a recovery." The reporter thanked her and went off after the rest.

Sam knelt beside Charlie. "Charlie, I'm sorry I missed you yesterday. I got tied up and I just couldn't get away to come see you." She was talking to him now, leaning against the wheel of his chair. "The attendants told me you sat out in the lobby all afternoon waiting for me. They said you didn't want to eat dinner or anything because you were waiting for me. That was not very nice of you. Just because I didn't come or call, that doesn't mean that you can't behave and cooperate with the attendants. You mustn't regress if I don't come to see you as often as I did at first. You mustn't depend on other people. Do you understand?"

He did understand. She was almost through with him.

"Charlie, there is someone here who wants to see you. Elizabeth is here. Her mother asked me if it would be all right for Elizabeth to come and say hello to you. She wanted to be here today to see her daddy get his medal. Would you like for her to come say hello?"

Little Bit. He must have smiled a little, because Sam patted his hand and went to get her. Charlie's ex-wife and the guy she was with stayed back; they did not seem to want to have anything to do with Charlie. Sam brought Little Bit over to see him, holding her by the hand. Bit smiled up at Charlie, and crawled up into his lap. Sam went to say something to his ex-wife.

"Daddy, how come your chair has wheels?"

"So I can take you for a ride, Little Bit."

"Daddy, you're the only one who calls me that."

"That's because you're my Little Bit, and nobody else's."

He pushed his chair across the patio, down a single step that bounced them and made Little Bit laugh, and out onto the jogging trail. He followed the trail as it curved to his left, past the pond with its fountain, past the willow with its bowed head, up the gentle slope toward the shadows of the stand of trees that ran across the low rise and down the other side, out of sight.

"I love you, Bit."

"I love you, too, Daddy."

And she laughed and laughed, as he went fast up the low hill.

About the Authors

Richard Abshire was born and raised in East Texas and like his writing partner, William Clair, is an author-cop. While serving with the Dallas Police Department, Abshire rapidly attained the rank of captain—at the time, the youngest captain ever in the history of the DPD. Later, he was placed in charge of the Tactical Section (S.W.A.T.) and in that capacity, was responsible for coordinating security for the White House in 1976. He has received a commendation from the Office of the President, and a Distinguished Police Commendation Bar for Valor. He is now a member of the police department of Southern Methodist University.

Currently, he is persuing a film degree at Southern Methodist University.

Abshire lives with his wife and two of his five children in Dallas, Texas.

William R. Clair is currently a Sergeant of Detectives in the Dallas Police Department, Criminal Investigation Division. He has been with the force for eighteen years, thirteen of those as a first-line supervisor in some of the roughest sections of Dallas, including East Dallas, where the story of *GANTS* is largely based. Along with numerous other awards and commendations, he has received the Dallas Police Medal of Valor, given only twelve times previously in the department's one hundred year history.

In addition to being cop and author, Clair is an artist of some reknown whose paintings and sculptures have been shown in galleries throughout the Southwest. He has even been used by the department as a police artist.

Bill Clair is married and has two daughters.